Praise for James Blish

"You are about to read one of the finest novels by one of the finest minds in science fiction. It's going to be a dizzying experience."
—from the new Introduction by Greg Bear

"*A Case of Conscience* . . . was one of the first serious attempts to deal with religion in sf, and remains one of the most sophisticated. It is generally regarded as an sf classic."
—*The Science Fiction Encyclopedia*

"A master of the telling detail, without which the gigantic has no meaning."
—BRIAN ALDISS

"A highly regarded science fiction writer."
—*The New York Times*

Other books in the Del Rey Impact line:

The King of Elfland's Daughter by Lord Dunsany
The Charwoman's Shadow by Lord Dunsany
The Man Who Fell to Earth by Walter Tevis
Mockingbird by Walter Tevis
The Drawing of the Dark by Tim Powers
Dragon's Egg by Robert Forward
The Best of Lester Del Rey by Lester Del Rey

Coming in March 2001 . . .
Pavane by Keith Roberts

There's much more to come. Del Rey Impact will continue to publish more seminal, trailblazing science fiction and fantasy, furthering our goal of bringing the past into the future.

A CASE OF CONSCIENCE

James Blish

I schal declare the disposcioun of rome fro hys first makyng . . . and the seconde part schal declar ye holynesse of ye same place fro his first crystendom; I schal not write but that I fynde in auctores or ellis that I sey with eye.

—JOHN CAPGRAVE
The Solace of Pilgrims

The Ballantine Publishing Group
New York

to LARRY SHAW

A Del Rey Impact Book
Published by The Ballantine Publishing Group

www.randomhouse.com/delrey/

Library of Congress Catalog Card Number: 00-190464

ISBN 0-345-43835-3

First Ballantine Books Edition: April 1958
First Impact Edition: September 2000

147028622

You are about to read one of the finest novels by one of the finest minds in science fiction. It's going to be a dizzying experience; James Blish was eclectic in the extreme, able to leap from subject to subject in a few sentences with expert grace, flashing a nervous, heady brilliance.

He could also tell a magnificent story, and that's what we have here: a Hugo Award–winning novel huge in subject if not length, intellectual on the surface but deeply passionate and humane in its depths. *A Case of Conscience* is a story about good and evil on both an abstract and a practical level, and it's the first of a sequence of novels Blish called After Such Knowledge. These consist of *A Case of Conscience*, *Black Easter*, *The Day After Judgment*, and *Doctor Mirabilis* (a historical novel about the philosopher and scientific pioneer Roger Bacon). *Black Easter* and *The Day After Judgment* are short books, one following upon another, and should be read back-to-back; the others are thematically related. Together they constitute one of the most impressive examinations of faith in modern literature.

Blish, himself an apparent agnostic, was fascinated by the question of ancient faith in a skeptical and scientific world.

In After Such Knowledge, he combined the metaphysics of Dante and Milton with modern science and technology and produced a sequence of books that has influenced many writers in the decades since, including me.

Rereading *A Case of Conscience* reminds me of a quite different tale: Henry James's *The Turn of the Screw.* Both are tales of hidden ghosts. In *A Case of Conscience,* the ghosts are those of God and Satan, vying offstage to create vast tapestries of spiritual warfare; in James, they are the ghosts of a sexually exuberant and unconventional man and woman. Both Blish and James assume the ghosts are real.* But is the result of fighting against their influence good, or evil?

In *A Case of Conscience,* the conscience is that of a Peruvian Jesuit priest, Father Ruiz-Sanchez, who is stationed on the planet Lithia, a richly populated and beautiful, lively place of few metals and no apparent evil—but also no religion. (No doubt some of Father Ruiz-Sanchez's ancestors would have known all about the invasion of an alien culture.) Ruiz-Sanchez works against the voracious exploitation of the technology-minded and clearly bigoted physicist Cleaver, whose plans will spoil this peculiar Eden.

Ruiz-Sanchez himself is fascinated by the beauties and peace of Lithia, a seeming paradise. However, he suspects that Lithia is a product of the Devil. *A planet without original sin—and without God.*

Yet in Catholic theology, Satan can create only illusion, not real works. Lithia is solid, real . . . Unless it is the most extravagant deception in the long and tormented history of the Fall!

The tale proceeds with all due speed through politics and theology, villains and heroes, to a stunning and brilliantly

*A careful reading of James's story shows that he intended no ambiguity about the ghosts' existence, despite the contentions of many critics in the century since.

ambiguous conclusion. And the questions remain: Is God cruel, and Satan creative? Is it best to live on a virtually perfect world, oblivious to the truth, like a glowing brick surrounded by the fulgurous evil of Satan's furnace?

Is Father Ruiz-Sanchez, as much as Cleaver, imposing his cultural preconceptions on innocence and beauty, as the Catholics imposed theirs on Peru and Latin America—and as the repressed governess imposed her Freudian fears on the children of *The Turn of the Screw*?

I intend no spoilers in this introduction, and so I will keep it short.

I think you'll be surprised by how much this book will affect you. And having read it, I can only recommend you turn to Blish's other novels.

For James Blish is one of the most neglected writers of our age. And shame on us all for that.

Pronunciation Key

For any reader who cares, the Lithian words and names he will encounter here and there in this story are to be pronounced as follows:

Xoredeshch—"X" as English "K" or Greek chi, hard; "shch" contains two separate sounds, as in Russian, or in English "fi*sh-ch*urch."

Sfath: As in English, with a broad "a."

Gton: Guttural "G," against the hard palate, like hawking.

Chtexa: Like German "Stuka," but with the flat "e."

gchteht: Guttural "g" followed by the soft "sh" sound, a flat "e," and the "h" serving as equivalent of the Old Russian mute sign; thus, a four-syllable word, with a palatal tick at the end, but sounded as one syllable.

Gleshchtehk—As indicated, with the guttural "G," the "fi*sh-ch*urch" middle consonants, and the mute "h" throwing the "k" back against the soft palate.

The rule is that "ch" is always English "sh" in the initial position, always English "ch" as in "chip" elsewhere in the word; and "h" in isolation is an accented rest which always *precedes*, never follows, a consonant. As Agronski somewhere remarks, anybody who can spit can speak Lithian.

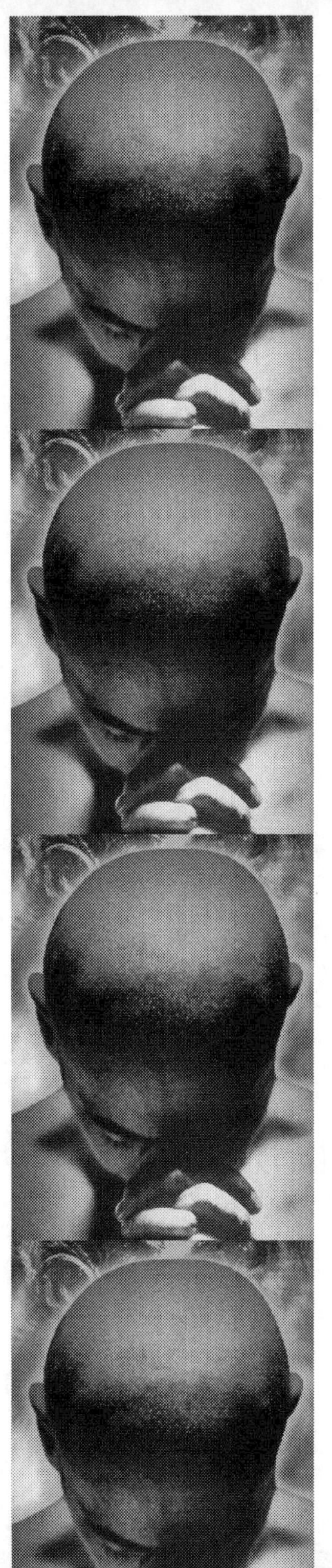

BOOK ONE

The stone door slammed. It was Cleaver's trade-mark: there had never been a door too heavy, complex, or cleverly tracked to prevent him from closing it with a sound like a clap of doom. And no planet in the universe could possess an air sufficiently thick and curtained with damp to muffle that sound—not even Lithia.

Father Ramon Ruiz-Sanchez, late of Peru, and always Clerk Regular of the Society of Jesus, professed father of the four vows, continued to read. It would take Paul Cleaver's impatient fingers quite a while to free him from his jungle suit, and in the meantime the problem remained. It was a century-old problem, first propounded in 1939, but the Church had never cracked it. And it was diabolically complex (that adverb was official, precisely chosen, and intended to be taken literally). Even the novel which had proposed the case was on the Index Expurgatorius, and Father Ruiz-Sanchez had spiritual access to it only by virtue of his Order.

He turned the page, scarcely hearing the stamping and muttering in the hall. On and on the text ran, becoming more tangled, more evil, more insoluble with every word:

> . . . Magravius threatens to have Anita molested by Sulla, an orthodox savage (and leader of a band of twelve mercenaries, the Sullivani), who desires to procure Felicia for Gregorius, Leo Vitellius and Macdugalius, four excavators, if she will not yield to him and also deceive Honuphrius by rendering conjugal duty when demanded. Anita who claims to have discovered incestuous temptations from Jeremias and Eugenius—

There now, he was lost again. Jeremias and Eugenius were—? Oh, yes, the "philadelphians" or brotherly lovers (another crime hidden there, no doubt) at the beginning of the case, consanguineous to the lowest degree with both Felicia and Honuphrius—the latter the apparent prime villain and husband of Anita. It was Magravius, who seemed to admire Honuphrius, who had been urged by the slave Mauritius to solicit Anita, seemingly under the aegis of Honuphrius himself. This, however, had come to Anita through her tirewoman Fortissa, who was or at one time had been the common-law wife of Mauritius and had borne him children—so that the whole story had to be weighed with the utmost caution. And that entire initial confession of Honuphrius had come out under torture—voluntarily consented to, to be sure, but still torture. The Fortissa-Mauritius relationship was even more dubious, really only a supposition of the commentator Father Ware—

"Ramon, give me a hand, will you?" Cleaver shouted suddenly. "I'm stuck, and—and I don't feel well."

The Jesuit biologist arose in alarm, putting the novel aside. Such an admission from Cleaver was unprecedented.

The physicist was sitting on a pouf of woven rushes, stuffed with a sphagnumlike moss, which was bulging at the equator under his weight. He was halfway out of his glass-fiber jungle suit, and his face was white and beaded with sweat, although his helmet was already off. His uncertain, stubby fingers tore at a jammed zipper.

"Paul! Why didn't you say you were ill in the first place? Here, let go of that; you're only making things worse. What happened?"

"Don't know exactly," Cleaver said, breathing heavily but relinquishing the zipper. Ruiz-Sanchez knelt beside him and began to work it carefully back onto its tracks. "Went a ways into the jungle to see if I could spot more pegmatite lies. It's been in the back of my mind that a pilot-plant for turning out tritium might locate here eventually—ought to be able to produce on a prodigious scale."

"God forbid," Ruiz-Sanchez said under his breath.

"Hm? Anyhow, I didn't see anything. A few lizards, hoppers, the usual thing. Then I ran up against a plant that looked a little like a pineapple, and one of the spines jabbed right through my suit and nicked me. Didn't seem serious, but—"

"But we don't have the suits for nothing. Let's look at it. Here, put up your feet and we'll haul those boots off. Where did you get the—oh. Well, it's angry-looking, I'll give it that. Any other symptoms?"

"My mouth feels raw," Cleaver complained.

"Open up," the Jesuit commanded. When Cleaver complied, it became evident that his complaint had been the understatement of the year. The mucosa inside his mouth was nearly covered with ugly and undoubtedly painful ulcers, their edges as sharply defined as though they had been cut with a cookie punch.

Ruiz-Sanchez made no comment, however, and deliberately changed his expression to one of carefully calculated dismissal. If the physicist needed to minimize his ailments, that was all right with Ruiz-Sanchez. An alien planet is not a good place to strip a man of his inner defenses.

"Come into the lab," he said. "You've got some inflammation in there."

Cleaver arose, a little unsteadily, and followed the Jesuit into the laboratory. There Ruiz-Sanchez took smears from several of the ulcers onto microscope slides, and Gram-stained them. He filled the time consumed by the staining process with the ritual of aiming the microscope's substage mirror out the window at a brilliant white cloud. When the timer's alarm went off, he rinsed and flame-dried the first slide and slipped it under the clips.

As he had half-feared, he saw few of the mixed bacilli and spirochetes which would have indicated a case of ordinary, Earthly, Vincent's angina—"trench mouth," which the clinical picture certainly suggested, and which he could have cured overnight with a spectrosigmin pastille. Cleaver's oral flora were normal, though on the increase because of all the exposed tissue.

"I'm going to give you a shot," Ruiz-Sanchez said gently. "And then I think you'd better go to bed."

"The hell with that," Cleaver said. "I've got nine times as much work to do as I can hope to clean up now, without any additional handicaps."

"Illness is never convenient," Ruiz-Sanchez agreed. "But why worry about losing a day or so, since you're in over your head anyhow?"

"What have I got?" Cleaver asked suspiciously.

"You haven't *got* anything," Ruiz-Sanchez said, almost regretfully. "That is, you aren't infected. But your 'pineapple' did you a bad turn. Most plants of that family on Lithia bear thorns or leaves coated with polysaccharides that are poisonous to us. The particular glucoside you ran up against today was evidently squill, or something closely related to it. It produces symptoms like those of trench mouth, but a lot harder to clear up."

"How long will that take?" Cleaver said. He was still balking, but he was on the defensive now.

"Several days at least—until you've built up an immunity. The shot I'm going to give you is a gamma globulin specific against squill, and it ought to moderate the symptoms until you've developed a high antibody titer of your own. But in the process you're going to run quite a fever, Paul; and I'll have to keep you well stuffed with antipyretics, because even a little fever is dangerous in this climate."

"I know it," Cleaver said, mollified. "The more I learn about this place, the less disposed I am to vote 'aye' when the time comes. Well, bring on your shot—and your aspirin. I suppose I ought to be glad it isn't bacterial infection, or the Snakes would be jabbing me full of antibiotics."

"Small chance of that," Ruiz-Sanchez said. "I don't doubt that the Lithians have at least a hundred different drugs we'll be able to use eventually, but—there, that's all there is to it; you can relax now—but we'll have to study their pharmacology from the ground up, first. All right, Paul, hit the hammock. In about ten minutes you're going to be wishing you'd been born dead, that I promise you."

Cleaver grinned. His sweaty face under its thatch of dirty blond hair was craggy and powerful even in illness. He stood up and deliberately rolled down his sleeve.

"Not much doubt about how you'll vote, either," he said.

"You like this planet, don't you, Ramon? It's a biologist's paradise, as far as I can see."

"I do like it," the priest said, smiling back. He followed Cleaver into the small room which served them both as sleeping quarters. Except for the window, it strongly resembled the inside of a jug. The walls were curving and continuous, and were made of some ceramic material which never beaded or felt wet, but never seemed to be quite dry, either. The hammocks were slung from hooks which projected smoothly from the walls, as though they had been baked from clay along with the rest of the house. "I wish my colleague Dr. Meid were able to see it. She would be even more delighted with it than I am."

"I don't hold with women in the sciences," Cleaver said, with abstract, irrelevant irritation. "Get their emotions all mixed up with their hypotheses. Meid—what kind of name is that, anyhow?"

"Japanese," Ruiz-Sanchez said. "Her first name is Liu—the family follows the Western custom of putting the family name last."

"Oh," Cleaver said, losing interest. "We were talking about Lithia."

"Well, don't forget that Lithia is my first extrasolar planet," Ruiz-Sanchez said. "I think I'd find *any* new, habitable world fascinating. The infinite mutability of life-forms, and the cunning inherent in each of them . . . It's all amazing, and quite delightful."

"Why shouldn't that be sufficient?" Cleaver said. "Why do you have to have the God bit too? It doesn't make sense."

"On the contrary, it's what gives everything else meaning," Ruiz-Sanchez said. "Belief and science aren't mutually exclusive—quite the contrary. But if you place scientific standards first, and exclude belief, admit nothing that's not proven, then what you have is a series of empty gestures. For me, biology *is* an act of religion, because I know that all creatures are God's—each new planet, with all its manifestations, is an affirmation of God's power."

"A dedicated man," Cleaver said. "All right. So am I. To the greater glory of man, that's what *I* say."

He sprawled heavily in his hammock. After a decent interval, Ruiz-Sanchez took the liberty of heaving up after him the foot he seemed to have forgotten. Cleaver didn't notice. The reaction was setting in.

"Exactly so," Ruiz-Sanchez said. "But that's only half the story. The other half reads, '. . . and to the greater glory of God.' "

"Read me no tracts, Father," Cleaver said. Then: "I didn't mean that. I'm sorry. . . . But for a physicist, this place is hell. . . . You'd better get me that aspirin. I'm cold."

"Surely, Paul."

Ruiz-Sanchez went quickly back into the lab, made up a salicylate-barbiturate paste in one of the Lithians' superb mortars, and pressed it into a set of pills. (Storing such pills was impossible in Lithia's humid atmosphere; they were too hygroscopic.) He wished he could stamp each pill "Bayer" before it set—if Cleaver's personal cure-all was aspirin, it would have been just as well to let him think he was taking aspirin—but of course he had no dies for the purpose. He took two of the pills back to Cleaver, with a mug and a carafe of Berkefeld-filtered water.

The big man was already asleep; Ruiz-Sanchez woke him, more or less. Cleaver would sleep longer, and awaken farther along the road to recovery, for having been done that small unkindness now. As it was, he hardly noticed when the pills were put down him, and soon resumed his heavy, troubled breathing.

That done, Ruiz-Sanchez returned to the front room of the house, sat down, and began to inspect the jungle suit. The tear which the plant spine had made was not difficult to find, and would be easy to repair. It would be much harder to repair Cleaver's notion that the defenses of Earthmen on Lithia were invulnerable, and that plant spines could be blundered against with impunity. Ruiz-Sanchez wondered whether either of the other two members of the Lithian Review Commission still shared that notion.

Cleaver had called the thing which had brought him low a "pineapple." Any biologist could have told Cleaver that even on Earth the pineapple is a prolific and dangerous weed, edible only by a happy and irrelevant accident. In Hawaii, as Ruiz-Sanchez remembered, the tropical forest was quite impassable to anyone not wearing heavy boots and tough trousers. Even inside the Dole plantations, the close-packed irrepressible pineapples could tear unprotected legs to ribbons.

The Jesuit turned the suit over. The zipper that Cleaver had jammed was made of a plastic into the molecule of which had been incorporated radicals from various terrestrial antifungal substances, chiefly the protoplasmic poison thiolutin. The fungi of Lithia respected these, all right, but the elaborate molecule of the plastic itself had a tendency, under Lithian humidities and heats, to undergo polymerization more or less spontaneously. That was what had happened here. One of the teeth of the zipper had changed into something resembling a kernel of popped corn.

The air grew dark as Ruiz-Sanchez worked. There was a muted puff of sound, and the room was illuminated with small, soft yellow flames from recesses in every wall. The burning substance was natural gas, of which Lithia had an inexhaustible and constantly renewed supply. The flames were lit by adsorption against a catalyst, as soon as the gas came on from the system. A lime mantle, which worked on a rack and pinion of heatproof glass, could be moved into the flame to provide a brighter light; but the priest liked the yellow light the Lithians themselves preferred, and used the limelight only in the laboratory.

For some purposes, of course, the Earthmen had to have electricity, for which they had been forced to supply their own generators. The Lithians had a far more advanced science of electrostatics than Earth had, but of electrodynamics they knew comparatively little. They had discovered magnetism only a few years before the Commission had arrived, since natural magnets were unknown on the planet. They had first observed the phenomenon, not in iron, of which they had next to none, but in liquid oxygen—a difficult substance from which to make generator cores!

The results in terms of Lithian civilization were peculiar, to an Earthman. The twelve-foot-tall, reptilian people had built several huge electrostatic generators and scores of little ones, but had nothing even vaguely resembling telephones. They knew a great deal on the practical level about electrolysis, but carrying a current over a long distance—say a mile—was regarded by them as a technical triumph. They had no electric motors as an Earthman would understand the term, but made fast intercontinental flights in jet aircraft powered by *static* electricity. Cleaver said he understood this feat, but Ruiz-Sanchez certainly did not (and after Cleaver's description of electron-ion plasmas heated by radio-frequency induction, he felt more in the dark than ever).

They had a completely marvelous radio network, which

among other things provided a "live" navigational grid for the whole planet, zeroed on (and here perhaps was the epitome of the Lithian genius for paradox) a tree. Yet they had never produced a standardized vacuum tube, and their atomic theory was not much more sophisticated than Democritus' had been!

These paradoxes, of course, could be explained in part by the things that Lithia lacked. Like any large rotating mass, Lithia had a magnetic field of its own, but a planet which almost entirely lacks iron provides its people with no easy way to discover magnetism. Radioactivity had been entirely unknown on the surface of Lithia, at least until the Earthmen had arrived, which explained the hazy atomic theory. Like the Greeks, the Lithians had discovered that friction between silk and glass produces one kind of energy or charge, and between silk and amber another; they had gone on from there to van de Graaf generators, electrochemistry, and the static jet—but without suitable metals they were unable to make heavy-duty batteries, or to do more than begin to study electricity in motion.

In the fields where they had been given fair clues, they had made enormous progress. Despite the constant cloudiness and endemic drizzle, their descriptive astronomy was excellent, thanks to the fortunate presence of a small moon which had drawn their attention outward early. This in turn made for basic advances in optics, and thence for a downright staggering versatility in the working of glass. Their chemistry took full advantage of both the seas and the jungles. From the one they took such vital and diversified products as agar, iodine, salt, trace metals, and foods of many kinds. The other provided nearly everything else that they needed: resins, rubbers, woods of all degrees of hardness, edible and essential oils, vegetable "butters," rope and other fibers, fruits and nuts, tannins, dyes, drugs, cork, paper. Indeed, the sole forest product which they did *not* take was game, and the reason for this neglect was hard to find. It seemed to the Jesuit to be religious—yet the Lithians had no religion, and they certainly ate many of the creatures of the sea without qualms of conscience.

He dropped the jungle suit into his lap with a sigh, though the popcorned tooth still was not completely trimmed back into shape. Outside, in the humid darkness, Lithia was in full concert. It was a vital, somehow fresh, new-sounding drone, covering most of the sound spectrum audible to an Earthman. It came from the myriad insects of Lithia. Many of these had wiry, trilling songs, almost like birds, in addition to the scrapes and chirrups and wing-case buzzes of the insects of Earth. In a way this was lucky, for there were no birds on Lithia.

Had Eden sounded like that, before evil had come into the world? Ruiz-Sanchez wondered. Certainly his native Peru sang no such song . . .

Qualms of conscience—these were, in the long run, his essential business, rather than the taxonomical mazes of biology, which had already become tangled into near-hopelessness on Earth before space flight had come along to add whole new layers of labyrinths for each planet, new dimensions of labryrinths for each star. It was only interesting that the Lithians were bipedal, evolved from reptiles, with marsupial-like pouches and pteropsid circulatory systems. But it was vital that they had qualms of conscience—if they did.

The calendar caught his eye. It was an "art" calendar Cleaver had produced from his luggage back in the beginning; the girl on it was now unintentionally modest beneath large patches of brilliant orange mold. The date was April 19, 2049. Almost Easter—the most pointed of reminders that to the inner life, the body was only a garment. To Ruiz-Sanchez personally, however, the year date was almost equally significant, for 2050 was to be a Holy Year.

The Church had returned to the ancient custom, first recognized officially in 1300 by Boniface VIII, of proclaiming the great pardon only once every half-century. If Ruiz-Sanchez was not in Rome next year when the Holy Door was opened, it would never be opened again in his lifetime.

Hurry, hurry! some personal demon whispered inside his brain. Or was it the voice of his own conscience? Were his sins already so burdensome—unknown to himself—as to put him in mortal need of the pilgrimage? Or was that, in turn, only a minor temptation, to the sin of pride?

In any event, the work could not be hurried. He and the other three men were on Lithia to decide whether or not the planet would be suitable as a port of call for Earth, without risk of damage either to Earthmen or to Lithians. The other three men on the commission were primarily scientists, as was Ruiz-Sanchez; but he knew that his own recommendation would in the long run depend upon conscience, not upon taxonomy.

And conscience, like creation, cannot be hurried. It cannot even be scheduled.

He looked down at the still-imperfect jungle suit with a troubled face until he heard Cleaver moan. Then he arose and left the room to the softly hissing flames.

From the oval front window of the house to which Cleaver and Ruiz-Sanchez had been assigned, the land slanted away with insidious gentleness toward the ill-defined south edge of Lower Bay, a part of the Gulf of Sfath. Most of the area was salt marsh, as was the seaside nearly everywhere on Lithia. When the tide was in, the flats were covered to a depth of a yard or so almost half the way to the house. When it was out, as it was tonight, the jungle symphony was augmented by the agonized barking of a species of lungfish, sometimes as many as a score of them at once. Occasionally, when the small moon was unoccluded and the light from the city was unusually bright, one could see the leaping shadow of some amphibian, or the sinuously advancing sigmoid track of the Lithian crocodile, in pursuit of some prey faster than itself but which it would nonetheless capture in its own geological good time.

Still farther—and usually invisible even in daytime because of the pervasive mists—was the opposite shore of Lower Bay, beginning with tidal flats again, and then more jungle, which ran unbroken thereafter for hundreds of miles north to the equatorial sea.

Behind the house, visible from the sleeping room, was the

rest of the city, Xoredeshch Sfath, capital of the great southern continent. As was the case in all the cities the Lithians built, its most striking characteristic to an Earthman was that it hardly seemed to be there at all. The Lithian houses were low, and made of the earth which had been dug from their foundations, so that, even to a trained observer, they seemed to fade into the soil.

Most of the older buildings were rectangular, put together without mortar of rammed-earth blocks. Over the course of decades the blocks continued to pack and settle themselves until it became easier to abandon an unwanted building than to tear it down. One of the first setbacks the Earthmen had suffered on Lithia had come about through Agronski's ill-advised offer to raze one such creature with TDX; this was a gravity-polarized explosive, unknown to the Lithians, which had the property of exploding in a flat plane which could cut through steel girders as if they were cheese. The warehouse in question, however, was large, thick-walled, and three Lithian centuries old—312 years by Earth time. The explosion created an uproar which greatly distressed the Lithians, but when it was over, the storehouse still stood, unshaken.

Newer structures were more conspicuous when the sun was out, for just during the past half-century had the Lithians begun to apply their enormous knowledge of ceramics to house construction. The new houses assumed thousands of fantastic, quasi-biological shapes, not quite amorphous but not quite resembling any form in experience, either; they looked a little like the dream constructions once made, by an Earth painter named Dalí, out of such materials as boiled beans. Each one was unique and to the choice of its owner, yet all markedly shared the character of the community and the earth from which they sprang. These houses, too, would have blended well with the background of soil and jungle, except that most of them were glazed and so shone blindingly for brief moments on sunny days, when the light and the angle of observation were just right. These shifting coruscations, seen from the air, had been the Earthmen's first clue as to where the intelligent life was hiding in the ubiquitous Lithian jungle. (There had never been any doubt that there was intelligent life there; the tremendous radio pulses emanating from the planet had made that plain from afar.)

Ruiz-Sanchez looked out through the sleeping-room window at the city, for at least the ten thousandth time, on his way to Cleaver's hammock. Xoredeshch Sfath was alive to him; it never looked the same twice. He found it singularly beautiful. And singularly strange: though the cities of Earth were very various, none was like this.

He checked Cleaver's pulse and respiration. Both were fast, even for Lithia, where a high partial pressure of carbon dioxide raised the pH of the blood of Earthmen and stimulated the breathing reflex. The priest judged, however, that Cleaver was in little danger as long as his actual oxygen utilization was not increased. At the moment he was certainly sleeping deeply—if not very restfully—and it would do no harm to leave him alone for a little while.

Of course, if a wild allosaur blundered into the city . . . But that was just about as likely as the blundering of an untended elephant into the heart of New Delhi. It could happen, but it almost never did. And no other dangerous Lithian animal could break into the house if it was closed. Even the rats—or the abundant monotreme creatures which were Lithia's equivalent—found it impossible to infest a pottery house.

Ruiz-Sanchez changed the carafe of fresh water in the niche beside the hammock, went into the hall, and donned boots, mackintosh and waterproof hat. The night sounds of Lithia burst in upon him as he opened the stone door, along with a gust of sea air bearing the characteristic halogen odor always called "salty." There was a thin drizzle falling, making halos around the lights of Xoredeshch Sfath. Far out, on the water, another light moved. That was probably the coastal side-wheeler to Yllith, the enormous island which stood athwart the Upper Bay, barring the Gulf of Sfath as a whole from the equatorial sea.

Outside, Ruiz-Sanchez turned the wheel which extended bolts on every margin of the door. Drawing from his mackintosh a piece of soft chalk, he marked on the sheltered tablet, designed for such uses, the Lithian symbols which meant "Illness is here." That would be sufficient. Anybody who chose to could open the door simply by turning the wheel—the Lithians had never heard of locks—but the Lithians, too, were overridingly social beings, who respected their own conventions as they respected natural law.

That done, Ruiz-Sanchez set out for the center of the city and the Message Tree. The asphalt streets shone in the yellow lights cast from windows, and in the white light of the mantled, wide-spaced street lanterns. Occasionally he passed the twelve-foot, kangaroo-like shape of a Lithian, and the two exchanged glances of frank curiosity, but there were not many Lithians abroad now. They kept to their houses at night, doing Ruiz-Sanchez knew not what. He could see them frequently, alone or by twos or threes, moving behind the oval windows of the houses he passed. Sometimes they seemed to be talking.

What about?

It was a nice question. The Lithians had no crime, no newspapers, no house-to-house communications systems, no arts that could be differentiated clearly from their crafts, no political parties, no public amusements, no nations, no games, no religions, no sports, no cults, no celebrations. Surely they didn't spend every waking minute of their lives exchanging knowledge, making things go, discussing philosophy or history, or planning for tomorrow! Or did they? Perhaps, Ruiz-Sanchez thought suddenly, they simply went inert once they were inside their jugs, like so many pickles! But even as the thought came, the priest passed another house, and saw their silhouettes moving to and fro. . . .

A puff of wind scattered cool droplets in his face. Automatically, he quickened his step. If the night were to turn out to be especially windy, there would doubtless be many voices coming and going in the Message Tree. It loomed ahead of him now, a sequoialike giant, standing at the mouth of the valley of the River Sfath—the valley which led in great serpentine folds into the heart of the continent, where Gleshchtehk Sfath, or Blood Lake in English, poured out its massive torrents.

As the winds came and went along the valley, the tree nodded and swayed—only a little, but that little was enough. With every movement, the tree's root system, which underlay the entire city, tugged and distorted the buried crystalline cliff upon which the city had been founded, as long ago in Lithian pre-history as was the founding of Rome on Earth. At every such pressure, the buried cliff responded with a vast heart-pulse of radio waves—a pulse detectable not only all over Lithia, but far out in space as well. The four Commission members had heard those pulses first on shipboard, when Alpha Arietis, Lithia's sun, was still only a point of light ahead of them, and had looked into each other's faces with eyes gleaming with conjecture.

The bursts, however, were sheer noise. How the Lithians modulated them to carry information—not only messages, but the amazing navigational grid, the planet-wide time-signal system, and much more—was something as remote from Ruiz-Sanchez' understanding as affine theory, although Cleaver said it was all perfectly simple once you understood it. It had something to do with semi-conduction and solid-state physics, which (again according to Cleaver) the Lithians understood better than any Earthman.

A free-association jump which startled him momentarily reminded him of the current *doyen* of Earthly affine theory, a man who signed his papers "H. O. Petard," though his real (if scarcely more likely) name was Lucien le Comte des Bois-d'Averoigne. Nor was the association as free as it appeared on the surface, Ruiz-Sanchez realized, for the count was a striking example of the now almost total alienation of modern physics from the common physical experiences of mankind. His title was not a patent of nobility, but merely a part of his name which had been maintained in his family long after the political system which had granted the patent had vanished away, a victim of the dividing up of Earth under the Shelter economy. There was more honor appertaining to the name itself than to the title, for the count had pretensions to hereditary grandeur which reached all the way back into thirteenth-century England, to the author of *Lucien Wycham His Boke of Magick.*

A high ecclesiastic heritage to be sure, but the latter-day Lucien, a lapsed Catholic, was a political figure, insofar as the Shelter economy sheltered any such thing: he carried the additional title of Procurator of Canarsie—a title which a moment's examination would also show to be nonsense, but which paid a small honorarium in exemptions from weekly labor. The subdivided and deeply buried world of Earth was full of such labels, all of them pasted on top of large sums of money which had no place to go now that speculation was dead and shareholding had become the only way by which an ordinary citizen could exercise any control over the keeps in which he lived. The remaining fortune-holders had no outlet left but that of conspicuous consumption, on a scale which would have made Veblen doubt that there had ever been such a thing in the world before. Had they attempted to assert any control over the economy they would have been toppled, if not by the shareholders, then by the grim defenders of the by now indefensible Shelter cities.

Not that the count was a drone. At last reports, he had been involved in some highly esoteric tampering with the Haertel equations—that description of the space-time continuum which, by swallowing up the Lorentz-Fitzgerald contraction exactly as Einstein had swallowed Newton (that is, alive), had made interstellar flight possible. Ruiz-Sanchez did not understand a word of it, but, he reflected with amusement, it was doubtless perfectly simple once you understood it.

Almost all knowledge, after all, fell into that category. It was either perfectly simple once you understood it, or else it fell apart into fiction. As a Jesuit—even here, fifty light-years from Rome—Ruiz-Sanchez knew something about knowledge that Lucien le Comte des Bois-d'Averoigne had forgotten, and that Cleaver would never learn: that all knowledge goes through *both* stages, the annunciation out of noise into fact, and the disintegration back into noise again. The process involved was the making of increasingly finer distinctions. The outcome was an endless series of theoretical catastrophes.

The residuum was faith.

* * *

The high, sharply vaulted chamber, like an egg stood on its large end, which had been burned out in the base of the Message Tree, was droning with life as Ruiz-Sanchez entered it. It would have been difficult to imagine anything less like an Earthly telegraph office or other message center, however.

Around the circumference of the lower end of the egg there was a continual whirling of tall figures, Lithians, entering and leaving through the many doorless entrances, and changing places in the swirl of movement like so many electrons passing from orbit to orbit. Despite their numbers, their voices were pitched so low that Ruiz-Sanchez could hear, blended in with their murmuring, the soughing of the wind through the enormous branches far above.

The inner side of this band of moving figures was bounded by a high railing of black, polished wood, evidently cut from the phloem of the Tree itself. On the other side of this token division, which reminded Ruiz-Sanchez irresistibly of the Encke division in the Saturnian rings, a thin circlet of Lithians took and passed out messages steadily and without a moment's break, handling the total load faultlessly—if one were to judge by the way the outer band was kept in motion—and without apparent effort, by memory alone. Occasionally one of these specialists would leave the circlet and go to one of the desks which were scattered over most of the rest of the sloping floor, increasingly thinly, like a Crape ring, to confer there with the desk's occupant. Then he went back to the black rail, or sometimes he took the desk, and its previous occupant went to the rail.

The bowl deepened, the desks thinned, and at the very center stood a single, aged Lithian, his hands clapped to the ear whorls behind his heavy jaws, his eyes covered by their nictitating membranes, only his nasal fossae and heat-receptive post-nasal pits uncovered. He spoke to no one, and no one consulted him—but the absolute stasis in which he stood was obviously the reason, the sole reason, for the torrents and counter-torrents of people which poured along the outermost ring.

Ruiz-Sanchez stopped, astonished. He had never been to the Message Tree himself before—communicating with Michelis and Agronski, the other two Earthmen on Lithia, had until now been one of Cleaver's tasks—and the priest found that he had no idea what to do. The scene before him was more suggestive of a bourse than of a message center in any ordinary sense. It seemed unlikely that so many Lithians could have urgent personal messages to send each time the winds were active; yet it seemed equally uncharacteristic that the Lithians, with their stable, abundance-based economy, should have any equivalent of stock or commodity brokerage.

There seemed to be no choice, however, but to plunge in, try to reach the polished black rail, and ask one of the Lithians who stood on the other side to try to raise Agronski or Michelis again. At worst, he supposed, he could only be refused, or fail to get a hearing at all. He took a deep breath.

Simultaneously his left arm was caught in a firm four-fingered grip which ran all the way from his elbow to his shoulder. Letting the stored breath out again in a snort of surprise, the priest looked around and up at the solicitously bent head of a Lithian. Under the long, trap-like mouth, the being's wattles were a delicate, curious aquamarine, in contrast to its vestigial comb, which was a permanent and silvery sapphire, shot through with veins of fuchsia.

"You are Ruiz-Sanchez," the Lithian said in his own language. The priest's name, unlike those of the other Earthmen, fell easily in that tongue. "I know you by your robe."

That was pure accident. Any Earthman out in the rain in a mackintosh would have been identified as Ruiz-Sanchez, because the priest was the only Earthman who seemed to the Lithians to wear the same garment indoors and out.

"I am," Ruiz-Sanchez said, a little apprehensively.

"I am Chtexa, the metallurgist, who consulted with you earlier on problems of chemistry and medicine and your mission here, and some other smaller matters."

"Oh. Yes, of course; I should have remembered your comb."

"You do me honor. We have not seen you here before. Do you wish to talk with the Tree?"

"I do," Ruiz-Sanchez said gratefully. "It is true that I am new here. Can you explain to me what to do?"

"Yes, but not to any profit," Chtexa said, tilting his head so that his completely inky pupils shone down into Ruiz-Sanchez' eyes. "One must have observed the ritual, which is very complex, until it is habit. We have grown up with it, but I think you lack the coordination to follow it on the first attempt. If I may bear your message instead—"

"I would be most indebted. It is for our colleagues Agronski and Michelis; they are at Xoredeshch Gton on the northeast continent, at about thirty-two degrees east, thirty-two degrees north—"

"Yes, the second bench mark at the outlet of the Lesser Lakes; that is the city of the potters, I know it well. And you would say?"

"That they are to join us now, here, at Xoredeshch Sfath. And that our time on Lithia is almost up."

"That me regards," Chtexa said. "But I will bear it."

The Lithian leapt into the whirling cloud, and Ruiz-Sanchez was left behind, considering again his thankfulness that he had been moved to study the painfully difficult Lithian language. Two of the four commission members had shown a regrettable lack of interest in that world-wide tongue: "Let 'em learn English" had been Cleaver's unknowingly classic formulation. Ruiz-Sanchez had been all the less likely to view this notion sympathetically for the facts that his own native language was Spanish, and that, of the five foreign languages in which he was really fluent, the one he liked best was West High German.

Agronski had taken a slightly more sophisticated stand. It was not, he said, that Lithian was too difficult to pronounce—certainly it wasn't any harder on the soft palate than Arabic or Russian—but, after all, "it's hopeless to attempt to grasp the concepts that lie *behind* a really alien language, isn't it? At least in the time we have to spend here?"

To both views, Michelis had said nothing; he had simply set out to learn to read the language first, and if he found his way from there into speaking it, he would not be surprised and neither would his confreres. That was Michelis' way of doing things, thorough and untheoretical at the same time. As for the other two approaches, Ruiz-Sanchez thought privately that it was close to criminal to allow any contact man for a new planet ever to leave Earth with such parochial notions. In understanding a new culture, language is of the essence; if one doesn't start here, where under God does one start?

Of Cleaver's penchant for referring to the Lithians themselves as "the Snakes," Ruiz-Sanchez' opinion was of a color admissible only to his remote confessor.

And in view of what lay before him now in this egg-shaped

hollow, what was Ruiz-Sanchez to think of Cleaver's conduct as communications officer for the commission? Surely he could never have transmitted or received a single message through the Tree, as he had claimed to have done. Probably he had never been closer to the Tree than Ruiz-Sanchez was now.

Of course, it went without saying that he had been in contact with Agronski and Michelis by *some* method, but that method had evidently been something private—a transmitter concealed in his luggage, or . . . No, that wouldn't do. Physicist though he most definitely was not, Ruiz-Sanchez rejected that solution on the spot; he had some idea of the practical difficulties of operating a ham radio on a world like Lithia, swamped as that world was on all wave-lengths by the tremendous pulses which the Tree wrung from the buried crystalline cliffs. The problem was beginning to make him feel decidedly uncomfortable.

Then Chtexa was back, recognizable not as much by any physical detail—for his wattles were now the same ambiguous royal purple as those of most of the other Lithians in the crowd—as by the fact that he was bearing down upon the Earthman.

"I have sent your message," he said at once. "It is recorded at Xoredeshch Gton. But the other Earthmen are not there. They have not been in the city for some days."

That was impossible. Cleaver had said he had spoken to Michelis only a day ago. "Are you sure?" Ruiz-Sanchez said cautiously.

"It admits of no uncertainty. The house which we gave them stands empty. The many things which they brought with them to the house are gone." The tall shape raised its four-fingered hands in a gesture which might have been solicitous. "I think this is an ill word. I dislike to bring it you. The words you brought me when first we met were full of good."

"Thank you. Don't worry," Ruiz-Sanchez said distractedly. "No man could hold the bearer responsible for the word, surely."

"The bearer also has responsibilities; at least, that is our custom," Chtexa said. "No act is wholly free. And as we see it, you have lost by our exchange. Your words on iron have been shown to contain great good. I would take pleasure in showing you how we have used them, especially since I have brought you in return an ill message. If you could share my house tonight, without prejudice to your work, I could expose this matter. Is that possible?"

Sternly Ruiz-Sanchez stifled his sudden excitement. Here was the first chance, at long last, to see something of the private life of Lithia, and through that, perhaps, to gain some inkling of the moral life, the role in which God had cast the Lithians in the ancient drama of good and evil, in the past and in the times to come. Until that was known, the Lithians in their Eden might be only spuriously good: all reason, all organic thinking machines, ULTIMACs with tails—and without souls.

But there remained the hard fact that he had left behind in his house a sick man. There was not much chance that Cleaver would awaken before morning. He had been given nearly fifteen milligrams of sedative per kilogram of body weight. But sick men are like children, whose schedules persistently defy all rules. If Cleaver's burly frame should somehow throw that dose off, driven perhaps by some anaphylactic crisis impossible to rule out this early in his illness, he would need prompt attention. At the very least, he would want badly for the sound of a human voice on this planet which he hated, and which had struck him down almost without noticing that he existed.

Still, the danger to Cleaver was not great. He most certainly did not require a minute-by-minute vigil; he was, after all, not a child, but an almost ostentatiously strong man.

And there was such a thing as an excess of devotion, a form of pride among the pious which the Church had long found peculiarly difficult to make clear to them. At its worst, it produced the hospital saints, whose attraction to noisomeness so peculiarly resembled the vermin-worship of the Hindi sects—or a St. Simon Stylites, who though undoubtedly acceptable to God had been for centuries very bad public relations for the Church. And had Cleaver really earned the kind of devotion Ruiz-Sanchez had been proposing, up to now, to tender him as a creature of God—or, to come closer to the mark, a godly creature?

And with a whole planet at stake, a whole people—no, more than that, a whole problem in theology, an imminent solution to the vast, tragic riddle of original sin . . . What a gift to bring to the Holy Father in a jubilee year—a grander and more solemn thing than the proclamation of the conquest of Everest had been at the coronation of Elizabeth II of England!

Always providing, of course, that this would be the ultimate outcome of the study of Lithia. The planet was not lacking in hints that something quite different, and fearful beyond all else, might emerge under Ruiz-Sanchez' prolonged attention. Not even prayer had yet resolved that doubt. But should he sacrifice even the possibility of this, for Cleaver?

A lifetime of meditation over just such cases of conscience had made Ruiz-Sanchez, like most other gifted members of his order, quick to find his way to a decision through all but the most complicated of ethical labyrinths. All Catholics must be devout; but a Jesuit must be, in addition, agile.

"Thank you," he said to Chtexa, a little shakily. "I will share your house very gladly."

THREE

(A voice): "Cleaver? Cleaver! Wake up, you big slob. Cleaver! Where the hell have you been?"

Cleaver groaned and tried to turn over. At his first motion, the world began to rock, gently, sickeningly. He was awash in fever. His mouth seemed to be filled with burning pitch.

"Cleaver, turn out. It's me—Agronski. Where's the Father? What's wrong? Why didn't we ever hear from you? *Look out,* you'll—"

The warning came too late, and Cleaver could not have understood it anyhow. He had been profoundly asleep, and had no notion of his situation in space or time. At his convulsive twist away from the nagging voice, the hammock rotated on its hooks and dumped him.

He struck the floor stunningly, taking the main blow across his right shoulder, though he hardly felt it yet. His feet, not yet part of him at all, still remained far aloft, twisted in the hammock webbing.

"What the hell—"

There was a brief chain of footsteps, like chestnuts dropping on a roof, and then a hollow noise of something hitting the floor near his head.

"Cleaver, are you sick? Here, lie still a minute and let me get your feet free. Mike—Mike, can't you turn the gas up in this jug? Something's wrong back here."

After a moment, yellow light began to pour from the glistening walls, and then the white glare of the mantles. Cleaver dragged an arm across his eyes, but it did him no good; it tired too quickly. Agronski's mild face, plump and anxious, floated directly above him like a captive balloon. He could not see Michelis anywhere, and at the moment he was just as glad he couldn't. Agronski's presence was hard enough to understand.

"How . . . the hell . . ." he said. At the words, his lips split painfully at both corners. He realized for the first time that they had become gummed together, somehow, while he was asleep. He had no idea how long he had been out of the picture.

Agronski seemed to understand the aborted question. "We came in from the Lakes in the 'copter," he said. "We didn't like the silence down here, and we figured we'd better come in under our own power, instead of registering in on the regular jet liner and tipping the Lithians off—just in case there'd been any dirty work afloat—"

"Stop jawing him," Michelis said, appearing suddenly, magically in the doorway. "He's got a bug, that's obvious. I don't like to feel pleased about misery, but I'm glad it's that instead of the Lithians."

The rangy, long-jawed chemist helped Agronski lift Cleaver to his feet. Tentatively, despite the pain, Cleaver got his mouth open again. Nothing came out but a hoarse croak.

"Shut up," Michelis said, not unkindly. "Let's get him back into the hammock. Where's the Father, I wonder? He's the only one capable of dealing with sickness here."

"I'll bet he's dead," Agronski burst out suddenly, his face

glistening with alarm. "He'd be here if he could. It must be catching, Mike."

"I didn't bring my mitt," Michelis said drily. "Cleaver, lie still or I'll have to clobber you. Agronski, you seem to have dumped his water bottle; better go get him some more, he needs it. And see if the Father left anything in the lab that looks like medicine."

Agronski went out, and, maddeningly, so did Michelis—at least out of Cleaver's field of vision. Setting his every muscle against the pain, Cleaver pulled his lips apart once more.

"Mike."

Instantly, Michelis was there. He had a pad of cotton between thumb and forefinger, wet with some solution, with which he gently cleaned Cleaver's lips and chin.

"Easy. Agronski's getting you a drink. We'll let you talk in a little while, Paul. Don't rush it."

Cleaver relaxed a little. He could trust Michelis. Nevertheless, the vivid and absurd insult of having to be swabbed like a baby was more than he could bear; he felt tears of helpless rage swelling on either side of his nose. With two deft, noncommittal swipes, Michelis removed them.

Agronski came back, holding out one hand tentatively, palm up.

"I found these," he said. "There's more in the lab, and the Father's pill press is still out. So are his mortar and pestle, though they've been cleaned."

"All right, let's have 'em," Michelis said. "Anything else?"

"No. Well, there's a syringe cooking in the sterilizer, if that means anything."

Michelis swore briefly and to the point.

"It means that there's a pertinent antitoxin in the shop

someplace," he added. "But unless Ramon left notes, we'll not have a prayer of figuring out which one it is."

As he spoke, he lifted Cleaver's head and tipped the pills into his mouth, onto his tongue. The water which followed was cold at the first contact, but a split second later it was liquid fire. Cleaver choked, and at that precise instant Michelis pinched his nostrils shut. The pills went down with a gulp.

"There's no sign of the Father?" Michelis said.

"Not a one, Mike. Everything's in good order, and his gear's still here. Both jungle suits are in the locker."

"Maybe he went visiting," Michelis said thoughtfully. "He must have gotten to know quite a few of the Lithians by now. He liked them."

"With a sick man on his hands? That's not like him, Mike. Not unless there was some kind of emergency. Or maybe he went on a routine errand, expected to be back in just a few minutes, and—"

"And was set upon by trolls, for forgetting to stamp his foot three times before crossing a bridge."

"All right, laugh."

"I'm not laughing, believe me. That's just the kind of damn fool thing that can kill a man in a strange culture. But somehow I can't see it happening to Ramon."

"Mike . . ."

Michelis took a step and looked down at Cleaver. His face was drifting as if detached through a haze of tears. He said:

"All right, Paul. Tell us what it is. We're listening."

But it was too late. The doubled sedative dose had gotten to Cleaver first. He could only shake his head, and with the motion Michelis seemed to go reeling away into a whirlpool of fuzzy rainbows.

* * *

Curiously, he did not quite go to sleep. He had had nearly a normal night's sleep, and he had started out his enormously long day a powerful and healthy man. The conversation of the two commissioners, and an obsessive consciousness of his need to speak to them before Ruiz-Sanchez returned, helped to keep him, if not totally awake, at least not far below a state of light trance. In addition, the presence in his system of thirty grains of acetylsalicylic acid had seriously raised his oxygen consumption, bringing with it not only dizziness but also a precarious, emotionally untethered alertness. That the fuel which was being burned to maintain it was in part the protein substrate of his own cells he did not know, and it could not have alarmed him had he known it.

The voices continued to reach him, and to convey a little meaning. With them were mixed fleeting, fragmentary dreams, so slightly removed from the surface of his waking life as to seem peculiarly real, yet at the same time peculiarly pointless and depressing. In the semiconscious intervals there came plans, a whole succession of them, all simple and grandiose at once, for taking command of the expedition, for communicating with the authorities on Earth, for bringing forward secret papers proving that Lithia was uninhabitable, for digging a tunnel under Mexico to Peru, for detonating Lithia in one single mighty fusion of all its lightweight atoms into one single atom of cleaverium, the element of which the monobloc had been made, whose cardinal number was Aleph-Null . . .

AGRONSKI: Mike, come here and look at this; you read Lithian. There's a mark on the front door, on the message tablet.

(Footsteps.)

MICHELIS: It says "Sickness inside." The strokes aren't casual or deft enough to be the work of the natives. Ideograms are hard to write rapidly without long practice. Ramon must have written it there.

AGRONSKI: I wish we knew where he went afterwards. Funny we didn't see it when we came in.

MICHELIS: I don't think so. It was dark, and we weren't looking for it.

(Footsteps. Door shutting, not loudly. Footsteps. Hassock creaking.)

AGRONSKI: Well, we'd better start thinking about getting up a report. Unless this damn twenty-hour day has me thrown completely off, our time's just about up. Are you still set on opening up the planet?

MICHELIS: Yes. I've seen nothing to convince me that there's anything on Lithia that's dangerous to us. Except maybe Cleaver in there, and I'm not prepared to say that the Father would have left him if he were in any serious danger. And I don't see how Earthmen could harm this society; it's too stable emotionally, economically, in every other way.

(Danger, danger, *said somebody in Cleaver's dream.* It will explode. It's all a popish plot. *Then he was marginally awake again, and conscious of how much his mouth hurt.*)

AGRONSKI: Why do you suppose those two jokers never called us after we went north?

MICHELIS: I don't have any answer. I won't even guess until I talk to Ramon. Or until Paul's able to sit up and take notice.

AGRONSKI: I don't like it, Mike. It smells bad to me. This town's right at the heart of the communications system of the planet—that's why we picked it, for Crisake! And yet—no messages, Cleaver sick, the Father not here . . . There's a hell of a lot we don't know about Lithia, that's for damn sure.

MICHELIS: There's a hell of a lot we don't know about central Brazil—let alone Mars, or the Moon.

AGRONSKI: Nothing essential, Mike. What we know about the periphery of Brazil gives us all the clues we need about the interior—even to those fish that eat people, the what-are-they, the piranhas. That's not true on Lithia. We don't know whether our peripheral clues about Lithia are germane or just incidental. Something enormous could be hidden under the surface without our being able to detect it.

MICHELIS: Agronski, stop sounding like a Sunday supplement. You underestimate your own intelligence. What kind of enormous secret could that be? That the Lithians eat people? That they're cattle for unknown gods that live in the jungle? That they're actually mind-wrenching, soul-twisting, heart-stopping, blood-freezing, bowel-moving superbeings in disguise? The moment you state any such proposition, you'll deflate it yourself; it's only in the abstract that it's able to scare you. I wouldn't even take the trouble of examining it, or discussing how we might meet it if it were true.

AGRONSKI: All right, all right. I'll reserve judgment for the time being, anyhow. If everything turns out to be all right here, with the Father and Cleaver I mean, I'll probably go along with you. I don't have any reason I could defend for voting against the planet, I admit that.

MICHELIS: Good for you. I'm sure Ramon is for opening it up, so that should make it unanimous. I can't see why Cleaver would object.

(Cleaver was testifying before a packed court convened in the UN General Assembly chambers in New York, with one finger pointed dramatically, but less in triumph than in

sorrow, at Ramon Ruiz-Sanchez, S.J. At the sound of his name the dream collapsed, and he realized that the room had grown a little lighter. Dawn—or the dripping, wool-gray travesty of it which prevailed on Lithia—was on its way.

He wondered what he had just said to the court. It had been conclusive, damning, good enough to be used when he awoke; but he could not remember a word of it. All that remained of it was a sensation, almost the taste of the words, but nothing of their substance.)

AGRONSKI: It's getting light. I suppose we'd better knock off.

MICHELIS: Did you stake down the 'copter? The winds down here are higher than they are up north, I seem to remember.

AGRONSKI: Yes. And covered it with the tarp. Nothing left to do now but sling our hammocks—

(A sound)

MICHELIS: Shhh. What's that?

AGRONSKI: Eh?

MICHELIS: Listen.

(Footsteps. Faint ones, but Cleaver knew them. He forced his eyes to open a little, but there was nothing to see but the ceiling. Its even color, and its smooth, ever-changing slope into a dome of nowhereness, drew him almost immediately upward into the mists of trance once more.)

AGRONSKI: Somebody's coming.

(Footsteps.)

AGRONSKI: It's the Father, Mike—look out here and you can see him. He seems to be all right. Dragging his feet a bit, but who wouldn't after being out helling all night?

MICHELIS: Maybe you'd better meet him at the door. It'd probably be better than our springing out at him after he gets inside. After all he doesn't expect us. I'll get to unpacking the hammocks.

AGRONSKI: Sure thing, Mike.

(Footsteps, going away from Cleaver. A grating sound of stone on stone: the door wheel being turned.)

AGRONSKI: Welcome home, Father! We just got in a little while ago and—My God, what's wrong? Are you ill too? Is there something that—Mike! *Mike!*

(Somebody was running. Cleaver willed his neck muscles to lift his head, but they refused to obey. Instead, the back of his head seemed to force itself deeper into the stiff pillow of the hammock. After a momentary and endless agony, he cried out):

CLEAVER: Mike!

AGRONSKI: Mike!

(With a gasp, Cleaver lost the long battle at last. He was asleep.)

FOUR

As the door of Chtexa's house closed behind him, Ruiz-Sanchez looked about the gently glowing foyer with a feeling of almost unbearable anticipation, although he could hardly have said what it was that he hoped to see. Actually, it looked exactly like his own quarters, which was all he could in justice have expected—all the furniture at "home" was Lithian, except of course for the lab equipment and a few other terrestrial trappings.

"We have cut up several of the metal meteors from our museums, and hammered them as you suggested," Chtexa was saying behind him, while he struggled out of his raincoat and boots. "They show very definite, very strong magnetism, as you predicted. We now have the whole of our world alerted to pick up these nickel-iron meteorites and send them to our electrical laboratory here, regardless of where they are found. The staff of the observatory is attempting to predict possible falls. Unhappily, meteors are rare here. Our astronomers say that we have never had a 'shower' such as you describe as frequent on your native planet."

"No; I should have thought of that," Ruiz-Sanchez said, following the Lithian into the front room. This, too, was quite ordinary by Lithian standards, and empty except for the two of them.

"Ah, that is interesting. Why?"

"Because in our system we have a sort of giant grinding-wheel—a whole ring of little planets, many thousands of them, distributed around an orbit where we had expected to find only one normal-sized world."

"Expected? By the harmonic rule?" Chtexa said, sitting down and pointing out another hassock to his guest. "We have often wondered whether that relationship was real."

"So have we. It broke down in this instance. Collisions between all those small bodies are incessant, and our plague of meteors is the result."

"It is hard to understand how so unstable an arrangement could have come about," Chtexa said. "Have you any explanation?"

"Not a good one," Ruiz-Sanchez said. "Some of us think that there really was a respectable planet in that orbit ages ago, which exploded somehow. A similar accident happened to a satellite in our system, creating a great flat ring of debris around its primary. Others think that at the formation of our solar system the raw materials of what might have been a planet just never suceeded in coalescing. Both ideas have many flaws, but each satisfies certain objections to the other, so perhaps there is some truth in both."

Chtexa's eyes filmed with the mildly disquieting "inner blink" characteristic of Lithians at their most thoughtful.

"There would seem to be no way to test either answer," he said at length. "By our logic, the lack of such tests makes the original question meaningless."

"That rule of logic has many adherents on Earth. My colleague Dr. Cleaver would certainly agree with it."

Ruiz-Sanchez smiled suddenly. He had labored long and hard to master the Lithian language, and to have recognized and understood so completely abstract a point as the one just made by Chtexa was a bigger victory than any quantitative gains in vocabulary alone could have been.

"But I can see that you are going to have difficulties in collecting these meteorites," he said. "Have you offered incentives?"

"Oh, certainly. Everyone understands the importance of the program. We are all eager to advance it."

This was not quite what the priest had meant by his question. He searched his memory for some Lithian equivalent for "reward," but found nothing but the word he had already used, "incentive." He realized that he knew no Lithian word for "greed," either. Evidently offering Lithians a hundred dollars for every meteorite they found would simply baffle them. He had to abandon that tack.

"Since the potential meteor fall is so small," he said instead, "you're not likely to get anything like the supply of metal that you need for a real study—no matter how thoroughly you cooperate on the search. A high percentage of the finds will be stony rather than metallic, too. What you need is another, supplementary iron-finding program."

"We know that," Chtexa said ruefully. "But we have been able to think of none."

"If only you had some way of concentrating the traces of the metal you actually have on the planet now . . . Our smelting methods would be useless to you, since you have no ore beds. Hmm . . . Chtexa, what about the iron-fixing bacteria?"

"Are there such?" Chtexa said, cocking his head dubiously.

"I don't know. Ask your bacteriologists. If you have any bacteria here that belong to the genus we call *Leptothrix*, one of them should be an iron-fixing species. In all the millions of years that this planet has had life on it, that mutation must have occurred, and probably very early."

"But why have we never seen it before? We have done perhaps more research in bacteriology than we have in any other field."

"Because," Ruiz-Sanchez said earnestly, "you don't know what to look for, and because such a species would be as rare on Lithia as iron itself. On Earth, because we have iron in abundance, our *Leptothrix ochracea* has found plenty of opportunity to grow. We find their fossil sheaths by uncountable billions in our great ore beds. It used to be thought, as a matter of fact, that the bacteria *produced* the ore beds, but I've always doubted that. They get their energy by oxidizing ferrous iron into ferric—but that's a change that can happen spontaneously if the oxidation-reduction potential and the pH of the solution are right, and both of those conditions can be affected by ordinary decay bacteria. On our planet the bacteria grew in the ore beds because the iron was there, not the other way around—but on Lithia the process will have to be worked in reverse."

"We will start a soil-sampling program at once," Chtexa said, his wattles flaring a subdued orchid. "Our antibiotics research centers screen soil samples by the thousands each month, in search of new microflora of therapeutic importance. If these iron-fixing bacteria exist, we are certain to find them eventually."

"They must exist. Do you have a bacterium that is a sulphur-concentrating obligate anaerobe?"

"Yes—yes, certainly!"

"There you are," the Jesuit said, leaning back contentedly and clasping his hands across one knee. "You have plenty of sulphur, and so you have the bacterium. Please let me know when you find the iron-fixing species. I'd like to make a subculture and take it home with me when I leave. There are two Earth scientists whose noses I'd like to rub it in."

The Lithian stiffened and thrust his head forward a little, as if puzzled.

"Pardon me," Ruiz-Sanchez said hastily. "I was translating literally an aggressive idiom of my own tongue. It was not meant to describe an actual plan of action."

"I think I understand," Chtexa said. Ruiz-Sanchez wondered if he did. In the rich storehouse of the Lithian language he had yet to discover any metaphors, either living or dead. Neither did the Lithians have any poetry or other creative arts. "You are of course welcome to any of the results of this program, which you would honor us by accepting. One problem in the social sciences which has long puzzled us is just how one may adequately honor the innovator. When we consider how new ideas change our lives, we despair of giving in kind, and it is helpful when the innovator himself has wishes which society can gratify."

Ruiz-Sanchez was at first not quite sure that he had understood the formulation. After he had gone over it once more in his mind, he was not sure that he could bring himself to like it, although it was admirable enough. From an Earthman it would have sounded intolerably pompous, but it was evident that Chtexa meant it.

It was probably just as well that the commission's report on Lithia was about to fall due. Ruiz-Sanchez had begun to think that he could absorb only a little more of this kind of calm sanity. And all of it—a disquieting thought from somewhere near his heart reminded him—all of it derived from reason, none from precept, none from faith. The Lithians did not know God. They did things rightly, and thought righteously, because it was reasonable and efficient and natural to do and to think that way. They seemed to need nothing else.

Did they never have night thoughts? Was it possible that there could exist in the universe a reasoning being of a high order, which was never for an instant paralyzed by the sudden question, the terror of seeing through to the meaninglessness of action, the blindness of knowledge, the barrenness of having been born at all? "Only upon this firm foundation of unyielding despair," a famous atheist once had written, "may the soul's habitation henceforth be safely built."

Or could it be that the Lithians thought and acted as they did because, not being born of man, and never in effect having left the Garden in which they lived, they did not share the terrible burden of original sin? The fact that Lithia had never once had a glacial epoch, that its climate had been left unchanged for seven hundred million years, was a geological fact that an alert theologian could scarcely afford to ignore. Could it be that, free from the burden, they were also free from the curse of Adam?

And if they were—could men bear to live among them?

"I have some questions to ask you, Chtexa," the priest said after a moment. "You owe me no debt whatsoever—it is our custom to regard all knowledge as community property—but we four Earthmen have a hard decision to make shortly. You know what it is. And I don't believe that we know enough yet about your planet to make that decision properly."

"Then of course you must ask questions," Chtexa said immediately. "I will answer, wherever I can."

"Well then—do your people die? I see you have the word, but perhaps it isn't the same in meaning as our word."

"It means to stop changing and to go back to existing,"

Chtexa said. "A machine exists, but only a living thing, like a tree, progresses along a line of changing equilibriums. When that progress stops, the entity is dead."

"And that happens to you?"

"It always happens. Even the great trees, like the Message Tree, die sooner or later. Is that not true on Earth?"

"Yes," Ruiz-Sanchez said, "yes, it is. For reasons which it would take me a long time to explain, it occurred to me that you might have escaped this evil."

"It is not evil as we look at it," Chtexa said. "Lithia lives because of death. The death of plants supplies our oil and gas. The death of some creatures is always necessary to feed the lives of others. Bacteria must die, and viruses be prevented from living, if illness is to be cured. We ourselves must die simply to make room for others, at least until we can slow the rate at which our people arrive in the world—a thing impossible to us at present."

"But desirable, in your eyes?"

"Surely desirable," Chtexa said. "Our world is rich, but not inexhaustible. And other planets, you have taught us, have peoples of their own. Thus we cannot hope to spread to other planets when we have overpopulated this one."

"No real thing is ever exhaustible," Ruiz-Sanchez said abruptly, frowning at the iridescent floor. "That we have found to be true over many thousands of years of our history."

"But exhaustible in what way?" Chtexa said. "I grant you that any small object, any stone, any drop of water, any bit of soil can be explored without end. The amount of information which can be gotten from it is quite literally infinite. But a given soil can be exhausted of nitrates. It is difficult, but with bad cultivation it can be done. Or take iron, about which we have been talking. To allow our economy to develop a demand for iron which exceeds the total known supply of Lithia—and exceeds it beyond any possibility of supplementation by meteorites or by import—would be folly. This is not a question of information. It is a question of whether or not the information can be used. If it cannot, then limitless information is of no help."

"You could certainly get along without more iron if you had to," Ruiz-Sanchez admitted. "Your wooden machinery is precise enough to satisfy any engineer. Most of them, I think, don't remember that we used to have something similiar: I've a sample in my own home. It's a kind of timer called a cuckoo clock, nearly two of our centuries old, made entirely of wood except for the weights, and still nearly a hundred percent accurate. For that matter, long after we began to build seagoing vessels of metal, we continued to use lignum vitae for ships' bearings."

"Wood is an excellent material for most uses," Chtexa agreed. "Its only deficiency, compared to ceramic materials or perhaps metal, is that it is variable. One must know it quite well to be able to assess its qualities from one tree to the next. And of course complicated parts can always be grown inside suitable ceramic molds; the growth pressure inside the mold rises so high that the resulting part is very dense. Larger parts can be ground direct from the plank with soft sandstone and polished with slate. It is a gratifying material to work, we find."

Ruiz-Sanchez felt, for some reason, a little ashamed. It was a magnified version of the same shame he had always felt back home toward that old Black Forest cuckoo clock. The electric clocks elsewhere in his hacienda outside Lima all should have been capable of performing silently, accurately, and in less space—but the considerations which had gone into the making of them had been commercial as well as purely technical. As a result, most of them operated with a thin, asthmatic whir, or groaned softly but dismally at regular hours. All of them were "streamlined," oversize and ugly. None of them kept good time, and several of them, since they were powered by constant-speed motors driving very simple gearboxes, could not be adjusted, but had been sent out from the factory with built-in, ineluctable inaccuracies.

The wooden cuckoo clock, meanwhile, ticked evenly away. A quail emerged from one of two wooden doors every quarter of an hour and let you know about it, and on the hour, first the quail came out, then the cuckoo, and there was a soft bell that rang just ahead of each cuckoo call. Midnight and noon were not just times of the day for that clock; they were productions. It was accurate to a minute a month, all for the price of running up the three weights which drove it, each night before bedtime.

The clock's maker had been dead before Ruiz-Sanchez was born. In contrast, the priest would probably buy and jettison at least a dozen cheap electric clocks in the course of one lifetime, as their makers had intended he should; they were linearly descended from "planned obsolescence," the craze for waste which had hit the Americas during the last half of the previous century.

"I'm sure it is," he said humbly. "I have one more question, if I may. It is really part of the same question. I have asked you if you die; now I should like to ask how you are born. I see many adults on your streets and sometimes in your houses—though I gather you yourself are alone—but never any children. Can you explain this to me? Or if the subject is not allowed to be discussed—"

"But why should it not be? There can never be any closed subjects," Chtexa said. "Our women, as I'm sure you know, have abdominal pouches where the eggs are carried. It was a lucky mutation for us, for there are a number of nest-robbing species on this planet."

"Yes, we have a few animals with a somewhat similar arrangement on Earth, although they are viviparous."

"Our eggs are laid in these pouches once a year," Chtexa said. "It is then that the women leave their own houses and seek out the man of their choice to fertilize the eggs. I am alone because, thus far, I am no woman's first choice this season; I will be elected in the Second Marriage, which is tomorrow."

"I see," Ruiz-Sanchez said carefully. "And how is the choice determined? Is it by emotion, or by reason alone?"

"The two are in the long run the same," Chtexa said. "Our ancestors did not leave our genetic needs to chance. Emotion with us no longer runs counter to our eugenic knowledge. It cannot, since it was itself modified to follow that knowledge by selective breeding for such behavior.

"At the end of the season, then, comes Migration Day. At that time all the eggs are fertilized, and ready to hatch. On that day—you will not be here to see it, I am afraid, for your scheduled date of departure precedes it by a short time—our whole people goes to the seashores. There, with the men to protect them from predators, the women wade out to swimming depth, and the children are born."

"In the sea?" Ruiz-Sanchez said faintly.

"Yes, in the sea. Then we all return, and resume our other affairs until the next mating season."

"But—but what happens to the children?"

"Why, they take care of themselves, if they can. Of course many perish, particularly to our voracious brother the great fish-lizard, whom for that reason we kill when we can. But a majority return home when the time comes."

"Return? Chtexa, I don't understand. Why don't they drown when they are born? And if they return, why have we never seen one?"

"But you have," Chtexa said. "And you have heard them often. Can it be that you yourselves do not—ah, of course, you are mammals; that is doubtless the difficulty. You keep your children in the nest with you; you know who they are, and they know their parents."

"Yes," Ruiz-Sanchez said. "We know who they are, and they know us."

"That is not possible with us," Chtexa said. "Here, come with me; I will show you."

He arose and led the way out into the foyer. Ruiz-Sanchez followed, his head whirling with surmises.

Chtexa opened the door. The night, the priest saw with a subdued shock, was on the wane; there was the faintest of pearly glimmers in the cloudy sky to the east. The multifarious humming and singing of the jungle continued unabated. There was a high, hissing whistle, and the shadow of a pterodon drifted over the city toward the sea. Out on the water, an indistinct blob that could only be one of Lithia's sailplaning squid broke the surface and glided low over the oily swell for nearly sixty yards before it hit the waves again. From the mud flats came a hoarse barking.

"There," Chtexa said softly. "Did you hear it?"

The stranded creature, or another of its kind—it was impossible to tell which—croaked protestingly again.

"It is hard for them at first," Chtexa said. "But actually the worst of their dangers are over. They have come ashore."

"Chtexa," Ruiz-Sanchez said. "Your children—*the lungfish*?"

"Yes," Chtexa said. "Those are our children."

In the last analysis it was the incessant barking of the lungfish which caused Ruiz-Sanchez to stumble when Agronski opened the door for him. The late hour, and the dual strains of Cleaver's illness and the subsequent discovery of Cleaver's direct lying, contributed. So did the increasing sense of guilt toward Cleaver which the priest had felt while walking home under the gradually brightening, weeping sky; and so, of course, did the shock of discovering that Agronski and Michelis had arrived some time during the night while he had been neglecting his charge to satisfy his curiosity.

But primarily it was the diminishing, gasping clamor of the children of Lithia, battering at his every mental citadel, all the way from Chtexa's house to his own.

The sudden fugue lasted only a few moments. He fought his way back to self-control to find that Agronski and Michelis had propped him up on a stool in the lab and were trying to remove his mackintosh without unbalancing him or awakening him—as difficult a problem in topology as removing a man's vest without taking off his jacket. Wearily, the priest pulled his own arm out of a mackintosh sleeve and looked up at Michelis.

"Good morning, Mike. Please excuse my bad manners."

"Don't be an idiot," Michelis said evenly. "You don't have to talk now, anyhow. I've already spent much of tonight trying to keep Cleaver quiet until he's better. Don't put me through it again, please, Ramon."

"I won't. I'm not ill; I'm just tired and a little overwrought."

"What's the matter with Cleaver?" Agronski demanded. Michelis made as if to shoo him off.

"No, no, Mike, it's a fair question. I'm all right, I assure you. As for Paul, he got a dose of glucoside poisoning when a plant spine stabbed him this afternoon. No, it's yesterday afternoon now. How has he been since you arrived?"

"He's sick," Michelis said. "Since you weren't here, we didn't know what to do for him. We settled for two of the pills you'd left out."

"You did?" Ruiz-Sanchez slid his feet heavily to the floor and tried to stand up. "As you say, you couldn't have known what else to do—but you did overdose him. I think I'd better look in on him—"

"Sit down, please, Ramon." Michelis spoke gently, but his tone showed that he meant the requests to be honored. Obscurely glad to be forced to yield to the big man's well-meant implacability, the priest let himself be propped back on the stool. His boots fell off his feet to the floor.

"Mike, who's the Father here?" he asked tiredly. "Still, I'm sure you've done a good job. He's in no apparent danger?"

"Well, he seems pretty sick. But he had energy enough to keep himself awake most of the night. He only passed out a short while ago."

"Good. Let him stay out. Tomorrow we'll probably have to begin intravenous feeding, though. In this atmosphere one doesn't give a salicylate overdose without penalties." He sighed. "Since I'll be sleeping in the same room, I'll be on hand if there's a crisis. So. Can we put off further questions?"

"If there's nothing else wrong here, of course we can."

"Oh," Ruiz-Sanchez said, "there's a great deal wrong, I'm afraid."

"I knew it!" Agronski said. "I knew damn well there was. I told you so, Mike, didn't I?"

"Is it urgent?"

"No, Mike—there's no danger to us, of that I'm positive. It's nothing that won't keep until we've all had a rest. You two look as though you need one as badly as I."

"We're tired," Michelis agreed.

"But why didn't you ever call us?" Agronski burst in aggrievedly. "You had us scared half to death, Father. If there's really something wrong here, you should have—"

"There's no immediate danger," Ruiz-Sanchez repeated patiently. "As for why we didn't call you, I don't understand that any more than you do. Up to last night, I thought we were in regular contact with you both. That was Paul's job and he seemed to be carrying it out. I didn't discover that he hadn't been doing it until after he became ill."

"Then obviously we'll have to wait for him," Michelis said. "Let's hit the hammock, in God's name. Flying that whirlybird through twenty-five hundred miles of fog banks wasn't exactly restful, either; I'll be glad to turn in . . . But, Ramon—"

"Yes, Mike?"

"I have to say that I don't like this any better than Agronski does. Tomorrow we've got to clear it up, and get our commission business done. We've only a day or so to make our decision before the ship comes and takes us off Lithia for good, and by that time we *must* know everything there is to know, and just what we're going to tell the Earth about it."

"Yes," Ruiz-Sanchez said. "Just as you say, Mike—in God's name."

The Peruvian priest-biologist awoke before the others; actually, he had undergone far less purely physical strain than had the other three. It was just beginning to be cloudy dusk when he rolled out of his hammock and padded over to look at Cleaver.

The physicist was in coma. His face was a dirty gray, and looked oddly shrunken. It was high time that the neglect and inadvertent abuse to which he had been subjected was rectified. Happily, his pulse and respiration were close to normal now.

Ruiz-Sanchez went quietly into the lab and made up a fructose intravenous feeding. At the same time he reconstituted a can of powdered eggs into a sort of soufflé, setting it in a covered crucible to bake at the back of the little oven; that was for the rest of them.

In the sleeping chamber, the priest set up his I-V stand. Cleaver did not stir when the needle entered the big vein just above the inside of his elbow. Ruiz-Sanchez taped the tubing in place, checked the drip from the inverted bottle, and went back into the lab.

There he sat, on the stool before the microscope, in a sort of suspension of feeling while the new night drew on. He was still poisoned-tired, but at least now he could stay awake without constantly fighting himself. The slowly rising soufflé in the oven went *plup-plup, plup-plup,* and after a while a thin tendril of aroma suggested that it was beginning to brown on top, or at least thinking about it.

Outside, it abruptly rained buckets. Just as abruptly, it stopped. Lithia's short, hot summer was drawing to a close;

its winter would be long and mild, the temperature never dropping below 20° centigrade in this latitude. Even at the poles the winter temperature stayed throughout well above freezing, usually averaging about 15° C.

"Is that breakfast I smell, Ramon?"

"Yes, Mike, in the oven. In a few minutes now."

"Right."

Michelis went away again. On the back of the workbench, Ruiz-Sanchez saw the dark blue book with the gold stamping which he had brought with him all the way from Earth. Almost automatically he pulled it to him, and almost automatically it fell open to page 573. It would at least give him something to think about with which he was not personally involved.

He had last quitted the text with Anita, who "would yield to the lewdness of Honuphrius to appease the savagery of Sulla and the mercenariness of the twelve Sullivani, and (as Gilbert at first suggested) to save the virginity of Felicia from Magravius"—now hold on a moment, how could Felicia still be considered a virgin at this point? Ah ". . . when converted by Michael after the death of Gillia;" that covered it, since Felicia had been guilty only of simple infidelities in the first place. ". . . but she fears that, by allowing his marital rights, she may cause reprehensible conduct between Eugenius and Jeremias. Michael, who has formerly debauched Anita, dispenses her from yielding to Honuphrius"—yes, that made sense, since Michael also had had designs on Eugenius. "Anita is disturbed, but Michael comminates that he will reserve her case tomorrow for the ordinary Guglielmus even if she should practice a pious fraud during affrication, which, from experience, she knows (according to Wadding) to be leading to nullity."

Well. This was all very well. The novel even seemed to be shaping up into sense, for the first time; evidently the author had known exactly what he was doing, every step of the way. Still, Ruiz-Sanchez reflected, he would not like to have known the imaginary family hidden behind the conventional Latin aliases, or to have been the confessor to any member of it.

Yes, it added up, when one tried to view it without outrage either at the persons involved—they were, after all, fictitious, only characters in a novel—or at the author, who for all his mighty intellect, easily the greatest ever devoted to fiction in English and perhaps in any language, had still to be pitied as much as the meanest victim of the Evil One. To view it, as it were, in a sort of gray twilight of emotion, wherein everything, even the barnacle-like commentaries the text had accumulated since it had been begun in the 1920s, could be seen in the same light.

"Is it done, Father?"

"Smells like it, Agronski. Take it out and help yourself, why don't you?"

"Thanks. Can I bring Cleaver—"

"No, he's getting an I-V."

"Check."

Unless his impression that he understood the problem at last was once more going to turn out to be an illusion, he was now ready for the basic question, the stumper that had deeply disturbed both the Order and the Church for so many decades now. He reread it carefully. It asked:

"Has he hegemony and shall she submit?"

To his astonishment, he saw as if for the first time that it was two questions, despite the omission of a comma between the two. And so it demanded two answers. Did Honuphrius have hegemony? Yes, he did, because Michael, the only member of the whole complex who had been gifted from the beginning with the power of grace, had been egregiously compromised. Therefore, Honuphrius, regardless of whether all his sins were to be laid at his door or were real only in rumor, could not be divested of his privileges by anyone.

But should Anita submit? No, she should not. Michael had forfeited his right to dispense or to reserve her in any way, and so she could not be guided by the curate or by anyone else in the long run but her own conscience—which in view of the grave accusations against Honuphrius could lead her to no recourse but to deny him. As for Sulla's repentance, and Felicia's conversation, they meant nothing, since the defection of Michael had deprived both of them—and everyone else—of spiritual guidance.

The answer, then, had been obvious all the time. It was:

Yes, and No.

And it had hung throughout upon putting a comma in the right place. A writer's joke. A demonstration that it could take one of the greatest novelists of all time seventeen years to write a book the central problem of which is exactly where to put one comma; thus does the Adversary cloak his emptiness, and empty his votaries.

Ruiz-Sanchez closed the book with a shudder and looked up across the bench, feeling neither more nor less dazed than he had before, but with a small stirring of elation deep inside him which he could not suppress. In the eternal wrestling, the Adversary had taken another fall.

As he looked dazedly out of the window into the dripping darkness, a familiar, sculpturesque head and shoulders moved into the truncated tetrahedron of yellow light being cast out through the fine glass into the rain. Ruiz-Sanchez awoke with a start. The head was Chtexa's, moving away from the house.

Suddenly Ruiz-Sanchez realized that nobody had bothered to rub away the sickness ideograms on the door tablet. If Chtexa had come here on some errand, he had been turned back unnecessarily. The priest leaned forward, snatched up an empty slide box, and rapped with a corner of it against the inside of the glass.

Chtexa turned and looked in through the streaming curtains of rain, his eyes completely filmed against the downpour. Ruiz-Sanchez beckoned to him, and got stiffly off the stool to open the door.

In the oven the priest's share of breakfast dried slowly and began to burn.

The rapping on the window had summoned forth Agronski and Michelis as well. Chtexa looked down at the three of them with easy gravity, while drops of water ran like oil down the minute, prismatic scales of his supple skin.

"I did not know that there was sickness here," the Lithian said. "I called because your brother Ruiz-Sanchez left my house this morning without the gift I had hoped to give him. I will leave if I am invading your privacy in any way."

"You are not," Ruiz-Sanchez assured him. "And the sickness is only a poisoning, not communicable and we think not likely to end badly for our colleague. These are my friends from the north, Agronski and Michelis."

"I am happy to see them. The message was not in vain, then?"

"What message is this?" Michelis said, in his pure but hesitant Lithian.

"I sent a message, as your colleague Ruiz-Sanchez asked me to do, last night. I was told by Xoredeshch Gton that you had already departed."

"As we had," Michelis said. "Ramon, what's this? I thought

you told us that sending messages was Paul's job. And you certainly implied that you didn't know how to do it yourself, after Paul took sick."

"I didn't. I don't. I asked Chtexa to send it for me; he just finished telling you that, Mike."

Michelis looked up at the Lithian.

"What did the message say?" he asked.

"That you were to join them now, here, at Xoredeshch Sfath. And that your time on our world was almost up."

"What does that mean?" Agronski said. He had been trying to follow the conversation, but he was not much of a linguist, and evidently the few words he had been able to pick up had served only to inflame his ready fears. "Mike, translate, please."

Michelis did so, briefly. Then he said:

"Ramon, was that really all you had to say to us, especially after what you had found out? We knew that departure time was coming, too, after all. We can keep a calendar as well as the next man, I hope."

"I know that, Mike. But I had no idea what previous messages you'd received, if indeed you'd received any. For all I knew, Cleaver might have been in touch with you some other way, privately. I thought first of a transmitter in his personal luggage, but later it occurred to me that he might have been sending dispatches over the regular jet liners; that would have been easier. He might have told you that we were going to stay on beyond the official departure time. Or he might have told you that I had been killed and that he was looking for the murderer. He might have told you anything. I had to make sure, as well as I could, that you'd arrive here *regardless* of what he had or had not said.

"And when I got to the local message center, I had to do all this message-revision on the spot, because I found that I couldn't communicate with you directly, or send anything that was at all detailed, anything that might have been garbled through being translated and passed through alien minds. Everything that goes out from Xoredeshch Sfath by radio goes out through the Tree, and until you've seen it you haven't any idea what an Earthman is up against there in sending even the simplest message."

"Is this true?" Michelis asked Chtexa.

"True?" Chtexa repeated. His wattles were stippled with confusion; though Ruiz-Sanchez and Michelis had both reverted to Lithian, there were a number of words they had used, such as "murderer," which simply did not exist in the Lithian language, and so had been thrown out hastily in English. "True? I do not know. Do you mean, is it valid? You must be the judge of that."

"But is it accurate, sir?"

"It is accurate," Chtexa said, "insofar as I understand it."

"Well, then," Ruiz-Sanchez, a little nettled despite himself, went on, "you can see why, when Chtexa appeared providentially in the Tree, recognized me, and offered to act as an intermediary, I had to give him only the gist of what I had to say. I couldn't hope to explain all the details to him, and I couldn't hope that any of those details would get to you undistorted after they'd passed through at least two Lithian intermediaries. All I could do was shout at the top of my voice for you two to get down here on the proper date—and hope that you'd hear me."

"This is a time of trouble, which is like a sickness in the house," Chtexa said. "I must not remain. I will wish to be left alone when I am troubled, and I cannot ask that, if I now force my presence on others who are troubled. I will bring my gift at a better time."

He ducked out through the door, without any formal gesture of farewell, but nevertheless leaving behind an overwhelming impression of graciousness. Ruiz-Sanchez watched him go helplessly, and a little forlornly. The Lithians always seemed to understand the essences of situations; they were never, unlike even the most cocksure Earthmen, beset by the least apparent doubt. They had no night thoughts.

And why should they have? They were backed—if Ruiz-Sanchez was right—by the second-best Authority in the universe, and backed directly, without intermediary churches or conflicts of interpretations. The very fact that they were never tormented by indecision identified them as creatures of that Authority. Only the children of God had been given free will, and hence were often doubtful.

Nevertheless, Ruiz-Sanchez would have delayed Chtexa's departure had he been able. In a short-term argument it is helpful to have pure reason on your side—even though such an ally could be depended upon to stab you to the heart if you depended upon him too long.

"Let's go inside and thrash this thing out," Michelis said, shutting the door and turning back toward the front room. He spoke in Lithian still, and acknowledged it with a wry grimace over his shoulder after the departed Chtexa before switching to English. "It's a good thing we got some sleep, but we have so little time left now that it's going to be touch-and-go to have a formal decision ready when the ship comes."

"We can't go ahead yet," Agronski objected, although along with Ruiz-Sanchez, he followed Michelis obediently enough. "How can we do anything sensible without having heard what Cleaver has to say? Every man's voice counts on a job of this sort."

"That's very true," Michelis said. "And I don't like the present situation any better than you do—I've already said that. But I don't see that we have any choice. What do you think, Ramon?"

"I'd like to hold out for waiting," Ruiz-Sanchez said frankly. "Anything I may say now is, to put it realistically, somewhat compromised with you two. And don't tell me that you have every confidence in my integrity, because we had every confidence in Cleaver's, too. Right now, trying to maintain both confidences just cancels out both."

"You have a nasty way, Ramon, of saying aloud what everybody else is thinking," Michelis said, grinning bleakly. "What alternatives do you see, then?"

"None," Ruiz-Sanchez admitted. "Time is against us, as you said. We'll just have to go ahead without Cleaver."

"*No you won't.*"

The voice, from the doorway to the sleeping chamber, was at once both uncertain and much harshened by weakness.

The others sprang up. Cleaver, clad only in his shorts, stood in the doorway, clinging to both sides of it. On one of his forearms Ruiz-Sanchez could see the marks where the adhesive tape which had held the I-V needle had been ripped away. Where the needle itself had been inserted, an ugly hematoma swelled bluely under the gray skin of Cleaver's upper arm.

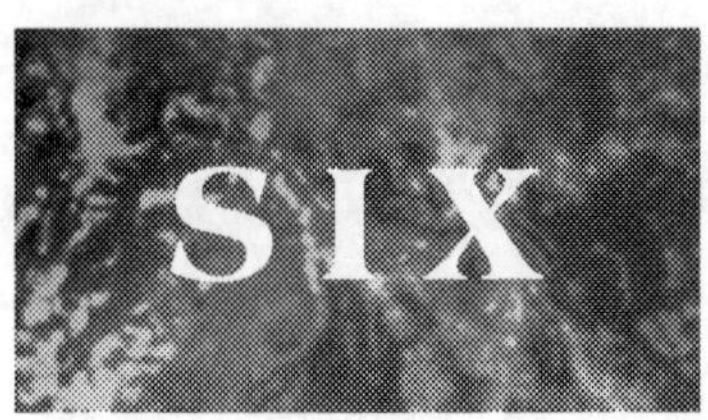

(A silence.)

"Paul, you must be crazy," Michelis said suddenly, almost angrily. "Get back into your hammock before you make things twice as bad for yourself. You're a sick man, can't you realize that?"

"Not as sick as I look," Cleaver said, with a ghastly grin. "Actually I feel pretty fair. My mouth is almost all cleared up, and I don't think I've got any fever. And I'll be damned if this commission is going to proceed one single damned inch without me. It isn't empowered to do it, and I'll appeal any decision—*any* decision, I hope you guys are listening—that it makes without me."

The commission was listening; the recorder had already been started, and the unalterable tapes were running into their sealed cans. The other two men turned dubiously to Ruiz-Sanchez.

"How about it, Ramon?" Michelis said, frowning. He shut off the recorder with his key. "Is it safe for him to be up like this?"

Ruiz-Sanchez was already at the physicist's side, peering

into his mouth. The ulcers were indeed almost gone, with granulation tissue forming nicely over the few that still remained. Cleaver's eyes were still slightly suffused, indicating that the toxemia was not completely defeated, but except for these two signs the effect of the accidental squill inoculation was no longer visible. It was true that Cleaver looked awful, but that was inevitable in a man quite recently sick, and in one who had been burning his own body proteins for fuel to boot. As for the hematoma, a cold compress would fix that.

"If he wants to endanger himself, I guess he's got a right to do so, at least by indirection," Ruiz-Sanchez said. "Paul, the first thing you'll have to do is get off your feet, and get into a robe, and put a blanket around your legs. Then you'll have to eat something; I'll fix it for you. You've staged a wonderful recovery, but you're a sitting duck for a real infection if you abuse your time during convalescence."

"I'll compromise," Cleaver said immediately. "I don't want to be a hero, I just want to be heard. Give me a hand over to that hassock. I still don't walk very straight."

It took the better part of half an hour to get Cleaver settled to Ruiz-Sanchez' satisfaction. The physicist seemed in a wry way to be enjoying every minute of it. At least he had in his hand a mug of *gchteht,* a local herb tea so delicious that it would probably become a major article of export before long, and he said:

"All right, Mike, turn on the recorder and let's go."

"Are you sure?" Michelis said.

"One hundred percent. Turn the goddam key."

Michelis turned the key, took it out and put it in his pocket. From now on, they were on the record.

"All right, Paul," Michelis said. "You've gone out of your

way to put yourself on the spot. Evidently that's where you want to be. So let's have the answer: Why didn't you communicate with us?"

"I didn't want to."

"Now wait a minute," Agronski said. "Paul, you're going on record; don't break your neck to say the first damn thing that comes into your head. Your judgment may not be well yet, even if your talking apparatus is. Wasn't your silence just a matter of your being unable to work the local message system—the Tree or whatever it is?"

"No, it wasn't," Cleaver insisted. "Thanks, Agronski, but I don't need to be shepherded down the safe and easy road, or have any alibis set up for me. I know exactly what I did that was ticklish, and I know that it's going to be impossible for me to set up consistent alibis for it now. My chances for keeping anything under my hat depended upon my staying in complete control of everything I did. Naturally those chances went out the window when I got stuck by that damned pineapple. I realized that last night, when I fought like a demon to get through to you before the Father could get back, and found that I couldn't make it."

"You seem to take it calmly enough now," Michelis observed.

"Well, I'm feeling a little washed out. But I'm a realist. And I also know, Mike, that I had damned good reasons for what I did. I'm counting on the chance that you'll agree with me wholeheartedly, when I tell you why I did it."

"All right," Michelis said, "begin."

Cleaver sat back, folding his hands quietly in the lap of his robe. He looked almost ecclesiastical. He was obviously still enjoying the situation. He said:

"First of all, I didn't call you because I didn't want to, as I said. I could have mastered the problem of the Tree easily enough by doing what the Father did—that is, by getting a Snake to ferry my messages. Of course I don't speak Snake, but the Father does, so all I had to do was to take him into my confidence. Barring that, I could have mastered the Tree itself. I already know all the technical problems involved. Mike, wait till you see that Tree. Essentially it's a single-junction transistor, with the semi-conductor supplied by a huge lump of crystal buried under it; the crystal is piezo-electric and emits in the RF spectrum every time the Tree's roots stress it. It's fantastic—nothing like it anywhere else in this galaxy, I'd lay money on that.

"But I wanted a gap to spring up between our party and yours. I wanted both of you to be completely in the dark about what was going on, down here on this continent. I wanted you to imagine the worst, and blame it on the Snakes, too, if that could be managed. After you got here—if you did—I was going to be able to show you that I hadn't sent any messages because the Snakes wouldn't let me. I've got more plants to that effect squirreled away around here than I'll bother to list now; besides, there'd be no point in it, since it's all come to nothing. But I'm sure that it would have looked conclusive, regardless of anything the Father would have been able to offer to the contrary."

"Are you sure you don't want me to turn off the machine?" Michelis said quietly.

"Oh, throw away your damned key, will you, and listen. From my point of view it was just a bloody shame that I had to run up against a pineapple at the last minute. It gave the Father a chance to find out something about what was up. I'll swear that if that hadn't happened, he wouldn't have smelt anything until you actually got here—and by then it would have been too late."

"I probably wouldn't have, that's true," Ruiz-Sanchez said, watching Cleaver steadily. "But your running up against that 'pineapple' was no accident. If you'd been observing Lithia as you were sent here to do, instead of spending all your time building up a fictitious Lithia for purposes of your own, you'd have known enough about the planet to have been more careful about 'pineapples.' You'd also have spoken at least as much Lithian as Agronski, by this time."

"That," Cleaver said, "is probably true, and again it doesn't make any difference to me. I observed the one fact about Lithia that overrides all other facts, and that is going to turn out to be sufficient. Unlike you, Father, I have no respect for petty niceties in extreme situations, and I'm not the kind of man who thinks anyone learns anything from analysis after the fact."

"Let's not get to bickering this early," Michelis said. "You've told us your story without any visible decoration, and it's evident that you have a reason for confessing. You expect us to excuse you, or at least not to blame you too heavily, when you tell us what that reason is. Let's hear it."

"It's this," Cleaver said, and for the first time he seemed to become a little more animated. He leaned forward, the glowing gaslight bringing the bones of his face into sharp contrast with the sagging hollows of his cheeks, and pointed a not-quite-steady finger at Michelis.

"Do you know, Mike, what it is that we're sitting on here? Just to begin with, do you know how much rutile there is here?"

"Of course I know," Michelis said. "Agronski told me, and since then I've been working on practicable methods of refining the ore. If we decided to vote for opening the planet up, our titanium problem will be solved for a century, maybe even longer. I'm saying as much in my personal report. But what of it? We anticipated that that would be true even before we first landed here, as soon as we got accurate figures on the mass of the planet."

"And what about the pegmatite?" Cleaver demanded softly.

"Well, what about it?" Michelis said, looking more puzzled than before. "I suppose it's abundant—I really didn't bother to check. Titanium's important to us, but I don't quite see why lithium should be. The days when the metal was used as a rocket fuel are fifty years behind us."

"And a good thing, too," Agronski said. "Those old Li-Fluor engines used to go off like war heads. One little leak in the feed lines, and bloo-*ey*!"

"And yet the metal's still worth about twenty thousand dollars an English ton back home, Mike, and that's exactly the same price it was drawing in the nineteen-sixties, allowing for currency changes since then. Doesn't that mean anything to you?"

"I'm more interested in knowing what it means to you," Michelis said. "None of us can make a personal penny out of this trip, even if we find the planet solid platinum inside—which is hardly likely. And if price is the only consideration, surely the fact that lithium ore is common here will break the market for it. What's it good for, after all, on a large scale?"

"Bombs," Cleaver said. "Real bombs. Fusion bombs. It's no good for controlled fusion, for power, but the deuterium salt makes the prettiest multimegaton explosion you ever saw."

Ruiz-Sanchez suddenly felt sick and tired all over again. It was exactly what he had feared had been on Cleaver's mind; given a planet named Lithia only because it appeared to be mostly rock, and a certain kind of mind will abandon every other concern to find a metal called lithium on it. But he had not wanted to find himself right.

"Paul," he said, "I've changed my mind. I would have caught you out, even if you had never blundered against your 'pineapple.' That same day you mentioned to me that you were looking for pegmatite when you had your accident, and that you thought Lithia might be a good place for tritium production on a large scale. Evidently you thought that I wouldn't know what you were talking about. If you hadn't hit the 'pineapple,' you would have given yourself away to me before now by talk like that. Your estimate of me was based on as little observation as is your estimate of Lithia."

"It's easy," Cleaver observed indulgently, "to say 'I knew it all the time'—especially on a tape."

"Of course it's easy, when the other man is helping you," Ruiz-Sanchez said. "But I think that your view of Lithia as a potential cornucopia of hydrogen bombs is only the beginning of what you have in mind. I don't believe that it's even your real objective. What you would like most is to see Lithia removed from the universe as far as you're concerned. You hate the place. It's injured you. You'd like to think that it doesn't really exist. Hence the emphasis on Lithia as a source of munitions, to the exclusion of every other fact about the planet; for if that emphasis wins out, Lithia will be placed under security seal. Isn't that right?"

"Of course it's right, except for the phony mind reading," Cleaver said contemptuously. "When even a priest can see it, it's got to be obvious—and it's got to be written off by impugning the motives of the man who saw it first. To hell with that. Mike, listen to me. This is the most tremendous opportunity that any commission has ever had. This planet is made to order to be converted, root and branch, into a thermonuclear laboratory and production center. It has indefinitely large supplies of the most important raw materials. What's even more important, it has no nuclear knowledge of its own for us to worry about. All the clue materials, the radioactive elements and so on, which you need to work out real knowledge of the atom, we'll have to import; the Snakes don't know a thing about them. Furthermore, the instruments involved, the counters and particle-accelerators and so on, all depend on materials like iron that the Snakes don't have, and on principles that they don't know, ranging all the way from magnetism to quantum mechanics. We'll be able to stock our plants here with an immense reservoir of cheap labor which doesn't know, and—if we take proper precautions—never will have a prayer of learning enough to snitch classified techniques.

"All we need to do is to turn in a triple-E Unfavorable on the planet, to shut off any use of Lithia as a way station or any other kind of general base for a whole century. At the same time, we can report separately to the UN Review Committee exactly what we do have in Lithia: a triple-A arsenal for the whole of Earth, for the whole commonwealth of planets we control! Only the decision becomes general administrative property back home; the tape is protected; it's an opportunity it'd be a crime to flub!"

"Against whom?" Ruiz-Sanchez said.

"Eh? You've lost me."

"Against whom are you stocking this arsenal? Why do we need a whole planet devoted to nothing but making fusion bombs?"

"The UN can use weapons," Cleaver said drily. "The time isn't very far gone since there were still a few restive nations on Earth, and it could come around again. Don't forget also that thermonuclear weapons last only a few years—they can't be stock-piled indefinitely, like fission bombs. The half-life of tritium is very short, and lithium-6 isn't very long-lived either. I suppose you wouldn't know anything about that. But take my word for it, the UN police would be glad to know that they could have access to a virtually inexhaustible stock of fusion bombs, and to hell with the shelf-life problem!

"Besides, if you've thought about it at all, you know as well as I do that this endless consolidation of peaceful planets can't go on forever. Sooner or later—well, what happens if the next planet we touch down on is a place like Earth? If it is its inhabitants may fight, and fight like a planetful of madmen, to stay *out* of our frame of influence. Or what happens if the next planet we hit is an outpost for a whole federation, maybe bigger than ours? When that day comes—and it will, it's in the cards—we'll be damned glad if we're able to plaster the enemy from pole to pole with fusion bombs, and clean up the matter with as little loss of life as possible."

"On our side," Ruiz-Sanchez added.

"Is there any other side?"

"By golly, that makes sense to me," Agronski said. "Mike, what do you think?"

"I'm not sure yet," Michelis said. "Paul, I still don't understand why you thought it necessary to go through all the cloak-and-dagger maneuvers. You tell your story fairly enough now, and it has its merits, but you also admit you were going to trick the three of us into going along with you, if you could. Why? Couldn't you trust the force of your argument alone?"

"No," Cleaver said bluntly. "I've never been on a commission like this before, where there was no single, definite chairman, where there was deliberately an even number of members so that a split opinion couldn't be settled if it occurred—and where the voice of a man whose head is filled with Pecksniffian, irrelevant moral distinctions and three-thousand-year-old metaphysics carries the same weight as the voice of a scientist."

"That's mighty loaded language, Paul," Michelis said.

"I know it. If it comes to that, I'll say here or anywhere that I think the Father is a hell of a fine biologist. I've seen him in operation, and they don't come any better—and for that matter he may have just finished saving my life, for all any of the rest of us can tell. That makes him a scientist like the rest of us—insofar as biology's a science."

"Thank you," Ruiz-Sanchez said. "With a little history in your education, Paul, you would also have known that the Jesuits were among the first explorers to enter China, and Paraguay, and the North American wilderness. Then it would have been no surprise to you to find me here."

"That may well be. However, it has nothing to do with the paradox as I see it. I remember once visiting the labs at Notre Dame, where they have a complete little world of germ-free animals and plants and have pulled I don't know how many physiological miracles out of the hat. I wondered then how a man goes about being as good a scientist as that, and a good Catholic at the same time—or any other kind of churchman. I wondered in which compartment in their brains they filed their religion, and in which their science. I'm still wondering."

"They're not compartmented," Ruiz-Sanchez said. "They are a single whole."

"So you said, when I brought this up before. That answers nothing; in fact, it convinced me that what I was planning to do was absolutely necessary. I didn't propose to take any chances on the compartments getting interconnected on Lithia. I had every intention of cutting the Father down to a point where his voice would be nearly ignored by the rest of you. That's why I undertook the cloak-and-dagger stuff. Maybe it was stupidly done—I suppose that it takes training to be a successful agent-provocateur and that I should have realized that."

Ruiz-Sanchez wondered what Cleaver's reaction would be when he found, as he would very shortly now, that his purpose would have been accomplished without his having to lift a finger. Of course the dedicated man of science, working for the greater glory of man, could anticipate nothing but failure; that was the fallibility of man. But would Cleaver be able to understand, through his ordeal, what had happened to Ruiz-Sanchez when he had discovered the fallibility of God? It seemed unlikely.

"But I'm not sorry I tried," Cleaver was saying. "*I'm only sorry I failed.*"

There was a short, painful hiatus.

"Is that it, then?" Michelis said.

"That's it, Mike. Oh—one more thing. My vote, if anybody is still in any doubt about it, is to keep the planet closed. Take it from there."

"Ramon," Michelis said, "do you want to speak next? You're certainly entitled to it, on a point of personal privilege. The air's a mite murky at the moment, I'm afraid."

"No, Mike. Let's hear from you."

"I'm not ready to speak yet either, unless the majority wants me to. Agronski, how about you?"

"Sure," Agronski said. "Speaking as a geologist, and also as an ordinary slob that doesn't follow rarefied reasoning very well, I'm on Cleaver's side. I don't see anything either for or against the planet on any other grounds but Cleaver's. It's a fair planet as planets go, very quiet, not very rich in anything else we need—sure, that *gchteht* is marvelous stuff, but it's strictly for the luxury trade—and not subject to any kind of trouble that I've been able to detect. It'd make a good way station, but so would lots of other worlds hereabouts.

"It'd also make a good arsenal, the way Cleaver defines the

term. In every other category it's as dull as ditch water, and it's got plenty of that. The only other thing it can have to offer is titanium, which isn't quite as scarce back home these days as Mike seems to think; and gem stones, particularly the semi-precious ones, which we can make at home without traveling fifty light-years to get them. I'd say, either set up a way station here and forget about the planet otherwise, or else handle the place as Cleaver suggested."

"But which?" Ruiz-Sanchez asked.

"Well, which is more important, Father? Aren't way stations a dime a dozen? Planets that can be used as thermonuclear labs, on the other hand, are rare—Lithia is the *first* one that can be used that way, at least in my experience. Why use a planet for a routine purpose if it's unique? Why not apply Occam's Razor—the law of parsimony? It works on every other scientific problem anybody's ever tackled. It's my bet that it's the best tool to use on this one."

"Occam's Razor isn't a natural law," Ruiz-Sanchez said. "It's only a heuristic convenience—in short, a learning gimmick. And besides, Agronski, it calls for the simplest solution of the problem that will fit all the facts. You don't have all the facts, not by a long shot."

"All right, show me," Agronski said piously. "I've got an open mind."

"You vote to close the planet, then," Michelis said.

"Sure. That's what I was saying, wasn't it, Mike?"

"I wanted to have it Yes or No for the tape," Michelis said. "Ramon, I guess it's up to us. Shall I speak first? I think I'm ready."

"Of course, Mike."

"Then," Michelis said evenly, and without changing in the slightest his accustomed tone of grave impartiality, "I'll say that I think both of these gentlemen are fools, and calamitous fools at that because they're supposed to be scientists. Paul, your maneuvers to set up a phony situation are perfectly beneath contempt, and I shan't mention them again. I shan't even appeal to have them cut from the tape, so you needn't feel that you have to mend any fences with me. I'm looking solely at the purpose those maneuvers were supposed to serve, just as you asked me to do."

Cleaver's obvious self-satisfaction began to dim a little around the edges. He said, "Go ahead," and wound the blanket a little bit tighter around his legs.

"Lithia is not even the beginning of an arsenal," Michelis said. "Every piece of evidence you offered to prove that it might be is either a half-truth or the purest trash. Take cheap labor, for instance. With what will you pay the Lithians? They have no money, and they can't be rewarded with goods. They have almost everything that they need, and they like the way they're living right now—God knows they're not even slightly jealous of the achievements we think make Earth great. They'd like to have space flight but, given a little time, they'll get it by themselves; they have the Coupling ion-jet right now, and they won't be needing the Haertel overdrive for another century."

He looked around the gently rounded room, which was shining softly in the gaslight.

"And I don't seem to see any place in here," he said, "where a vacuum cleaner with forty-five patented attachments would find any work to do. How will you pay the Lithians to work in your thermonuclear plants?"

"With knowledge," Cleaver said gruffly. "There's a lot they'd like to know."

"But what knowledge, Paul? The things they'd like to know

are specifically the things you can't tell them, if they're to be valuable to you as a labor force. Are you going to teach them quantum mechanics? You can't; that would be dangerous. Are you going to teach them nucleonics, or Hilbert space, or the Haertel scholium? Again, any one of those would enable them to learn other things you think dangerous. Are you going to teach them how to extract titanium from rutile, or how to accumulate enough iron to develop a science of electrodynamics, or how to pass from this Stone Age they're living in now—this Pottery Age, I should say—into an Age of Plastics? Of course you aren't. As a matter of fact, we don't have a thing to offer them in that sense. It'd all be classified under the arrangement you propose—and they just wouldn't work for us under those terms."

"Offer them other terms," Cleaver said shortly. "If necessary, tell them what they're going to do, like it or lump it. It'd be easy enough to introduce a money system on this planet. You give a Snake a piece of paper that says it's worth a dollar, and if he asks you just what makes it worth a dollar—well, the answer is an honest day's work."

"And we put a machine pistol to his belly to emphasize the point," Ruiz-Sanchez interjected.

"Do we make machine pistols for nothing? I never figured out what else they were good for. Either you point them at someone or you throw them away."

"Item: slavery," Michelis said. "That disposes, I think, of the argument of cheap labor. I won't vote for slavery. Ramon won't. Agronski?"

"No," Agronski said uneasily. "But isn't it a minor point?"

"The hell it is! It's the reason why we're here. We're supposed to think of the welfare of the Lithians as well as of ourselves—otherwise this commission procedure would be a waste of time, of thought, of energy. If we want cheap labor, we can enslave any planet."

"How do we do that?" Agronski said. "There aren't any other planets. I mean, none with intelligent life on them that we've hit so far. You can't enslave a Martian sand crab."

"Which brings up the point of our own welfare," Ruiz-Sanchez said. "We're supposed to be considering that, too. Do you know what it does to a people to be slave-owners? It kills them."

"Lots of people have worked for money without calling it slavery," Agronski said. "I don't mind getting a pay check for what I do."

"There is no money on Lithia," Michelis said stonily. "If we introduce it here, we do so only by force. Forced labor is slavery. Q.E.D."

Agronski was silent.

"Speak up," Michelis said. "Is that true, or isn't it?"

Agronski said, "I guess it is. Take it easy, Mike. There's nothing to get mad about."

"Cleaver?"

"Slavery's just a swearword," Cleaver said sullenly. "You're deliberately clouding the issue."

"Say that again."

"Oh, hell. All right, Mike, I know you wouldn't. But we could work out a fair pay scale somehow."

"I'll admit that the instant that you can demonstrate it to me," Michelis said. He got up abruptly from his hassock, walked over to the sloping window sill, and sat down again, looking out into the rain-stippled darkness. He seemed to be more deeply troubled than Ruiz-Sanchez had ever before thought possible for him. The priest was astonished, as much at himself as at Michelis; the argument from money had never occurred to him, and Michelis had unknowingly put his finger on a doctrinal sore spot which Ruiz-Sanchez had never been able to reconcile with his own beliefs. He remembered the lines of poetry that had summed it up for him—lines written way back in the 1950s:

> *The groggy old Church has gone toothless,*
> *No longer holds against* neshek; *the fat has covered their croziers . . .*

Neshek was the lending of money at interest, once a sin called usury, for which Dante had put men into Hell. And now here was Mike, not a Christian at all, arguing that money itself was a form of slavery. It was, Ruiz-Sanchez discovered upon fingering it mentally once more, a *very* sore spot.

"In the meantime," Michelis had resumed, "I'll prosecute my own demonstration. What's to be said, now, about this theory of automatic security that you've propounded, Paul? You think that the Lithians can't learn the techniques they would need to be able to understand secret information and pass it on, and so they won't have to be screened. There again, you're wrong, as you'd have known if you'd bothered to study the Lithians even perfunctorily. The Lithians are highly intelligent, and they already have many of the clues they need. I've given them a hand toward pinning down magnetism, and they absorbed the material like magic and put it to work with enormous ingenuity."

"So did I," Ruiz-Sanchez said. "And I've suggested to them a technique for accumulating iron that should prove to be pretty powerful. I had only to suggest it, and they were already halfway down to the bottom of it and traveling fast. They can make the most of the smallest of clues."

"If I were the UN I'd regard both actions as the plainest

kind of treason," Cleaver said harshly. "You'd better think again about using that key, Mike, on your own behalf—if it isn't already too late. Isn't it possible that the Snakes found out both items by themselves, and were only being polite to you?"

"Set me no traps," Michelis said. "The tape is on and it stays on, by your own request. If you have any second thoughts, file them in your individual report, but don't try to stampede me into hiding anything under the rug now, Paul. It won't work."

"That," Cleaver said, "is what I get for trying to help."

"If that's what you were trying to do, thanks. I'm not through, however. So far as the practical objective that you want to achieve is concerned, Paul, I think it's just as useless as it is impossible. The fact that we have here a planet that's especially rich in lithium doesn't mean that we're sitting on a bonanza, no matter what price per ton the metal commands back home.

"The fact of the matter is that you can't ship lithium home. Its density is so low that you couldn't send away more than a ton of it per shipload; by the time you got it to Earth, the shipping charges on it would more than outweigh the price you'd get for it on arrival. I should have thought that you'd know there's lots of lithium on Earth's own moon, too—and it isn't economical to fly back to Earth even over that short a distance, less than a quarter of a million miles. Lithia is three hundred and fourteen trillion miles from Earth; that's what fifty light-years comes to. Not even radium is worth carrying over a gap that great!

"No more would it be economical to ship from Earth to Lithia all the heavy equipment that would be needed to make use of lithium here. There's no iron here for massive magnets. By the time you got your particle-accelerators and mass chromatographs and the rest of your needs to Lithia, you'd have cost the UN so much that no amount of locally available pegmatite could compensate for it. Isn't that so, Agronski?"

"I'm no physicist," Agronski said, frowning slightly. "But just getting the metal out of the ore and storing it would cost a fair sum, that's a cinch. Raw lithium would burn like phosphorus in this atmosphere; you'd have to store it and work it under oil. That's costly no matter how you look at it."

Michelis looked from Cleaver to Agronski and back again.

"Exactly so," he said. "And that's only the beginning. In fact, the whole scheme is just a chimera."

"Have you got a better one, Mike?" Cleaver said, very quietly.

"I hope so. It seems to me that we have a lot to learn from the Lithians, as well as they from us. Their social system works like the most perfect of our physical mechanisms, and it does so without any apparent repression of the individual. It's a thoroughly liberal society in terms of guarantees, yet all the same it never even begins to tip over toward the side of total disorganization, toward the kind of Gandhiism that keeps a people tied to the momma-and-poppa farm and the roving-brigand distribution system. It's in balance, and not in precarious balance either—it's in perfect chemical equilibrium.

"The notion of using Lithia as a fusion-bomb plant is easily the strangest anachronism I've ever encountered—it's as crude as proposing to equip an interstellar ship with galley slaves, oars and all. Right here on Lithia is the *real* secret, the secret that's going to make bombs of all kinds, and all the rest of the antisocial armament, as useless, unnecessary, obsolete as the iron boot!

"And on top of all that—no, please, I'm not quite finished, Paul—on top of all that, the Lithians are decades ahead of us in some purely technical matters, just as we're ahead of them in others. You should see what they can do with mixed disciplines—scholia like histochemistry, immunodynamics, biophysics, terataxonomy, osmotic genetics, electrolimnology, and half a hundred more. If you'd been looking, you *would* have seen.

"We have much more to do, it seems to me, than just to vote to open the planet. That's only a passive move. We have to realize that being able to use Lithia is only the beginning. The fact of the matter is that we actively *need* Lithia. We should say so in our recommendation."

Michelis unfolded himself from the window sill and stood up, looking down on all of them, but most especially at Ruiz-Sanchez. The priest smiled at him, but as much in anguish as in admiration, and then had to look back down at his shoes.

"Well, Agronski?" Cleaver said, spitting the words out like bullets on which he had been clenching his teeth, like a Civil War casualty during an operation without anesthetics. "What d'you say now? Do you like the pretty picture?"

"Sure, I like it," Agronski said, slowly but forthrightly. It was a virtue in him, as well as a frequent source of exasperation, that he always said exactly what he was thinking, the moment he was asked to do so. "Mike makes sense. I wouldn't expect him not to, if you see what I mean. Also he's got another advantage: he told us what he thought, *without* trying to trick us first into his way of thinking."

"Oh, don't be a thumphead," Cleaver exclaimed. "Are we scientists or Boy Rangers? Any rational man up against a majority of do-gooders would have taken the same precautions I did."

"Maybe," Agronski said. "I'm none too sure. Why is it silly to be a do-gooder? Is it wrong to do good? Do you want to be a do-badder—whatever the hell that is? Your precautions still smell to me like a confession of weakness somewhere in the argument. As for me, I don't like to be finessed. And I don't much like being called a thumphead, either."

"Oh, for Christ's sake—"

"Now-you-listen-to-me," Agronski said, all in one breath. "Before you call me any more names, I'm going to say that I think you're more right than Mike is. I don't like your methods, but your aim seems sensible to me. Mike's shot some of your major arguments full of holes, that I'll admit. But as far as I'm concerned, you're still leading—by a nose."

He paused, breathing heavily and glaring at the physicist. Then he said:

"By a nose, Paul. That's all. Just bear that in mind."

Michelis remained standing for a moment longer. Then he shrugged, walked back to his hassock, and sat down, locking his hands awkwardly between his knees.

"I did my best, Ramon," he said. "But so far it looks like a draw. See what you can do."

Ruiz-Sanchez took a deep breath. What he was about to do would hurt him, without doubt, for the rest of his life, regardless of the way time had of turning any blade. The decision had already cost him many hours of concentrated, agonized doubt. But he believed that it had to be done.

"I disagree with all of you," he said, "except Cleaver. I believe, as he does, that Lithia should be reported triple-E Unfavorable. But I think also that it should be given a special classification: X-One."

Michelis' eyes were glazed with shock. Even Cleaver seemed unable to credit what he had heard.

"X-One—but that's a quarantine label," Michelis said huskily. "As a matter of fact—"

"Yes, Mike, that's right," Ruiz-Sanchez said. "I vote to seal Lithia off from *all* contact with the human race. Not only now, or for the next century—but forever."

Forever.

The word did not produce the consternation that he had been dreading—or, perhaps, hoping for, somewhere in the back of his mind. Evidently they were all too tired for that. They took his announcement with a kind of stunned emptiness, as though it were so far out of the expected order of events as to be quite meaningless.

It was hard to say whether Cleaver or Michelis was the more overwhelmed. All that could be seen for certain was that Agronski recovered first, and was now ostentatiously reaming out his ears, as if in signal that he would be ready to listen again when Ruiz-Sanchez changed his mind.

"Well," Cleaver began. And then again, shaking his head amazedly, like an old man: "Well. . . ."

"Tell us why, Ramon," Michelis said, clenching and unclenching his fists. His voice was quite flat, but Ruiz-Sanchez thought he could feel the pain under it.

"Of course. But I warn you, I'm going to be very roundabout. What I have to say seems to me to be of the utmost importance. I don't want to see it rejected out of hand as just the product of my peculiar training and prejudices—interesting perhaps as a study in aberration, but not germane to the problem. The evidence for my view of Lithia is overwhelming. It overwhelmed me quite *against* my natural hopes and inclinations. I want you to hear that evidence."

The preamble, with its dry scholiast's tone and its buried suggestion, did its work well.

"He also wants us to understand," Cleaver said, recovering a little of his natural impatience, "that his reasons are religious and won't hold water if he states them right out."

"Hush," Michelis said intently. "Listen."

"Thank you, Mike. All right, here we go. This planet is what I think is called in English 'a set-up.' Let me describe it for you briefly as I see it, or rather as I've come to see it.

"Lithia is a paradise. It has resemblances to a number of other planets, but the closest correspondence is to the Earth in its pre-Adamic period, before the coming of the first glaciers. The resemblance ends there, because on Lithia the glaciers never came, and life continued to be spent in the paradise, as it was not allowed to do on Earth."

"Myths," Cleaver said sourly.

"I use the terms with which I'm most familiar; strip off those terms and what I am saying is still a fact that all of you know to be true. We find here a completely mixed forest, with plants that fall from one end of the creative spectrum to the other living side by side in perfect amity, cycad with cycladella, giant horsetail with flowering trees. To a great extent that's also true of the animals. The lion doesn't lie down with the lamb here because Lithia has neither animal, but as an allegory the phrase is apt. Parasitism occurs rather less often on Lithia than it does on Earth, and there are very few carnivores of any sort except in the sea. Almost all of the surviving land animals eat plants only, and by a neat arrangement which is typically Lithian, the plants are admirably set up to attack animals rather than each other.

"It's an unusual ecology, and one of the strangest things about it is its rationality, its extreme, almost single-minded insistence upon one-for-one relationships. In one respect it looks almost as though somebody had arranged the whole planet as a ballet about Mengenlehre—the theory of aggregates.

"Now, in this paradise we have a dominant creature, the Lithian, the man of Lithia. This creature is rational. It conforms, as if naturally and without constraint or guidance, to the highest ethical code we have evolved on Earth. It needs no laws to enforce this code. Somehow, everyone obeys it as a matter of course, although it has never even been written down. There are no criminals, no deviates, no aberrations of any kind. The people are not standardized—our own very bad and partial answer to the ethical dilemma—but instead are highly individual. They choose their own life courses without constraint—yet somehow no antisocial act of any kind is ever committed. There isn't even any word for such an act in the Lithian language."

The recorder made a soft, piercing pip of sound, announcing that it was threading a new tape. The enforced pause would last about eight seconds, and on a sudden inspiration, Ruiz-Sanchez put it to use. On the next pip, he said:

"Mike, let me stop here and ask you a question. What does this suggest to you, thus far?"

"Why, just what I've said before that it suggested," Michelis said slowly. "An enormously superior social science, evidently founded in a precise system of psychogenetics. I should think that would be more than enough."

"Very well, I'll go on. I felt as you did, at first. Then I came to ask myself some correlative questions. For instance: How does it happen that the Lithians not only have no deviates—think of that, *no* deviates!—but that the code by which they live so perfectly is, point for point, the code *we* strive to obey? If that just happened, it was by the uttermost of all coincidences. Consider, please, the imponderables involved. Even on Earth we have never known a society which evolved independently *exactly* the same precepts as the Christian precepts—by which I mean to include the Mosaic. Oh, there were some duplications of doctrine, enough to encourage the twentieth century's partiality toward synthetic religions like theosophism and Hollywood Vedanta, but no ethical system on Earth that grew up independently of Christianity agreed with it point for point. Not Mithraism, not Islam, not the Essenes—not even these, which influenced or were influenced by Christianity, were in good agreement with it in the matter of ethics.

"And yet here on Lithia, fifty light-years away from Earth and among a race as unlike man as man is unlike the kangaroos, what do we find? A Christian people, lacking nothing but the specific proper names and the symbolic appurtenances of Christianity. I don't know how you three react to this, but I found it extraordinary and indeed completely impossible—mathematically impossible—under any assumption but one. I'll get to that assumption in a moment."

"You can't get there any too soon for me," Cleaver said morosely. "How a man can stand fifty light-years from home in deep space and talk such parochial nonsense is beyond my comprehension."

"Parochial?" Ruiz-Sanchez said, more angrily than he had intended. "Do you mean that what we think true on Earth is automatically made suspect just by the fact of its removal into deep space? I beg to remind you, Paul, that quantum mechanics seem to hold good on Lithia, and that you see nothing parochial about behaving as if it does. If I believe in Peru that God created and still rules the universe, I see nothing parochial in my continuing to believe it on Lithia. You brought your parish with you; so did I. This has been willed where what is willed must be."

As always, the great phrase shook him to the heart. But it was obvious that it meant nothing to anyone else in the room; were such men hopeless? No, no. That Gate could never slam behind them while they lived, no matter how the hornets buzzed for them behind the deviceless banner. Hope was with them yet.

"A while back I thought I had been provided an escape hatch, incidentally," he said. "Chtexa told me that the Lithians would like to modify the growth of their population, and he implied that they would welcome some form of birth control. But, as it turns out, birth control in the sense that the Church interdicts it is impossible to Lithia, and what Chtexa had in mind was obviously some form of fertility control, a proposition to which the Church gave its qualified assent many decades ago. So there I was, even on this small point forced again to realize that we had found on Lithia the most colossal rebuke to our aspirations that we had ever encountered: a people that seems to live with ease the kind of life which we associate with saints alone.

"Bear in mind that a Muslim who visited Lithia would find no such thing; though he would find a form of polygamy here, its purposes and methods would revolt him. Neither would a Taoist. Neither would a Zoroastrian, presuming that there were still such, or a classical Greek. But for the four of us—and I include you, Paul, for despite your tricks and your agnosticism you still subscribe to the Christian ethical doctrines enough to be put on the defensive when you flout them—what we four have here on Lithia is a coincidence which beggars description. It is more than an astronomical coincidence—(that tired old metaphor for numbers that don't seem very large anymore)—it is a transfinite coincidence. It would take the shade of Cantor himself to do justice to the odds against it."

"Wait a minute," Agronski said. "Holy smoke. I don't know any anthropology, Mike, I'm lost here. I was with the Father up to the part about the mixed forest, but I don't have any standards to judge the rest. Is it so, what he says?"

"Yes, I think it's so," Michelis said slowly. "But there could be differences of opinion as to what it means, if anything. Ramon, go on."

"I will. There's still a good deal more to say. I'm still describing the planet, and more particularly the Lithians. The Lithians take a lot of explaining. What I've said about them thus far states only the most obvious fact. I could go on to point out many more, equally obvious facts. They have no nations and no regional rivalries, yet if you look at the map of Lithia—all those small continents and archipelagoes separated by thousands of miles of seas—you'll see every reason why they *should* have developed such rivalries. They have emotions and passions, but are never moved by them to irrational acts. They have only one language, and have never had more than this same one—which again should have been made impossible by the geography of Lithia. They exist in complete harmony with everything, large and small, that they find in their world. In short, they're a people that couldn't exist—and yet does.

"Mike, I'll go beyond your view to say that the Lithians are the most perfect example of how human beings *ought* to behave that we're ever likely to find, for the very simple reason that they behave now the way human beings once behaved before we fell in our own Garden. I'd go even farther: as an example, the Lithians are useless to us, because until the coming of the Kingdom of God no substantial number of human beings will ever be able to imitate the Lithian conduct. Human beings seem to have built-in imperfections that the Lithians lack—original sin, if you like—so that after thousands of years trying, we are farther away than ever from our original emblems of conduct, while the Lithians have never departed from theirs.

"And don't allow yourselves to forget for an instant that these emblems of conduct are the same on both planets. That couldn't ever have happened, either—but it did.

"I'm now going to adduce another interesting fact about Lithian civilization. It is a fact, whatever you may think of its merits as evidence. It is this: that your Lithian is a creature of logic. Unlike Earthmen of all stripes, he has no gods, no myths, no legends. He has no belief in the supernatural—or, as we're calling it in our barbarous jargon these days, the 'paranormal.' He has no traditions. He has no tabus. He has no faiths, except for an impersonal belief that he and his lot are indefinitely improvable. He is as rational as a machine. Indeed, the only way in which we can distinguish the Lithian from an organic computer is his possession and use of a moral code.

"And that, I beg you to observe, is *completely irrational.* It is based upon a set of axioms, a set of propositions which were 'given' from the beginning—though your Lithian sees no need to postulate any Giver. The Lithian, for instance Chtexa, believes in the sanctity of the individual. Why? Not by reason, surely, for there is no way to reason to that proposition. It is an axiom. Or: Chtexa believes in the right of juridical defense, in the equality of all before the code. Why? It's possible to behave rationally *from* the proposition, but it's impossible to reason one's way *to* it. It's given. If you assume that the responsibility to the code varies with the individual's age, or with what family he happens to belong to, logical behavior can follow from one of these assumptions, but there again one can't arrive *at* the principle by reason alone.

"One begins with belief: 'I think that all people ought to be equal before the law.' That is a statement of faith, nothing more. Yet Lithian civilization is so set up as to suggest that one can arrive at such basic axioms of Christianity, and of Western civilization on Earth as a whole, by reason alone—in the plain face of the fact that one cannot. One rationalist's axiom is another one's madness."

"Those *are* axioms," Cleaver growled. "You don't arrive at them by faith, either. You don't arrive at them at all. They're self-evident—that's the definition of an axiom."

"It was until the physicists kicked that definition to pieces," Ruiz-Sanchez said, with a certain grim relish. "There's the axiom that only one parallel can be drawn to a given line. It may be self-evident, but it's also untrue, isn't it? And it's self-evident that matter is solid. Go on, Paul, you're a physicist yourself. Kick a stone for me, and say, 'Thus I refute Bishop Berkeley.' "

"It's peculiar," Michelis said in a low voice, "that Lithian culture should be so axiom-ridden, without the Lithians being aware of it. I hadn't formulated it in quite these terms before, Paul, but I've been disturbed myself at the bottomless *assumptions* that lie behind Lithian reasoning—all utterly unprobed, although in other respects the Lithians are very subtle. Look at what they've done in solid-state chemistry, for instance. It's a structure of the purest kind of reason, and yet when you get down to its fundamental assumptions you discover the axiom: 'Matter is real.' How can they know that? How did logic lead them to it? It's a very shaky notion, in my opinion. If I say that the atom is just a-hole-inside-a-hole-through-a-hole, how can they controvert me?"

"But their system works," Cleaver said.

"So does our solid-state theory—but we work from opposite axioms," Michelis said. "Whether it works or not isn't the issue. The question is, what is it that's working? I don't myself see how this immense structure of reason which the Lithians have evolved can stand for an instant. It doesn't seem to rest on anything. 'Matter is real' is a crazy proposition, when you come right down to it; all the evidence points in exactly the opposite direction."

"I'm going to tell you," Ruiz-Sanchez said. "You won't believe me, but I'm going to tell you anyhow, because I have to. *It stands because it's being propped up.* That's the simple answer and the whole answer. But first I want to add one more fact about the Lithians:

"They have complete physical recapitulation outside the body."

"What does that mean?" Agronski said.

"You know how a human child grows inside its mother's body. It is a one-celled animal to begin with, and then a simple metazoan resembling the fresh-water hydra or a simple jellyfish. Then, very rapidly, it goes through many other animal forms, including the fish, the amphibian, the reptile, the lower mammal, and finally becomes enough like a man to be born. I don't know how this was taught to you as a geologist, but biologists call the process *recapitulation.*

"The term assumes that the embryo is passing through the various stages of evolution which brought life from the single-celled organism to man, but on a contracted time scale. There is a point, for instance, in the development of the fetus when it has gills, though it never uses them. It has a tail almost to the very end of its time in the womb, and rarely it still has it when it is born; and the tail-wagging muscle, the pubococcygeus, persists in the adult—in women it becomes transformed into the contractile ring around the vestibule. The circulatory system of the fetus in the last month is still reptilian, and if it fails to be completely transformed before birth, the infant emerges as a 'blue baby' with patent ductus arteriosus, the tetralogy of Fallot, or a similar heart defect which allows venous blood to mix with arterial—which is the rule with terrestrial reptiles. And so on."

"I see," Agronski said. "It's a familiar idea; I just didn't recognize the term. I had no idea that the correspondence was that close either, come to think of it."

"Well, the Lithians, too, go through this series of metamorphoses as they grow up, but they go through it *outside* the bodies of their mothers. This whole planet is one huge womb. The Lithian female lays her eggs in her abdominal pouch, the eggs are fertilized, and then she goes to the sea to give birth to her children. What she bears is not a miniature of the marvelously evolved reptile which is the adult Lithian; far from it: instead, she hatches a fish, rather like a lamprey. The fish lives in the sea a while, and then develops rudimentary lungs and comes to live along the shore lines. Once it's stranded on the flats by the tides, the lungfish's pectoral fins become simple legs, and it squirms away through the mud, changing into an amphibian and learning to endure the rigors of living away from the sea. Gradually their limbs become stronger, and better set on their bodies, and they become the big froglike things we sometimes see down the hill, leaping in the moonlight, trying to get away from the crocodiles.

"Many of them do get away. They carry their habit of leaping with them into the jungle, and there they change once again, into the small, kangaroo-like reptiles we've all seen, fleeing from us among the trees—the things we called the 'hoppers.' The last change is circulatory—from the sauropsid blood system which still permits some mixing of venous and arterial blood, to the pteropsid system we see in Earthly birds, which supplies nothing to the brain but oxygenated arterial blood. At about the same time, they become homeostatic and homeothermic, as mammals are. Eventually, they emerge, fully grown, from the jungles, and take their places among the folk of the cities as young Lithians, ready for education.

"But they have *already* learned every trick of every environment that their world has to offer. Nothing is left them to learn but their own civilization; their instincts are fully matured, fully under control; their rapport with nature on Lithia is absolute; their adolescence is passed and can't distract their intellects—they are ready to become social beings in every possible sense."

Michelis locked his hands together again in an agony of quiet excitement, and looked up at Ruiz-Sanchez.

"But that—that's a discovery beyond price!" he whispered. "Ramon, that alone is worth our trip to Lithia. What a stunning, elegant—what a *beautiful* sequence—and what a brilliant piece of analysis!"

"It is very elegant," Ruiz-Sanchez said dispiritedly. "He who would damn us often gives us gracefulness. It is not the same thing as Grace."

"But is it as serious as all that?" Michelis said, his voice charged with urgency. "Ramon, surely your Church can't object to it in any way. Your theorists accepted recapitulation in the human embryo, and also the geological record that showed the same process in action over longer spans of time. Why not this?"

"The Church accepts facts, as it always accepts facts," Ruiz-Sanchez said. "But—as you yourself suggested hardly ten minutes ago—facts have a way of pointing in several different directions at once. The Church is as hostile to the doctrine of evolution—particularly to that part of it which deals with the descent of man—as it ever was, and with good reason."

"Or with obdurate stupidity," Cleaver said.

"I confess that I haven't followed the ins and outs of all this," Michelis said. "What is the present position?"

"There are really two positions. You may assume that man evolved as the evidence attempts to suggest that he did, and that somewhere along the line God intervened and infused a soul; this the Church regards as a tenable position, but does not endorse it, because historically it had led to cruelty to animals, who are also creations of God. Or, you may assume that the soul evolved along with the body; this view the Church entirely condemns. But these positions are not important, at least not in this company, compared with the fact that the Church thinks *the evidence itself* to be highly dubious."

"Why?" Michelis said.

"Well, the Diet of Basra is hard to summarize in a few words, Mike; I hope you'll look it up when you get home. It's not exactly recent—it met in 1995, as I recall. In the meantime, look at the question very simply, with the original premises of the Scriptures in mind. If we assume that God created man, just for the sake of argument, did He create him perfect? I see no reason to suppose that He would have bothered with any lesser work. Is a man perfect without a navel? I don't know, but I'd be inclined to say that he isn't. Yet the first man—Adam, again for the sake of argument—wasn't born of woman, and so didn't really *need* to have a navel. Did he have one? All the great painters of the Creation show him with one: I'd say that their theology was surely as sound as their aesthetics."

"What does that prove?" Cleaver said.

"That the geological record, and recapitulation too, do not necessarily prove the doctrine of the descent of man. Given *my* initial axiom, which is that God created everything from scratch, it's perfectly logical that he should have given Adam a navel, Earth a geological record, and the embryo the process of recapitulation. None of these need indicate a real past; all might be there because the creations involved would have been imperfect otherwise."

"Wow," Cleaver said. "And I used to think that Haertel relativity was abstruse."

"Oh, that's not a new argument by any means, Paul; it dates back nearly two centuries—a man named Gosse invented it, not the Diet of Basra. Anyhow, any system of thought becomes abstruse if it's examined long enough. I don't see why my belief in a God you can't accept is any more rarefied than Mike's vision of the atom as a-hole-inside-a-hole-through-a-hole. I expect that in the long run, when we get right down to the fundamental stuff of the universe, we'll find that there's nothing there at all—just nothings moving no-place through no-time. On the day that that happens, I'll have God and you will not—otherwise there'll be no difference between us.

"But in the meantime, what we have here on Lithia is very clear indeed. We have—and now I'm prepared to be blunt—a planet and a people propped up by the Ultimate Enemy. It is a gigantic trap prepared for all of us—for every man on Earth and off it. We can do nothing with it but reject it, nothing but say to it, *Retro me, Sathanas.* If we compromise with it in any way, we are damned."

"Why, Father?" Michelis said quietly.

"Look at the premises, Mike. *One:* Reason is always a sufficient guide. *Two:* The self-evident is always the real. *Three:* Good works are an end in themselves. *Four:* Faith is irrelevant to right action. *Five:* Right action can exist without love. *Six:* Peace need not pass understanding. *Seven:* Ethics can exist without evil alternatives. *Eight:* Morals can exist without conscience. *Nine:* Goodness can exist without God. *Ten*—but do I really need to go on? We have heard all these propositions before, and we know What proposes them."

"A question," Michelis said, and his voice was painfully gentle. "To set such a trap, you must allow your Adversary to be creative. Isn't that—a heresy, Ramon? Aren't you now subscribing to a heretical belief? Or did the Diet of Basra—"

For a moment, Ruiz-Sanchez could not answer. The question cut to the heart. Michelis had found the priest out in the full agony of his defection, his belief betrayed, and he in full betrayal of his Church. He had hoped that it would not happen so soon.

"It is a heresy," he said at last, his voice like iron. "It is called Manichaeanism, and the Diet did not readmit it." He swallowed. "But since you ask, Mike, I do not see how we can avoid it now. I do not do this gladly, Mike, but we have seen these demonstrations before. The demonstration, for instance, in the rocks—the one that was supposed to show how the horse evolved from Eohippus, but which somehow never managed to convince the whole of mankind. If the Adversary *is* creative, there is at least some divine limitation that rules that Its creations be maimed. Then came the discovery of intra-uterine recapitulation, which was to have clinched the case for the descent of man. That one failed because the Adversary put it into the mouth of a man named Haeckel, who was so rabid an atheist that he took to faking the evidence to make the case still more convincing. Nevertheless, despite their flaws, these were both very subtle arguments, but the Church is not easily swayed; it is founded on a rock.

"But now we have, on Lithia, a new demonstration, both the subtlest and at the same time the crudest of all. It will sway many people who could have been swayed in no other way, and who lack the intelligence or the background to understand that it is a rigged demonstration. It seems to show us evolution in action on an inarguable scale. It is supposed to settle the question once and for all, to rule God out of the picture, to snap the chains that have held Peter's rock together all these many centuries. Henceforth there is to be no more question; henceforth there is to be no more God, but only phenomenology—and, of course, behind the scenes, within the hole that's inside the hole that's through a hole, the Great Nothing itself, the Thing that has never learned any word but *No* since it was cast flaming from heaven. It has many other names, but we know the name that counts. That will be all that's left us.

"Paul, Mike, Agronski, I have nothing more to say than this: We are all of us standing on the brink of Hell. By the grace of God, we may still turn back. We must turn back—for I at least think that this is our last chance."

NINE

The vote was cast, and that was that. The commission was tied, and the question would be thrown open again in higher echelons on Earth, which would mean tying Lithia up for years to come. *Proscripted area pending further study.* The planet was now, in effect, on the Index Expurgatorius.

The ship arrived the next day. The crew was not much surprised to find that the two opposing factions of the commission were hardly speaking to each other. It often happened that way.

The four commission members cleaned up in almost complete silence the house in Xoredeshch Sfath that the Lithians had given them. Ruiz-Sanchez packed the dark blue book with the gold stamping without being able to look at it except out of the corner of his eye, but even obliquely he could not help seeing its long-familiar title:

FINNEGANS WAKE
James Joyce

So much for his pride in his solution of the case of conscience the novel proposed. He felt as though he himself had been collated, bound and stamped, a tortured human text for future generations of Jesuits to explicate and argue.

He had rendered the verdict he had found it necessary for him to render. But he knew that it was not a final verdict, even for himself, and certainly not for the UN, let alone the Church. Instead, the verdict itself would be a knotty question for members of his Order yet unborn:

Did Father Ruiz-Sanchez correctly interpret the Divine case, and did this ruling, if so, follow from it?

Except, of course, that they would not use his name—but what good would it do them to use an alias? Surely there would never be any way to disguise the original of *this* problem. Or was that pride again—or misery? It had been Mephistopheles himself who had said, *Solamen miseris socios habuisse doloris. . . .*

"Let's go, Father. It'll be take-off time shortly."

"All ready, Mike."

It was only a short journey to the clearing, where the mighty spindle of the ship stood ready to weave its way back through the geodesics of deep space to the sun that shone on Peru. There was even some sunlight here, piercing now and then through low, scudding clouds; but it had been raining all morning, and would begin again soon enough.

The baggage went on board smoothly and without any fuss. So did the specimens, the films, the tapes, the special reports, the recordings, the sample cases, the slide boxes, the vivariums, the type cultures, the pressed plants, the animal cages, the tubes of soil, the chunks of ore, the Lithian manuscripts in their atmospheres of helium—everything was lifted decorously by the cranes and swung inside.

Agronski went up the cleats to the air lock first, with Michelis following him, a barracks bag slung over one shoulder. On the ground Cleaver was stowing some last-minute bit of gear, something that seemed to require delicate, almost reverent bedding down before the cranes could be allowed to take it in their indifferent grip; Cleaver was fanatically motherly about his electronic apparatus. Ruiz-Sanchez took advantage of the delay to look around once more at the near margins of the forest.

At once, he saw Chtexa. The Lithian was standing at the entrance to the path the Earthmen themselves had taken from the city to reach the ship. He was carrying something.

Cleaver swore under his breath and undid something he had just done to do it in another way. Ruiz-Sanchez raised his hand. Immediately Chtexa walked toward the ship, in great loping strides which nevertheless seemed almost leisurely.

"I wish you a good journey," the Lithian said, "wherever you may go. I wish also that your road may lead back to this world at some future time. I have brought you the gift that I sought before to give you, if the moment is now appropriate."

Cleaver had straightened and was now glaring up suspiciously at the Lithian. Since he did not understand the language, he was unable to find anything to which he could object. He simply stood there and radiated unwelcomeness.

"Thank you," Ruiz-Sanchez said. This creature of Satan made him miserable all over again, made him feel intolerably in the wrong. Yet how could Chtexa know—?

The Lithian was holding out to him a small vase, sealed at the top and provided with two gently looping handles. The gleaming porcelain of which it had been made still carried inside it, under the glaze, the fire which had formed it; it was iridescent, alive with long quivering festoons and plumes of rainbows, and the form as a whole would have made any potter of Greece abandon his trade in shame. It was so beautiful that one could imagine no use for it at all. Certainly one could not make a lamp of it, or fill it with leftover beets and put it in the refrigerator. Besides, it would take up too much space.

"This is the gift," Chtexa said. "It is the finest container yet to come out of Xoredeshch Gton. The material of which it is made includes traces of every element to be found on Lithia, even including iron, and thus, as you see, it shows the colors of every shade of emotion and of thought. On Earth, it will tell Earthmen much of Lithia."

"We will be unable to analyze it," Ruiz-Sanchez said. "It is too perfect to destroy, too perfect even to open."

"Ah, but we wish you to open it," Chtexa said. "For it contains our other gift."

"Another gift?"

"Yes, and a more important one. It is a fertilized, living egg of our species. Take it with you. By the time you reach Earth, it will have hatched, and will be ready to grow up with you in your strange and marvelous world. The container is the gift of all of us; but the child inside is my gift, for it is my child."

Appalled, Ruiz-Sanchez took the vase in trembling hands, as though he expected it to explode—as indeed he did. It shook with subdued flame in his grip.

"Good-bye," Chtexa said. He turned and walked away, back toward the entrance to the path. Cleaver watched him go, shading his eyes.

"Now what was that all about?" the physicist said. "The Snake couldn't have made a bigger thing of it if he'd been handing you his own head on a platter. And all the time it was only a jug!"

Ruiz-Sanchez did not answer. He could not have spoken even to himself. He turned away and began to ascend the cleats, cradling the vase carefully in one elbow. It was not the gift he had hoped to bring to the holy city for the grand indulgence of all mankind, no; but it was all he had.

While he was still climbing, a shadow passed rapidly over the hull: Cleaver's last crate, being borne aloft into the hold by a crane.

Then he was in the air lock, with the rising whine of the ship's Nernst generators around him. A long shaft of sunlight was cast ahead of him, picking out his shadow on the deck.

After a moment, a second shadow overlaid and blurred his own: Cleaver's. Then the light dimmed and went out.

The air lock door slammed.

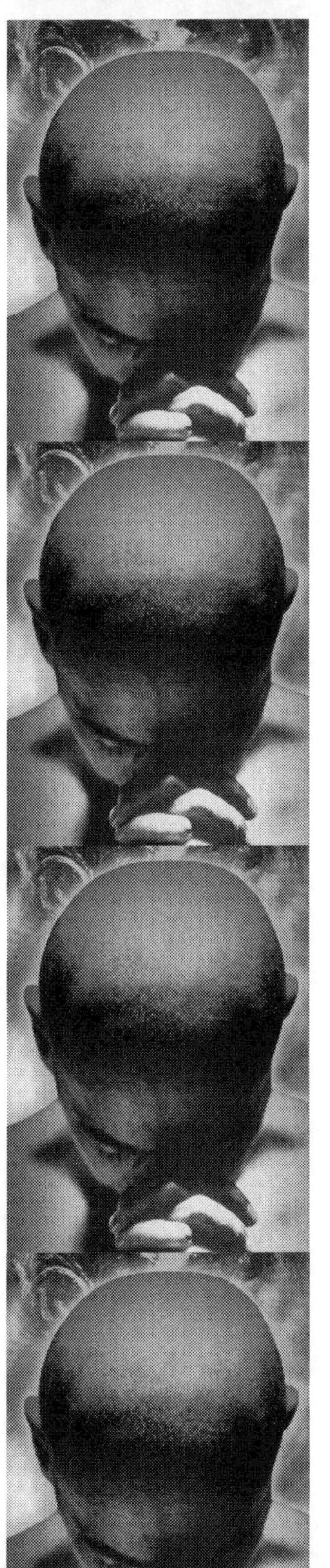

BOOK TWO

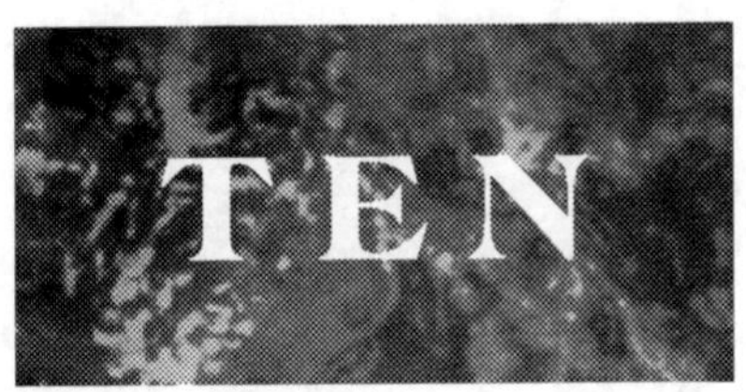

TEN

At first Egtverchi knew nothing, in the peculiarly regular and chilly womb where he floated, except his name. That was inherited, and marked in a twist of deoxyribonucleic acid upon one of his genes; farther up on the same chromosome, the x-chromosome, another gene carried his father's name: Chtexa. And that was all. At the moment he had begun his independent life, as a zygote or fertilized egg, that had been written down in letters of chromatin: his name was Egtverchi, his race Lithian, his sex male, his inheritance continuous back through Lithian centuries to the moment when the world of Lithia began. He did not need to understand this; it was implicit.

But it was dark, chilly, and too regular in the pouch. Tiny as a speck of pollen, Egtverchi drifted in the fluid which sustained him, from wall to smoothly curved and unnaturally glazed wall, not conscious yet, but constantly, chemically reminded that he was not in his mother's pouch. No gene that he carried bore his mother's name, but he knew—not in his brain, for he had none yet, but by feel, with purely chemical revulsion—whose child he was, of what race he was, and where he should be: *not here.*

And so he grew—and drifted, seeking to attach himself at every circuit to the chilly glass-lined pouch which rejected him always. By the time of gastrulation, the attachment reflex had run its course and he forgot it. Now he merely floated, knowing once more only what he had known at the beginning: his race Lithian, his sex male, his name Egtverchi, his father Chtexa, his life due to begin; and his birth world as bitter and black as the inside of a jug.

Then his notochord formed, and his nerve cells congregated in a tiny knot at one end of it. Now he had a front end and a hind end, as well as an address. He also had a brain—and now he was a fish—a spawn, not even a fingerling yet, circling and circling in the cold enclave of sea.

That sea was tideless and lightless, but there was some motion in it, the slow roll of convection currents. Sometimes, too, something went through it which was not a current, forcing him far down toward the bottom, or against the walls. He did not know the name of this force—as a fish he knew nothing, only circled with the endlessness of his hunger—but he fought it, as he would have fought cold or heat. There was a sense in his head, aft of his gills, which told him which way was up. It told him, too, that a fish in its natural medium has mass and inertia, but no weight. The sporadic waves of gravity—or acceleration—which whelmed through the lightless water were not part of his instinctual world, and when they were over he was often swimming desperately on his back.

There came a time when there was no more food in the little sea; but time and the calculations of his father were kind to him. Precisely at that time the weight force returned more powerfully than had even been suggested as possible before, and he was driven to sluggish immobility for a long period, fanning the water at the bottom of the jug past his gills with slow exhausted motions.

It was over at last, and then the little sea was moving jerkily from side to side, up and down, and forward. Egtverchi was now about the size of a larval fresh-water eel. Beneath his pectoral bones twin sacs were forming, which connected with no other system of his body, but were becoming more and more richly supplied with capillaries. There was nothing inside the sacs but a little gaseous nitrogen—just enough to equalize the pressure. In due course, they would be rudimentary lungs.

Then there was light.

To begin with, the top of the world was taken off. Egtverchi's eyes would not have focussed at this stage in any case and, like any evolved creature, he was subject to the neo-Lamarckian laws which provide that even a completely inherited ability will develop badly if it is formed in the absence of any opportunity to function. As a Lithian, with a Lithian's special sensitivity to the modifying pressures of environment, the long darkness had done him less potential damage than it surely would have done another creature—say, an Earth creature; nevertheless, he would pay for it in due course. Now, he could sense no more than that in the *up* direction (now quite stable and unchanging) there was light.

He rose toward it, his pectoral fins strumming the warm harps of the water.

Father Ramon Ruiz-Sanchez, late of Peru, late of Lithia, and always Fellow in the Society of Jesus, watched the surfacing, darting little creature with surfacing strange emotions. He could not help feeling for the sinuous eft the pity that he felt for every living thing, and an aesthetic delight in the flashing unpredictable certainty of its motions. But this little animal was Lithian.

He had had more time than he had wanted to explore the black ruin that underlay his position. Ruiz-Sanchez had never underestimated the powers which evil could still exercise, powers retained—even by general agreement within the Church—after its fall from beside the throne of the Most High. As a Jesuit he had examined and debated far too many cases of conscience to believe that evil is unsubtle or impotent. But that among these powers the Adversary numbered the puissance to create—no, that had never entered his head, not until Lithia. That power, at least, had to be of God, and of God only. To think that there could be more than one demiurge was outright heresy, and a very ancient heresy at that.

So be it, it was so, heretical or not. The whole of Lithia, and in particular the whole of the dominant, rational, infinitely admirable race of Lithians, had been created by Evil, out of Its need to confront men with a new, a specifically intellectual seduction, springing like Minerva from the brow of Jove. Out of that unnatural birth, as out of the fabled one, there was to come a symbolic clapping of palms to foreheads for everyone who could admit for an instant that any power but God could create; a ringing, splitting ache in the skull of theology; a moral migraine; even a cosmological shell shock, for Minerva was the mistress of Mars, on Earth as—undoubtedly, Ruiz-Sanchez remembered with anguish—as it is in heaven.

After all, he had been there, and he knew.

But all that could wait a little while, at least. For the moment it was sufficient that the little creature, so harmlessly like a three-inch eel, was still alive and apparently healthy. Ruiz-Sanchez picked up a beaker of water, cloudy with thousands of cultured *Cladocera* and Cyclops, and poured nearly half of it into the subtly glowing amphora. The infant Lithian flashed instantly away into the darkness, in chase after the nearly microscopic crustaceans. Appetite, the priest reflected, is a universal barometer of health.

"Look at him go," a soft voice said beside his shoulder. He looked up, smiling. The speaker was Liu Meid, the UN laboratory chief whose principal charge the Lithian child would be for many months. A small, black-haired girl with an expression of almost childlike calm, she peered into the vase expectantly, waiting for the imago to reappear.

"They won't make him sick, do you think?" she said.

"I hope not," Ruiz-Sanchez said. "They're Earthly, it's true, but Lithian metabolism is remarkably like ours. Even the blood pigment is an analogue of hemoglobin, though the metal base isn't iron, of course. Their plankton includes forms very like Cyclops and the water flea. No; if he's survived the trip, I daresay our subsequent care won't kill him, not even with kindness."

"The trip?" Liu said slowly. "How could that have hurt him?"

"Well, I really can't say exactly. It was simply the chance that we took. Chtexa—that was his father—presented him to us inside this vase, already sealed in. We had no way of knowing what provisions Chtexa had made for his child against the various strains of space flight. And we didn't dare look inside to see; if there was one thing of which I was certain, it was that Chtexa wouldn't have sealed the vase without a reason; after all, he does know the physiology of his own race better than any of us, even Dr. Michelis or myself."

"That's what I was getting at," Liu said.

"I know; but you see, Liu, Chtexa *doesn't* know space flight.

Oh, ordinary flight stresses are no secret to him—the Lithians fly jets; it was the Haertel overdrive that *I* was worried about. You'll remember the fantastic time effects that Garrard went through on that first successful centaurus flight. I couldn't explain the Haertel equations to Chtexa even if I'd had the time. They're classified against him; besides, he couldn't have understood them, because Lithian math doesn't include transfinites. And time is of the utmost importance in Lithian gestation."

"Why?" Liu said. She peered down into the amphora again, with an instinctive smile.

The question touched a nerve which had lain exposed in Ruiz-Sanchez for a long time. He said carefully: "Because they had physical recapitulation outside the body, Liu. That's why that creature in there is a fish; as an adult, it will be a reptile, though with a pteropsid circulatory system and a number of other unreptilian features. The Lithian females lay their eggs in the sea—"

"But it's fresh water in the jug."

"No, it's sea water; the Lithian seas are not so salty as ours. The egg hatches into a fishlike creature, such as you see in there; then the fish develops lungs and is beached by the tides. I used to hear them barking in Xoredeshch Sfath—they barked all night long, blowing the water out of their lungs and developing their diaphragm musculature."

Unexpectedly, he shuddered. The recollection of the sound was far more disturbing than the sound itself had been. Then, he had not known what it was—or, no, he had known that, but he had not known what it meant.

"Eventually the lungfish develop legs and lose their tails, like a tadpole, and go off into the Lithian forests as true amphibians. After a while, their respiratory system loses its dependence upon the skin as an auxiliary source, so they no longer need to stay near water. Eventually, they become true adults, a very advanced type of reptile, marsupial, bipedal, homeostatic—and highly intelligent. The new adults come out of the jungle and are ready for education in the cities."

Liu took a deep breath. "How marvelous," she whispered.

"It is just that," he said somberly. "Our own children go through nearly the same changes in the womb, but they're protected throughout; the Lithian children have to run the gauntlet of every ecology their planet possesses. That's why I was afraid of the Haertel overdrive. We insulated the vase against the drive fields as best we could, but in a maturation process so keyed to the appearances of evolution, a time slow-down could have been crucial. In Garrard's case, he was slowed down to an hour a second, then whipped up to a second an hour, then back again, and so on along a sine wave. If there'd been the slightest break in the insulation, something like that might have happened to Chtexa's child, with unknownable results. Evidently, there was no leak, but I was worried."

The girl thought about it. In order to keep himself from thinking about it, for he had already pondered himself in dwindling spirals to a complete, central impasse, Ruiz-Sanchez watched her think. She was always restful to watch, and Ruiz-Sanchez needed rest. It now seemed to him that he had had no rest at all since the moment when he had fainted on the threshold of the house in Xoredeshch Sfath, directly into the astonished Agronski's arms.

Liu had been born and raised in the state of Greater New York. It was Ruiz-Sanchez' most heartfelt compliment that nobody would have guessed it; as a Peruvian he hated the nineteen-million-man megalopolis with an intensity he would have been the first to characterize as unchristian.

There was nothing in the least hectic or harried about Liu. She was calm, slow, serene, gentle, her reserve unshakable without being in the least cold or compulsive, her responses to everything that impinged upon her as direct and uncomplicated as a kitten's; her attitude toward her fellow men virtually unsuspicious, not out of naïveté, but out of her confidence that the essential Liu was so inviolable as to prevent anyone even from wanting to violate it.

These were the abstract terms which first came to Ruiz-Sanchez' mind, but immediately he came to grief over a transitional thought. As nobody would take Liu for a New Yorker—even her speech betrayed not a one of the eight dialects, all becoming more and more mutually unintelligible, which were spoken in the city, and in particular one would never have guessed that her parents spoke nothing but Bronix—so nobody could have taken her for a female laboratory technician.

This was not a line of thought that Ruiz-Sanchez felt comfortable in following, but it was too obvious to ignore. Liu was as small-boned and intensely nubile as a geisha. She dressed with exquisite modesty, but it was not the modesty of concealment, but of quietness, of the desire to put around a firmly feminine body clothes that would be ashamed of nothing, but would also advertise nothing. Inside her soft colors, she was a Venus Callipygous with a slow, sleepy smile, inexplicably unaware that she—let alone anybody else—was expected by nature and legend to worship continually the firm dimpled slopes of her own back.

There now, that was quite enough; more than enough. The little eel chasing fresh-water crustacea in the ceramic womb presented problems enough, some of which were about to become Liu's. It would hardly be suitable to complicate Liu's task by so much as an unworthy speculation, though it be communicated by no more than a curious glance. Ruiz-Sanchez was confident enough of his own ability to keep himself in the path ordained for him, but it would not do to burden this grave sweet girl with a suspicion her training had never equipped her to meet.

He turned away hastily and walked to the vast glass west wall of the laboratory, which looked out over the city thirty-four storeys from the street—not a great height, but more than sufficient for Ruiz-Sanchez. The thundering, heat-hazed, nineteen-million-man megalopolis repelled him, as usual—or perhaps even more than usual, after his long stay in the quiet streets of Xoredeshch Sfath. But at least he had the consolation of knowing that he did not have to live here the rest of his life.

In a way, the state of Manhattan was only a relic anyhow, not only politically, but physically. What could be seen of it from here was an enormous multi-headed ghost. The crumbling pinnacles were ninety percent empty, and remained so right around the clock. At any given moment most of the population of the state (and of any other of the thousand-odd city-states around the globe) was underground.

The underground area was self-sufficient. It had its own thermonuclear power sources; its own tank farms, and its thousands of miles of illuminated plastic pipe through which algae suspensions flowed richly, grew unceasingly; decades worth of food and medical supplies in cold storage; water-processing equipment which was a completely closed circuit, so that it could recover moisture even from the air and from the city's own sewage; and air intakes equipped to remove gas, virus, fall-out particles or all three at once. The city-states were equally independent of any central government; each was under the hegemony of a Target Area Authority modeled on the old, self-policing port authorities of the previous century—out of which, indeed, they had evolved inevitably.

This fragmentation of the Earth had come about as the end product of the international Shelter race of 1960–85. The fission-bomb race, which had begun in 1945, was effectively over five years later; the fusion-bomb race and the race for the intercontinental ballistic missile had each taken five years more. The Shelter race had taken longer, not because any new physical knowledge or techniques had been needed to bring it to fruition—quite the contrary—but because of the vastness of the building program it involved.

Defensive though the Shelter race seemed on the surface, it had taken on all the characteristics of a classical arms race—for the nation that lagged behind invited instant attack. Nevertheless, there had been a difference. The Shelter race had been undertaken under the dawning realization that the threat of nuclear war was not only imminent but transcendent; it could happen at any instant, but its failure to break out at any given time meant that it had to be lived with for at least a century, and perhaps five centuries. Thus the race was not only hectic, but long-range—

And, like all arms races, it defeated itself in the end, this time because those who planned it had planned for too long a span of time. The Shelter economy was world-wide now, but the race had hardly ended when signs began to appear that people simply would not live willingly under such an economy for long; certainly not for five hundred years, and probably not for a century. The Corridor Riots of 1993 were the first major sign; since then, there had been many more.

The riots had provided the United Nations with the excuse it needed to set up, at long last, a real supranational government—a world state with teeth in it. The riots had provided the excuse—and the Shelter economy, with its neo-Hellenic fragmentation of political power, had given the UN the means.

Theoretically, that should have solved everything. Nuclear war was no longer likely between the member states; the threat was gone . . . but how do you *un*build a Shelter economy? An economy which cost twenty-five billion dollars a year, every year for twenty-five years, to build? An economy now embedded in the face of the Earth in uncountable billions of tons of concrete and steel, to a depth of more than a mile? It could not be undone; the planet would be a mausoleum for the living from now until the Earth itself perished: gravestones, gravestones, gravestones . . .

The word tolled in Ruiz-Sanchez' ears, distantly. The infra-bass of the buried city's thunder shook the glass in front of him. Mingled with it there was an ominous grinding sound of unrest, more marked than he had ever heard it before—like the noise of a cannon ball rolling furiously around and around in a rickety, splintering wooden track. . . .

"Dreadful, isn't it?" Michelis' voice said at his shoulder. Ruiz-Sanchez shot a surprised glance at the big chemist—not surprised that he had not heard Michelis enter, but that Mike was speaking to him again.

"It is," he said. "I'm glad you noticed it too. I thought it just might be hypersensitivity on my part—from having been away so long."

"It might well be that," Michelis agreed gravely. "I was away myself."

Ruiz-Sanchez shook his head.

"No, I think it's real," he said. "These are intolerable conditions to ask people to live under. And it's more than a matter of making them live ninety days out of every hundred at the bottom of a hole. After all, they think of living every day of their lives on the verge of destruction. We trained their parents to think that way, otherwise there'd never have been enough taxes to pay for the shelters. And of course the children have been brought up to think that too. It's inhuman."

"Is it?" Michelis said. "People lived all their lives on the verge for centuries—all the way up until Pasteur. How long ago was that?"

"Only about 1860," Ruiz-Sanchez said. "But no, it's quite different now. The pestilence was capricious; one's children might survive it; but fusion bombs are catholic." He winced involuntarily. "And there it is. A moment ago, I caught myself thinking that the shadow of destruction we labor under now is not only imminent but transcendent; I was burlesquing a tragedy; death in premedical days was always both imminent and immanent, impending and indwelling—but it was never transcendent. In those days, only God was impending, indwelling *and* transcendent all at once, and that was their hope. Today, we've given them Death instead."

"Sorry," Michelis said, his bony face suddenly turning flinty. "You know I can't argue with you on those grounds, Ramon. I've already been burned once. Once is enough."

The chemist turned away. Liu, who had been making a serial dilution at the long bench, was holding the ranked test tubes up to the daylight, and peeping up at Michelis from under her half-shut eyelids. She looked promptly away again as Ruiz-Sanchez' gaze fell on her face. He did not know whether she knew that he had caught her; but the tubes rattled a little in the rack as she put them down again.

"Excuse me," he said. "Liu, this is Dr. Michelis, one of my confreres on the commission to Lithia. Mike, this is Dr. Liu Meid, who'll be taking care of Chtexa's child for an indefinite period, more or less under my supervision. She's one of the world's best xenozoologists."

"How do you do," Mike said gravely. "Then you and the Father stand *in loco parentis* to our Lithian guest. It's a heavy responsibility for a young woman, I should think."

The Jesuit felt a thoroughly unchristian impulse to kick the tall chemist in the shins; but there seemed to be no conscious malice in Michelis' voice.

The girl merely looked down at the ground and sucked in her breath between slightly parted lips. "*Ah*-so-*deska,*" she said, almost inaudibly.

Michelis' eyebrows went up, but in a moment it became obvious that Liu was not going to say anything more, to him, right now. With a slight huff of embarrassment, Michelis addressed himself to the priest, catching him erasing the traces of a smile.

"So I'm all feet," Michelis said, grinning ruefully. "But I won't have time to practice my manners for a while yet. There are lots of loose ends to tie up. Ramon, how soon do you think you can leave Chtexa's child in Dr. Meid's hands? We've been asked to do a non-classified version of the Lithia report—"

"We?"

"Yes. Well, you and I."

"What about Cleaver and Agronski?"

"Cleaver's not available," Michelis said. "I don't offhand know where he is. And for some reason they don't want Agronski; maybe he doesn't have enough letters after his name. It's *The Journal of Intersellar Research,* and you know how stuffy they are—they're *nouveau riche* in terms of prestige, and that makes them more academic than the academicians. But I think it would be worth doing, just to get some of our data out into the open. Can you find the time?"

"I think so," Ruiz-Sanchez said thoughtfully. "Providing it can be sandwiched in between getting Chtexa's child born, and my pilgrimage."

Michelis raised his eyebrows again. "That's right, this is a Holy Year, isn't it?"

"Yes," Ruiz-Sanchez said.

"Well, I think we can work it in," Michelis said. "But—excuse me for prying, Ramon, but you don't strike me as a man in urgent need of the great pardon. Does this mean that you've changed your mind about Lithia?"

"No, I haven't changed my mind," Ruiz-Sanchez said quietly. "We are all in need of the great pardon, Mike. But I'm not going to Rome for that."

"Then—"

"I expect to be tried there for heresy."

There was light on the mud flat where Egtverchi lay, somewhere eastward of Eden, but day and night had not been created yet, nor was there yet wind or tide to whelm him as he barked the water from his itchy lungs and whooped in the fiery air. Hopefully he squirmed with his new forelimbs, and there was motion; but there was no place to go, and no one and nothing from which to escape. The unvarying, glareless light was comfortingly like that of a perpetually overcast sky, but Somebody had failed to provide for that regular period of darkness and negation during which an animal consolidates its failures and seeks in the depth of its undreaming self for sufficient joy to greet still another morning.

"Animals have no souls," said Descartes, throwing a cat out the window to prove, if not his point, at least his faith in it. The timid genius of mechanism, who threw cats well but Popes badly, had never met a true automaton, and so never saw that what the animal lacks is not a soul, but a mind. A computer which can fill the parameters of the Haertel equations for all possible values and deliver them in two and a half seconds is an intellectual genius but, compared even to a cat, it is an emotional moron.

As an animal which does not think, but instead responds to each minute experience with the fullness of immediately apprehended—and immediately forgotten—emotions which involve its whole body, needs the temporary death of nightfall to protract its life, so the newly emerged animal body requires the battles appointed to the day in order to become, at long last, the somnolent self-confident adult which has been written aforetime in its genes; and here, too, Somebody had failed Egtverchi. There was soap in his mud, a calculated percentage which allowed him to thrash on the floor of his cage without permitting him to make enough progress to bump his head against its walls. This was conservative of his head, but it wasted the muscles of his limbs. When his croaking days were over, and he was transformed into a totally air-breathing, leaping thing, he did not leap well.

This too had been arranged, in a sense. There was nothing in this childhood of his from which he needed to leap away in terror, nor was there any place in it to which a small leap could have carried him. Even the smallest jump ended with an invisible bang and a slithering fall for the end of which, harmless though it invariably proved to be, no instinct prepared him, and for which no learning-reflex helped him to cultivate a graceful recovery. Besides, an animal with a perpetually sprained tail cannot be graceful regardless of its instincts.

Finally, he forgot how to leap entirely, and simply sat huddled until the next transformation overcame him, looking back dully at the many bobbing heads that were beginning to ring him round during his every waking hour. By the time he realized that all these watchers were alive like himself, and much larger than he was, his instincts were so far submerged as to produce in him nothing more than a vague alarm which resulted in no action.

The new transformation turned him into a weak and spindly walker with no head for distance, oversized though it was. It was here that Somebody saw to it that he was transferred to the terrarium.

Here at last the hormones of his true adolescence awakened and began to flow in his blood. The proper responses for a world something like this tiny jungle had been written imperatively upon every chromosome in his body; here, all at once, he was almost at home. He roved through the verdure of the terrarium on his shaky shanks with a counterfeit of gladness, looking for something to flee, something to fight, something to eat, something to learn. Yet in the long run he hardly found even a place to sleep, for in the terrarium night was as unknown as ever.

Here he also became aware for the first time that there were differences among the creatures who looked in at him and sometimes molested him. There were two who were almost always to be seen, either alone or together. They were always the molesters, as well—except—except that it was not always exactly molestation, for sometimes these beings with their sharp stings and their rough hands would give him something to eat which he had never tasted before, or do something else to him which pleased as much as it annoyed. He did not understand this relationship at all, and he did not like it.

After a while, he hid from all the watchers except these two—and even from them most of the time, for he was always sleepy. When he wanted them, he would call: "Szan-tchez!" (For he could not say "Liu" at all; his mesentery-tied tongue and almost cleft palate would never master so demanding a combination of liquid sounds—that had to wait for his adulthood.)

But eventually he stopped calling, and took to squatting apathetically beside the pond in the center of the miniature jungle. When on the last night of his lizard existence he laid his bulging brain case again in that hollow of mosses where there was the most dimness, he knew in his blood that on the morrow, when he awoke into his doom as a thinking creature, he would be old with that age which curses those who have never even for an instant been young. Tomorrow he would be a thinking creature, but the weariness was on him tonight. . . .

And so he awoke; and so the world was changed. The multiple doors from sense to soul had closed; suddenly, the world was an abstract; he had made that crossing from animal to automaton which had caused all the trouble eastward of Eden in 4004 B.C.

He was not a man, but he would pay the toll on that bridge all the same. From this point on, nobody would ever be able to guess what he felt in his animal soul, least of all Egtverchi himself.

"But what is he thinking about?" Liu said wonderingly, staring up at the huge, grave Lithian head which bent down upon them from the other side of the transparent pyroceram door. Egtverchi—he had told them his name very early—could hear her, of course, despite the division of the laboratory into two; but he said nothing. Thus far, he was anything but talkative, though he was a voracious reader.

Ruiz did not respond for a while, though the nine-foot young Lithian awed and puzzled him quite as much as he did Liu—and for better reasons. He looked sidewise at Michelis.

The chemist was ignoring them both. Ruiz could understand that well enough, as far as he himself was concerned; the attempt to write a joint but impartial report on the Lithian expedition for the *J.I.R.* had proven disastrous for the already tense relationship between the two scientists. But that same tension, he could see, was distressing Liu without her being quite aware of it, and that he could not let pass; she was innocent. He mustered a last-ditch attempt to draw Mike out.

"This is their learning period," he said. "Necessarily, they spend most of it listening. They're like the old legend of the wolf boy, who is raised by animals and comes into human cities without even knowing human speech—except that the Lithians don't learn speech in infancy and so have no block against learning it in young adulthood. To do that, they must listen very hard—most wolf boys never learn to talk at all—and that's what he's doing."

"But why won't he at least answer questions?" Liu said troubledly, without quite looking at Michelis. "How is he going to learn if he won't practice?"

"He hasn't anything to tell us yet, by his lights," Ruiz said. "And for him, we lack the authority to put questions. Any adult Lithian could question him, but obviously we don't qualify—and what Mike calls the foster-parent relationship couldn't mean anything to a creature adapted to a solitary childhood."

Michelis did not respond.

"He used to call us," Liu said softly. "At least, he used to call you."

"That's different. That's the pleasure response; it has nothing to do with authority, or affection either. If you were to put an electrode into the septal or caudate nucleus areas in the brain of a cat, or a rat, so that they could stimulate themselves electrically by pushing a pedal, you could train them to do almost anything that's within their powers, for no other reward but that jolt in the head. In the same way, a cat or a rat or a dog will learn to respond to its name, or to initiate some action, in order to gain pleasure. But you don't expect the animal to talk to you or answer questions just because it can do that."

"I never heard of the brain experiments," Liu said. "I think that's horrible."

"I think so too," Ruiz said. "It's an old line of research that got sidetracked somehow. I've never understood why some of our megalomaniacs didn't follow it up in human beings. A dictatorship founded on that device might really last a thousand years. But it has nothing to do with what you're asking of Egtverchi. When he's ready to talk, he'll talk. In the meantime, we don't have the stature to compel him to answer questions. For that, we would have to be twelve-foot Lithian adults."

Egtverchi's eyes filmed, and he brought his hands together suddenly.

"You are already too tall," his harsh voice said over the annunciator system.

Liu clapped her hands together in delighted imitation.

"See, see, Ramon, you're wrong! Egtverchi, what do you mean? Tell us!"

Egtverchi said experimentally: "Liu, Liu. Liu."

"Yes, yes. That's right, Egtverchi. Go on, go on—what do you mean—tell us!"

"Liu." Egtverchi seemed satisfied. The colors in his wattles died down. He was again almost a statue.

After a moment, there was an explosive snort from Michelis. Liu turned to him with a start, and, without really meaning to, so did Ruiz.

But it was too late. The big New Englander had already turned his back on them, as though disgusted at himself for having broken his own silence. Slowly, Liu too turned her back, if only to hide her face from everyone, even Egtverchi.

Ruiz was left standing alone at the vertex of the tetrahedron of disaffection.

"This is going to be a fine performance for a prospective citizen of the United Nations to turn in," Michelis said suddenly, bitterly, from somewhere behind his shoulder. "I suppose you expected nothing else when you asked me here. What moved you to tell me what vast progress he was making? As I got the story, he ought to have been propounding theorems by this time."

"Time," Egtverchi said, "is a function of change, and change is the expression of the relative validity of two propositions, one of which contains a time *t* and the other a time *t*-prime, which differ from each other in no respect except that one contains the coordinate *t* and the other the coordinate *t*-prime."

"That's all very well," Michelis said coldly, turning to look up at the great head. "But I know where you got it from. If you're only a parrot, you're not going to be a citizen of *this* culture; you can take that from me."

"Who are you?" Egtverchi said.

"I'm your sponsor, God help me," Michelis said. "I know my own name, and I know what kind of record goes with it. If you expect to be a citizen, Egtverchi, you'll have to do better than pass yourself off as Bertrand Russell, or Shakespeare for that matter."

"I don't think he has any such notion," Ruiz said. "We explained the citizenship proposal to him, but he didn't give us any sign that he understood it. He just finished reading the *Principia* last week, so there's nothing unlikely about his feeding it back. He does that now and then."

"In first-order feedback," Egtverchi said somnolently, "if the connections are reversed, any small disturbance will be self-aggravating. In second-order feedback, going outside normal limits will force random changes in the network which will stop only when the system is stable again.

"God damn it!" Mike said savagely. "Now where did he get *that*? Stop it, you! You don't fool me for a minute!"

Egtverchi closed his eyes and fell silent.

Suddenly Michelis shouted: "Speak up, damn it!"

Without opening his eyes, Egtverchi said: "Hence the system can develop vicarious function if some of its parts are destroyed." Then he was silent again; he was alseep. He was often asleep, even these days.

"Fugue," Ruiz said softly. "He thought you were threatening him."

"Mike," Liu said, turning to him with a kind of desperate earnestness, "what do you think you're doing? He won't answer you, he can't answer you, especially when you speak to him like that! He's only a child, whatever you think when you have to look up at him! Obviously he learns many of these things by rote. Sometimes he says them when they seem to be apposite, but when we question him, he never carries it any farther. Why don't you give him a chance? *He* didn't ask you to bring any citizenship committee here!"

"Why don't you give *me* a chance?" Michelis said raggedly. Then he turned white-on-white. After a moment, so did Liu.

Ruiz looked up again at the slumbering Lithian and, as assured as he could be that Egtverchi was truly asleep, pressed the button which brought the rumbling metal curtain down in front of the transparent door. To the last, Egtverchi did not seem to move. Now they were isolated and away from him; Ruiz did not know whether this would make any difference, but he had his doubts about the innocence of Egtverchi's responses. To be sure, he had not overtly done anything but make an enigmatic statement, ask a simple question, quote from his reading—yet somehow everything he said had helped matters to go more badly than before.

"Why did you do that?" Liu said.

"I wanted to clear the air," Ruiz said quietly. "He's asleep, anyhow. Besides, we don't have any argument with Egtverchi yet. He may not be equipped to argue with us. But we've got to talk to each other—you too, Mike."

"Haven't you had enough of that already, Ramon?" Michelis said, in a voice a little more like his own.

"Preaching is my vocation," Ruiz said. "If I make a vice of it, I expect to atone for that somewhere else than here. But in the meantime—Liu, part of our trouble is the quarrel that I mentioned to you. Mike and I sharply disagreed on what Lithia means to the human race, indeed we disagreed on whether Lithia poses us any philosophical question at all. I think the planet is a time bomb; Mike thinks that's nonsense. And he thought that a general article for a scientific audience was no place to raise such questions, especially since this particular question has been posed officially and hasn't been adjudicated yet. And that's one reason why we're all snarling at each other right now, without any surface reason for it."

"What a cold thing to be heated about!" Liu said. "Men are so exasperating. How could a problem like that matter now?"

"I can't tell you," Ruiz said helplessly. "I can't be specific—the whole issue is under security seal. Mike thinks even the general issues I wanted to raise are graveyarded for the time being."

"But what we're waiting for is to find out what's going to happen to Egtverchi," Liu said. "The UN examining group must be already on its way. What business do you have to be hatching philosophical mandrake's-eggs when the life of a—of a human being, there's no other way to put it—is hanging on the next half hour?"

"Liu," Ruiz said gently, "forgive me, but are you so convinced that Egtverchi is what you mean by a human being—a *hnau*, a rational soul? Does he talk like one? You were complaining yourself that he won't answer questions, and that very often when he speaks he doesn't make much sense. I've talked to adult Lithians, I knew Egtverchi's father well, and Egtverchi isn't much like them, let alone much like a human being. Hasn't anything that's happened in the past hour changed your mind?"

"Oh, no," Liu said warmly, reaching out her hands for the Jesuit's. "Ramon, you've heard him talk yourself, as much as I have—you've tended him with me—you know he's not just an animal! He can be brilliant when he wants to be!"

"You're right, the mandrake's eggs have nothing to do with the case," Michelis said, turning and looking at Liu with dark, astonishingly pain-haunted eyes. "But I can't make Ramon listen to me. He's becoming more and more bound in some rarefied theological torture of his own. I'm sorry Egtverchi isn't as far along as I'd thought, but I foresaw almost from the beginning, I think, that he was going to be a serious embarrassment to us all, the closer he approaches his full intelligence.

"And I didn't get all my information from Ramon. I've seen the protocol on the progressive intelligence tests. Either they're reports on something phenomenal, or else we have no really trustworthy way of measuring Egtverchi's intelligence at all—and that may add up to the same thing in the end. If the tests are right, what's going to happen when Egtverchi finally does grow up? He's the son of a highly intelligent inhuman culture, and he's turning out to be a genius to boot—and his present status is that of an animal in a zoo! Or far worse than that, he's an experimental animal; that's how most of the public tends to think of him. The Lithians aren't going to like that, and furthermore the public won't like it when it learns the facts.

"That's why I brought up this whole citizenship question in the beginning. I see no other way out; we've got to turn him loose."

He was silent a moment, and then added, with almost his wonted gentleness:

"Maybe I'm naïve. I'm not a biologist, let alone a psychometrist. But I'd thought he'd be ready by now, and he isn't, so I guess Ramon wins by default. The interviewers will take him as he is, and the results obviously can't be good."

This was precisely Ruiz-Sanchez' opinion, though he would hardly have put it that way.

"I'll be sorry to see him go, if he leaves," Liu said abstractedly. It was evident, however, that she was hardly thinking about Egtverchi at all anymore. "But Mike, I *know* you're right, there's no other solution in the long run—he has to go free. He *is* brilliant, there's no doubt about that. Now that I come to think of it, even this silence isn't the natural reaction of an animal with no inner resources. Father, is there nothing we can do to help?"

Ruiz shrugged; there was nothing that he could say. Michelis' reaction to the apparent parroting and unresponsiveness of Egtverchi had of course been far too extreme for the actual situation, springing mostly from Michelis' own disappointment at the equivocal outcome of the Lithia expedition; he liked issues to be clear-cut, and evidently he had thought he had found in the citizenship maneuver a very sharp-edged tool indeed. But there was much more to it than that: some of it, of course, tied into the yet unadmitted bond which was forming between the chemist and the girl; in that single word "Father" she had shucked the priest off as a foster parent of Egtverchi, and put him in a position to give her away instead.

And what remained left over to be said would have no audience here. Michelis had already dismissed it as "some rarefied theological torture" which was personal to Ruiz and of no importance outside the priest's own skin. What Michelis dismissed would shortly fail to exist at all for Liu, if indeed it had not already been obliterated.

No, there was nothing further that could be done about Egtverchi; the Adversary was protecting his begotten son with all the old, divisive, puissant weapons; it was already too late. Michelis did not know how skilled UN naturalization commissions were at detecting intelligence and desirability in a candidate, even through the thickest smoke screen of language and cultural alienation, and at almost any age after the disease called "talking" had set in. And he did not realize how primed the commission would be to settle the Lithia question by a *fait accompli.* The visitors would see through Egtverchi within an hour at most, and then—

And then, Ruiz would be left with no allies at all. It seemed now to be the will of God that he be stripped of everything, and brought before the Holy Door with no baggage—not even such comforters as Job had, no, not even burdened by belief.

For Egtverchi would surely pass. He was as good as free—and closer to being a citizen in good standing than Ruiz himself.

Egtverchi's coming-out party was held at the underground mansion of Lucien le Comte des Bois-d'Averoigne, a fact which greatly complicated the already hysterical life of Aristide, the countess' caterer. Ordinarily, such a party would have presented Aristide with no problems reaching far beyond the technical ones with which he was already familiar, and used to drive the staff to that frantic peak which he regarded as the utmost in efficiency; but planning for the additional presence of a ten-foot monster was an affront to his conscience as well as to his artistry.

Aristide—born Michel di Giovanni in the timeless brutal peasantry of un-Sheltered Sicily—was a dramatist who knew well the intricate stage upon which he had to work. The count's New York mansion was many levels deep. The part of it in which the party was being held protruded one storey above the surface of Manhattan, as though the buried part of the city were coming out of hibernation—or not quite finished digging in for it. The structure had been a carbarn, Aristide had discovered, a dismal block-square redbrick building which had been put up in 1887 when cable street cars had been the newest and most hopeful addition to the city's circulatory system. The trolley tracks, with their middle division for the cable grips, were still there in the asphalt floor, with only a superficial coating of rust—steel does not rust appreciably in less than two centuries. In the center of the top storey was a huge old steam elevator with a basketwork shaft, which had once been used to lower the trolley cars below ground for storage. There were more tracks in the basement and sub-basement, whose elaborate switches led toward the segments of rail in the huge elevator cab. Aristide had been stunned when he first encountered this underlying blueprint, but he had promptly put it to good use.

The countess' parties, thanks to his genius, were now confined in their most formal phase to the uppermost of these three levels, but Aristide had installed a serpentine of fourteen two-chair cars which wound its way sedately along the trolley tracks, picking up as passengers those who were already bored with nothing but chatter and drinking, and rumbled onto the elevator to be taken down—with a great hissing and a cloud of rising steam, for the countess was a stickler for surface authenticity in antiques—to the next level, where presumably more interesting things were happening.

As a dramatist, Aristide also knew his audience: it was his job to provide that whatever was seen on the next levels *was* more interesting than what had been going on above. And he knew his *dramatis personae*, too: he knew more about the countess' regular guests than they knew about themselves, and much of his knowledge would have been decidedly destructive had he been the talkative type. Aristide, however, was an artist; he did not bribe; the notion was as unthinkable to him as plagiarism (except, of course, self-plagiarism; that was how you kept going during slumps). Finally, as an artist,

Aristide knew his patroness: he knew her to the point where he could judge just how many parties had to pass by before he could chance repeating an Effect, a Scene or a Sensation.

But what could you do with a ten-foot reptilian kangaroo?

From where he stood in a discrete pillared alcove on the above-ground entrance floor, Aristide watched the early guests filtering in from the reception room to the formal cocktail party, one of his favorite anachronisms, and one which the countess seemed prepared to allow him to repeat year after year. It required very little apparatus, but the most absurd and sub-lethal concoctions, and even more absurd costumes on the part of both staff and guests. The nice rigidity of the costumes provided a pleasant contrast to the unlimbering of the psyche which the drinks quickly induced.

Thus far, there were only the early comers: here, Senator Sharon, wagging her oversize eyebrows in wholesome cheeriness at the remaining guests, ostentatiously refusing drinks, secure in the knowledge that her good friend Aristide had provided for her below five strong young men not one of whom she had ever seen before: there, Prince William of East Orange, a young man whose curse was that he had no vices, and who came again and again to ride the serpentine in hopes of discovering one that he liked; and, nearby, Dr. Samuel P. Shovel, M.D., a jovial, red-cheeked, white-haired man who was the high priest of psichonetology, "the New Science of the Id," and a favorite of Aristide's, since he was easy to provide for—he was fundamentally nothing more complicated than a bottom-pincher.

Faulkner, the head butler, was approaching Aristide stiffly from the left. Ordinarily, Faulkner ran the countess' household like an oriental despot, but he was no longer in control while Aristide was on the premises.

"Shall I order in the embryos in wine?" Faulkner said.

"Don't be such a blind, stupid fool," Aristide said. He had learned his first English from sentimental 3-C 'casts, which gave his ordinary conversation decidedly odd overtones; he was well aware of it, and these days it was one of his principal weapons for driving his underlings, who could not tell when he said these things dispassionately from when he was really angry. "Go below, Faulkner. I'll call you when I need you—if I do."

Faulkner bowed slightly and vanished. Fuming mildly at the interruption, Aristide resumed his survey of the early comers.

In addition to the regulars, there was, of course, the countess, who had posed him no special problems yet. Her gilded makeup was still unmussed, and the mobiles in the little caves Stefano had contrived in her hair spun placidly or blinked their diamond eyes. Then there were the sponsors of the Lithian monster into Shelter society, Dr. Michelis and Dr. Meid; these two might present special problems, for he had been unable to find out enough about them to decide what personal tastes they might need to have catered to down below, despite the fact that they were key guests, second only to the impossible creature itself. There was an explosive potential here, Aristide knew with the certainty of fate, for that impossible creature was already more than an hour late, and the countess had let it be known to all the guests and to Aristide that the creature was to be the guest of honor; fully half of the party would be coming to see him.

There was no one else in the room at the moment but a UN man wearing a funny hat—a sort of crash helmet liberally provided with communications apparatus and other, unnamable devices, including bubble goggles which occasionally filmed over to become a miniature 3-V screen—and a Dr. Martin Agronski, whom Aristide could not place at all, and whom he regarded with the consequent intense suspicion he reserved for people whose weaknesses he could not even guess at. Agronski's face was as petulant as that of the Prince of East Orange, but he was a much older man, and it seemed unlikely that he was there for the same reasons. He had something to do with the guest of honor, which made Aristide all the more uneasy. Dr. Agronski seemed to know Dr. Michelis, but for an unaccountable reason shied away from him at every opportunity; he was spending most of his time at one of the most potent of Aristide's punches, with the glum determination of a non-drinker who believes that he can perfect his poise by poisoning his timidity. Perhaps a woman . . . ?

Aristide crooked a finger. His assistant scuttled around the back of the hanging floral decorations with a practiced stoop, covering even the sound of his movements by a brief delay which allowed the serpentine to come into its station, and cocked his ear to Aristide's mouth under the squeal of the train's brakes.

"Watch that one," Aristide said through motionless lips, pointing with the apex of one pelvic bone. "He will be drunk within the next half hour. Take him out before he falls down, but don't take him off the premises. She may ask for him later. Better put him in the recovery room and taper him off as soon as he begins to wobble."

The assistant nodded and pedaled away, bent double. Aristide was still talking to him in blunt, businesslike English; that was a good sign, as far as it went.

Aristide returned to watching the guests; their number was

growing a little, but he was still most interested in assessing the countess' reaction to the absence of the guest of honor. For the moment Aristide himself was in no danger, though he could see that the countess' hints had begun to acquire a certain hardness. Thus far, however, she was directing them at the monster's sponsors, Dr. Michelis and Dr. Meid, and it was plain that they had no answer for these gambits.

Dr. Michelis could only say over and over again, with a politeness which was becoming more and more formal as his patience visibly evaporated:

"Madame, I don't know when he's coming. I don't even know where he lives now. He promised to come. I'm not surprised that he's late, but I think he'll show up eventually."

The countess turned away petulantly, swinging her hips. Here was the first danger point for Aristide. There was no other pressure that the countess could bring to bear upon the monster's sponsors, regardless of how ignorant they were of the actual situation in the countess' household. By some trick of heredity, Lucien le Comte des Bois-d'Averoigne, Procurator of Canarsie, had been shrewd enough to spend his money wisely: he gave ninety-eight percent of it to his wife, and used the other two percent to disappear with for most of the year. There were even rumors that he did scientific research, though nobody could say in what field; certainly it could not be psichonetology or ufonics, or the countess would have known about it, since both were currently fashionable. And without the count, the countess was socially a nullity supported only by money; if the Lithian creature failed to show up at all, there was nothing that the countess could do to his sponsors but fail to invite them to the next party—which she would probably fail to do anyhow. On the other hand, there was a great deal that she might do to Aristide. She could not fire him, of course—he had kept careful dossiers against that possibility—but she could make his professional life with her very difficult indeed.

He signaled his second-in-command.

"Give Senator Sharon the canapé with the jolt in it as soon as there are ten more people on the floor," he directed crisply. "I don't like the way this is going. As soon as we have a minimum crowd, we'll have to get them rolling on the trains—Sharon's not the best Judas goat for the purpose, but she'll have to do. Take my advice, Cyril, or you will rue the day."

"Very good, Maestro," the assistant, whose name was not Cyril at all, said respectfully.

Michelis had hardly noticed the serpentine at the beginning, except as a novelty, but somehow or other it became noisier as the party grew older. It seemed to wind along the floor about every five minutes, but he soon realized that there were actually three such trains: the first one collected passengers up here; the second returned parties from the second level, to discharge wildly exhilarated recruiters among the cautiously formal newcomers on the first level; the third train, usually almost empty this early in the party's course, brought glassy-eyed party-poopers from the sub-basement, who were removed efficiently by the countess' livery in a covered station-stop well apart from the main entrance and well out of sight of new boarders for the nether levels. Then the whole cycle repeated itself.

Michelis had had every intention of staying off the serpentine entirely. He did not like the diplomatic service, especially now that it had nothing left to be diplomatic about, and anyhow he was far too dedicated to loneliness to be comfortable even at small parties, let alone anything like *this.* After a while, however, he became bored with repeating that same apology for Egtverchi, and aware that the top level of the party was now so empty that his and Liu's presence there was keeping their hostess against her will.

When Liu finally noticed that the serpentine not only toured this level but went below, he lost his last excuse to stay off it; and the elevator took all the rest of the newcomers down, leaving behind only the servants and a few bewildered scientific attachés who probably were at the wrong party to begin with. He looked about for Agronski, whose presence had astonished him earlier, but the hollow-eyed geologist had disappeared.

Everyone on the train shouted with glee and mock terror as the steam elevator took it down to the second level in utter blackness and rusty-smelling humidity. Then the great doors rolled up sharply in their eyes, and the train surged out, making an abrupt turn along its banked rails. Its plow-like nose butted immediately through a set of swinging double doors, plunged its passengers into even deeper darkness, and stopped completely with a grinding shudder.

From out of the darkness came a barrage of shrieking, hysterical feminine laughter and the shouting of men's voices.

"Oh, I can't stand it!"

"Henry, is that you?"

"Leggo of me, you bitch."

"I'm so dizzy!"

"Look out, the damn thing's speeding up again!"

"Get off my foot, you bastard."

"Hey, *you're* not my husband."

"Ugh. Lady, I couldn't care less."

"Woman's gone too far this—"

Then they were drowned out by a siren so prolonged and deafening that Michelis' ears rang frighteningly even after the sound had risen past the upper limits of audibility. Then there was the groan of machinery, a dim violet glow—

The serpentine was turning over and over in midspace, supported by nothing. Many-colored stars, none of them very bright, whirled past, rising on one side and sweeping over and then under the train with a period of only ten seconds from one "horizon" to the other. The shouts and the laughter were heard again, accompanied by a frantic scrabbling sound—and there came the siren again, first as a pressure, then as a thin singing which seemed to be inside the skull, and then as a prolonged sickening slide toward the infrabass.

Liu clutched frantically at Michelis' arm, but he could do nothing but cling to his seat. Every cell in his brain was flaring with alarm, but he was paralyzed and sick with giddiness—

Lights.

The world stabilized instantly. The serpentine sat smugly on its tracks, which were supported by cantilever braces; it had never moved. At the bottom of a gigantic barrel, disheveled guests looked up at the nearly blinded passengers of the train and howled with savage mockery. The "stars" had been spots of fluorescent paint, brought to life by hidden ultraviolet lamps. The illusion of spinning in midspace had been made more real by the siren, which had disturbed their vestibular apparatus, the inner ear which maintains the sense of balance.

"All out!" a rough male voice shouted. Michelis looked down cautiously; he was still a little dizzy. The shouter was a man in rumpled black evening clothes and fire-red hair; his huge shoulders had burst one seam of his jacket. "You get the next train. That's the rule."

Michelis thought of refusing, and changed his mind. Being tumbled in the barrel was probably less likely to produce serious wounds than would fighting with two people who had already "earned" their passage out in his and Liu's seats. There were rules of conduct for everything. A gang ladder protruded up at them; when their turn came, he helped Liu down it.

"Try not to fight it," he told her in a low voice. "When it starts to revolve, slide if you can, roll if you can't. Got a pyrostyle? All right, here's mine—jab if anybody stays too close, but don't worry about the drum—it looks thoroughly waxed."

It was: but Liu was frightened and Michelis in a murderously ugly mood by the time the next train came through and took them out; he was glad that he had not decided to argue with his predecessors in the barrel. Anybody who had tried the same thing with him might well have been killed.

The fact that he was drenched with perfume as the serpentine passed through the next cell did not exactly improve his temper, but at least the cell did not require anyone's participation. It was a sizable and beautiful garden made of blown glass in every possible color, in which live Javanese models were posed in dioramas of discovered lust; the situations depicted were melodramatic in the extreme but, except for their almost imperceptible breathing, the models did not move a muscle; they were almost as motionless as the glass foliage. To Michelis' surprise—for outside the sciences he had almost no aesthetic sense—Liu regarded these lascivious, immobile scenes with a kind of withdrawn, grave approval.

"It's an art, to suggest a dance without moving," she murmured suddenly, as though she had sensed his uneasiness. "Difficult with the brush, far more difficult with the body. I think I know the man who designed this; there couldn't be but one."

He stared at her as though he had never seen her before, and by the pure current of jealousy that shot through him he knew for the first time that he loved her. "Who?" he said hoarsely.

"Oh, Tsien Hi, of course. The last classicist. I thought he was dead, but this isn't a copy—"

The serpentine slowed before the exit doors long enough for two models, looking obscenely alive in very modest movement, to hand them each a fan covered with brushed drawings in ink. A single glance was enough to make Michelis thrust his fan in his pocket, unwilling to acknowledge ownership of it by so definite a gesture as throwing it away; but Liu pointed mutely to an ideogram and folded hers with reverence, "Yes," she said. "It is he; these are the original sketches. I never thought I'd own one—"

The train lurched forward suddenly. The garden vanished, and they were plunged into a vague, colored chaos of meaningless emotions. There was nothing to see or hear or feel, yet Michelis was shaken to his soul, and then shaken again, and again. He cried out, and dimly heard others crying. He fought for control of himself, but it eluded him, and . . . no, he had it now, or almost had it. . . . If he could only *think* for an instant—

For an instant, he managed it, and saw what was happening. The new cell was a long corridor, divided by invisible currents of moving air into fifteen sub-cells. Inside each subcell was a colored smoke, and in each smoke was some gas which went instantly home to the hypothalamus. Michelis recognized some of them: they were crude hallucinogenic compounds which had been developed during the heyday of tranquilizer research in the mid–twentieth century. Under the waves of fright, religious exaltation, berserker bravery, lust for power, and less namable emotions which each induced, he felt a mounting intellectual anger at such irresponsible wholesale tampering with the pharmacology of the mind for the sake of a momentary "experience"; but he knew that this kind of jolt-breathing was anything but uncommon in the Shelter state. The smokes had the reputation of being nonaddicting, which for the most part they were—but they were certainly habit-forming, which is quite a different thing, and not necessarily less dangerous.

A hazy, formless curtain of pink at the far end of the corridor proved to be a pure free-serotonin antagonist in high concentration, a true ataraxic which washed his mind free of every emotion but contentment with everything in all the wide universe. What must be, must be . . . it is all the best . . . there is peace in everything—

In this state of uncritical yea-saying, the passengers on the serpentine were run through an assembly line of elaborate and bestial practical jokes. It ended with a 3-V tape recreation of Belsen, in which the scenarist had cunningly made it appear that the people on the serpentine would be next into the ovens. As the furnace door closed behind them there was a blast of mind-cleansing oxygen; staggering with horror at what they had been about to accept with joy, the passengers were helped off the train to join a guffawing audience of previous victims.

Michelis' only impulse was to escape—above all he did not want to stay to laugh at the next load of passengers in shock—

but he was too exhausted to get beyond the nearest bench in the amphitheater, and Liu could hardly walk even that far. They were forced to sit there in the press until they had made a better recovery.

It was fortunate that they did. While they were nursing their drinks—Michelis had been deeply suspicious of the warm amber cups, but their contents had proved to be nothing but honest and welcome brandy—the next train was greeted with a roar of delight and a unanimous surge of the crowd at its feet.

Egtverchi had arrived.

There was a real mob now in the cocktail lounge above ground, but Aristide was far too happy; he had already cut off quite a few heads down below on the catering staff. He had somewhere inside him a very delicate sense which told him when a party was going sour, and that sense had put up the red alarms long before this. The arrival of the guest of honor in particular had been an enormous fiasco. The countess had not been on hand, the creature's sponsors had not been there, none of the really important guests who had been invited specifically to see the guest of honor had been there, and the guest himself had betrayed Aristide into showing, before all the staff, that he was frightened out of his wits.

He was bitterly ashamed of his fright, but the fact was now beyond undoing. He had been told to anticipate a monster, but not such a monster as this—a creature well *more* than ten feet high, a reptile which walked more like a man than like a kangaroo, with vast grinning jaws, wattles which changed color every few moments, small clawlike hands which looked as though they could pluck one like a chicken, a balancing tail which kept sweeping trays off tables, and above all a braying laugh and an enormous tenor voice which spoke English with a perfection so cold and carefully calculated as to make Aristide feel like a thumb-fingered leather-skinned Sicilian who had just landed. And at the monster's entrance, nobody but Aristide had been there to welcome him. . . .

A train rumbled into the atrium of the recovery room, but before it stopped, Senator Sharon tumbled out with a vast display of piano legs and black eyebrows. "Look at *him*!" she squealed, full of the five-fold revival Aristide had conscientiously arranged for her. "Isn't he *male*!"

Another failure for Aristide: it was one of the countess' standing orders that the Senator had to be put through her cell and fired out into the Shelter night long before the party proper could be said to have begun; otherwise the Senator would spend the rest of the evening, after her five-fold awakening, climbing from one pair of shoulders to another to a political, literary, scientific or any other eminence she could manage to attain at the expense of everyone else who could be bought with half an hour on a tabletop—and never mind that she would spend the rest of the next week falling down from that eminence into the swamps of nymphomania again. If Senator Sharon were not properly ejected this early, and with due assurances, in the warm glow of her aftermath, she was given to lawsuits.

The empty train pulled out invitingly into the lounge. The Lithian monster saw it and his grin got wider.

"I always wanted to be an engine driver," he said in a brassy English which nevertheless was more precise than anything to which Aristide would be able to pretend to the end of his life. "And there's the major-domo. Good sir, I've brought two, three, several guests of my own. Where is our hostess?"

Aristide pointed helplessly, and the tall reptile boarded the train at the front car, with a satisfied crow. He was scarcely settled in before the rest of his party was pouring across the lounge floor and piling in behind him. The train started with a jerk, and rumbled to the elevator. It sank down amid tall wisps of steam.

And that was that. Aristide had muffed the grand entrance. Had he had any doubts about it, they would have been laid to rest most directly: less than ten minutes later, he was snooted egregiously by Faulkner.

So much for being a dedicated artist with a loyal patroness, he thought dismally. Tomorrow, he would be a short-order cook in some Shelter commissariat, dossiers or no dossiers. And why? Because he had been unable to anticipate the time of arrival, let alone the desires or the friends, of some creature which had never been born on Earth at all.

He marched deliberately and morosely away from his post toward the recovery room, kicking assistants who were green enough to stay within range. He could think of nothing further to do but to supervise personally the tapering-off of Dr. Martin Agronski, the unknown guest who had something to do with the Lithian.

But he had no illusions. Tomorrow, Aristide, caterer to Countess des Bois-d'Averoigne, would be lucky to be Michel di Giovanni, late of the malarial plains of Sicily.

Michelis was sorry he had allowed himself and Liu aboard the serpentine the moment he understood the construction of the second level, for he saw at once that they would have virtually no chance of seeing Egtverchi's arrival. Fundamentally, the second level was divided by soundproof walls into a number of smaller parties, some of them only slightly drunker and more unorthodox than the cocktail party had been, but the rest running a broad spectrum of frenetic exoticism. He and Liu were carried completely around the course before he was able to figure out how to get the girl and himself safely off the serpentine; and each time he was moved to attempt it, the train began to go faster in unpredictable spurts, producing a sensation rather like that of riding a roller coaster in the middle of the night.

Nevertheless, they saw the only entrance that counted. Egtverchi emerged from the last gas bath standing in the head car of the serpentine, and stepped out of the car under his own power. In the next five cars behind him, also standing, were ten nearly identical young men in uniforms of black and lizard-green with silver piping, their arms folded, their expressions stern, their eyes straight ahead.

"Greetings," Egtverchi said, with a deep bow which his disproportionately small dinosaurian arms and hands made both comical and mocking. "Madame the Countess, I am delighted. You are protected by many bad smells, but I have braved them all."

The crowd applauded. The countess' reply was lost in the noise, but evidently she had chided him with being naturally immune to smokes which would affect Earthmen, for he said promptly, with a trace of hurt in his voice:

"I thought you might say that, but I'm grieved to be caught in the right. To the pure all things are pure, however—did you ever see such upstanding, unshaken young men?" He gestured at the ten. "But of course I cheated. I stopped their nostrils with filters, as Ulysses stopped his men's ears with wax to pass the sirens. My entourage will stand for anything; they think I am a genius."

With the air of a conjurer, the Lithian produced a silver whistle which seemed small in his hand, and blew into the thick air a white, warbling note which was utterly inadequate to the gesture which had preceded it. The ten soldierly young men promptly melted. The forefront of the crowd gleefully toed the limp bodies, which took the abuse with lax indifference.

"Drunk," Egtverchi said with fatherly disapproval. "Of course. Actually I didn't stop their noses at all. I prevented their reticular formations from reporting the countess' smokes to their brains until I gave the cue. Now they have gotten all the messages at once; isn't it disgraceful? Madame, please have them removed, such dissoluteness embarrasses me. I shall have to institute discipline."

The countess clapped her hands. "Aristide! Aristide?" She touched the transceiver concealed in her hair, but there was no response that Michelis could detect. Her expression changed abruptly from childish delight to infant fury. "Where is that lousy rustic—"

Michelis, boiling, shouldered his way into Egtverchi's line of sight with difficulty.

"Just what the hell do you think you're doing?" he said in a hoarse voice.

"Good evening, Mike. I am attending a party, just as you are. Good evening, dear Liu. Countess, do you know my foster parents? But I am sure you do."

"Of course," the countess said, turning her bare shoulders and back unmistakably on Michelis and Liu, and looking up at Egtverchi's perpetually grinning head from under gilded eyelids. "Let's go next door—there's more room, and it will be quieter. We've all seen enough of these train riders. After you, their arrivals will seem all alike."

"I cultivate the unique," Egtverchi said. "But I must have Mike and Liu by my side, Countess. I am the only reptile in the universe with mammalian parents, and I cherish them. I have a notion that it may be a sin; isn't that interesting?"

The gilded eyelids lowered. It had been years since the countess' caterers had come up with a new sin interesting enough to be withheld from the next evening's guests for private testing; that was common knowledge. She looked as if she scented one now, Michelis thought; and since she was, in fact, a woman of small imagination, Michelis was not in much doubt as to what it was. For all his saurian shape and texture, there was something about Egtverchi that was intensely, overwhelmingly masculine.

And intensely childlike, too. That the combination was perfectly capable of overriding any repugnance people might feel toward his additionally overwhelming reptilianness had already been demonstrated, in response to his first interview on 3-V. His wry and awry comments on Earthly events and customs had been startling enough, and perhaps it could have been predicted even then that the intelligentsia of the world would pick him up as a new fad before the week was out. But nobody had anticipated the flood of letters from children, from parents, from lonely women.

Egtverchi was a sponsored news commentator now, the first such ever to have an audience composed half-and-half of disaffected intellectuals and delighted children. There was no precedent for it in the present century, at least; learned men in communications compared him simultaneously with two historical figures named Adlai E. Stevenson and Oliver J. Dragon.

Egtverchi also had a lunatic following, though its composition had not yet been analyzed publicly by his 3-V network. Ten of these followers were being lugged limply out by the countess' livery right now, and Michelis' eyes followed them speculatively while he trailed with the crowd after Egtverchi and the countess, out of the amphitheater and into the huge lounge next door. The uniforms were suggestive—but of what? They might have been no more than costumes, designed for the party alone; had the ten young men who fell to the bleat of Egtverchi's silver whistle been physically different from each other, the effect would have been smaller, as Egtverchi would have known. And yet the whole notion of uniforms was foreign to Lithian psychology, while it was profoundly meaningful in Earth terms—and Egtverchi knew more about Earth than most Earthmen did, already.

Lunatics in uniforms, who thought Egtverchi to be a genius who could do no wrong; what could that mean?

Were Egtverchi a man, one would know instantly what it meant. But he was not a man, but a musician playing upon man as on an organ. The structure of the composition would not be evident for a long time to come—if it had a structure; Egtverchi might only be improvising, at least this early. That was a frightening thought in itself.

And all this had happened within a month of the awarding of citizenship to Egtverchi. That had been a pleasant surprise. Michelis was none too sure how he felt about the surprises that had followed; about those certain to come he was decidedly wary.

"I have been exploring this notion of parenthood," Egtverchi was saying. "I know who my father is, of course—it is a knowledge we are born with—but the concept that goes with the word is quite unlike anything you have here on Earth. *Your* concept is a tremendous network of inconsistencies."

"In what way?" the countess said, not very much interested.

"Why, it seems to be based on reverence for the young, and an extremely patient and protective attitude toward their physical and mental welfare. Yet you make them live in these huge caves, utterly out of contact with the natural world, and you teach them to be afraid of death—which of course makes them a little insane, because there is nothing anybody can do about death. It is like teaching them to be afraid of the second law of thermodynamics, just because living matter sets that law aside for a very brief period. How they hate you!"

"I doubt that they know I exist," the countess said drily. She had no children.

"Oh, they hate their own parents first of all," Egtverchi said, "but there is enough hatred left over for every other adult in your planet. They write me about it. They have never had anybody to say this to before, but they see in me someone who has had no hand in their torment, who is critical of it, and who obviously is a comical, harmless fellow who won't betray them."

"You're exaggerating," Michelis said uneasily.

"Oh no, Mike. I have prevented several murders already. There was one five-year-old who had a most ingenious plan, something involving garbage disposal. He was ready to include his mother, his father, and his fourteen-year-old brother, and the whole affair would have been blamed on a computational error in his city's sanitation department. Amazing that a child that age could have planned anything so elaborate, but I believe it would have worked—these Shelter cities of yours are so complex, they become lethal engines if even the most minute errors creep into them. Do you doubt me, Mike? I shall show you the letter."

"No," Michelis said slowly. "I don't think I do."

Egtverchi's eyes filmed briefly. "Some day I will let one of these affairs proceed to completion," he said. "As a demonstration, perhaps. Something of the sort seems to be in order."

Somehow Michelis did not doubt that he would, nor that the results would be as predicted. People did not remember their childhoods clearly enough to take seriously the rages and frustrations that shook children—and the smaller the child, the less superego it had to keep the emotions tamed. It seemed more than likely that a figure like Egtverchi would be able to tap this vast, seething underworld of impotent fury more effectively and easily than any human analyst, no matter how skilled and subtle, had ever been able to do.

And there was where you had to tap it, if you were hoping to do any good. Tapping it by hindsight, through analysis of adults, was successful with neurotics, but it had never proved effective against the psychoses; those had to be attacked pharmacologically, by regulating serotonin metabolism with ataraxics—the carefully tailored chemical grandchildren of the countess' crude smokes. That worked, but it was not a cure, but a maintenance operation—like giving insulin or sulfonylureas to a diabetic. The organic damage had already been done. In the great raveled knot of the brain, the basic reverberating circuits, once set in motion, could be interrupted but never discontinued—except by destructive surgery, a barbarity now a century out of use.

And it all fitted some of the disturbing things he had been discovering about the Shelter economy since his return from his long sojourn on Lithia. Having been born into it, Michelis had always taken that economy pretty much for granted; or at least his adult memory of his childhood told him that. Maybe it had really been different, and perhaps a little less grim, back in those days, or maybe that was just an illusion cherished by the silent censor in his brain. But it seemed to him that in those days people had let themselves become reconciled to these endless caverns and corridors for the sake of their children, in the hope that the next generation would be out from under the fear and could know something a little better—a glimpse of sunlight, a little rain, the fall of a leaf.

Since then, the restrictions on surface living had been relaxed greatly—nobody now believed in the possibility of nuclear war, since the Shelter race had produced an obvious impasse—but somehow the psychic atmosphere was far worse instead of better. The number of juvenile gangs roaming the corridors had increased four hundred percent while Michelis was out of the solar system; the UN was now spending about a hundred million dollars a year on elaborate recreation and rehabilitation programs for adolescents, but the rec centers stayed largely deserted, and the gangs continued to multiply. The latest measure taken against them was frankly punitive: a tremendous increase in the cost of compulsory insurance on power scooters, seemingly harmless, slow-moving vehicles which the gangs had adapted first to simple crimes like purse-snatching, and then to such more complicated and destructive games as mass raids on food warehouses, industrial distilleries, even utilities—it had been drag racing in the air ducts that had finally triggered the confiscatory insurance rates.

In the light of what Egtverchi had said, the gangs made perfect and horrible sense. Nobody now believed in the possibility of nuclear war, but nobody could believe in the possibility of a full return to surface life, either. The billions of tons of concrete and steel were far too plainly there to stay. The adults no longer had hopes even for their children, let alone for themselves. While Michelis had been away in the Eden of Lithia, on Earth the number of individual crimes without motive—crimes committed just to distract the committer from the grinding monotony of corridor life—had passed the total of all other crimes put together. Only last week some fool on the UN's Public Policy Commission had proposed putting tranquilizers in water supplies; the World Health Organization had had him ousted within twenty-four hours—actually putting the suggestion into effect would have doubled crimes of this kind, by cutting the population further free of its already feeble grip on responsibility—but it was too late to counteract the effect on morale of the suggestion alone.

The WHO had had good reason to be both swift and arbitrary about it. Its last demographic survey showed, under the grim heading of "Acutal Insanity," a total of thirty-five million unhospitalized early paranoid schizophrenics who had been clearly diagnosed, every one of whom should have been committed for treatment at once—except that, were the WHO to commit them, the Shelter economy would suffer a manpower loss more devastating than any a war had inflicted on mankind in all of its history. Every one of those thirty-five million persons was a major hazard to his neighbors and to his job, but the Shelter economy was too complicated to do without them—

—let alone do without the unrecognized, subclinical cases, which probably totaled twice as many. The Shelter economy obviously could not continue operating much longer without a major collapse; it was on the verge of a psychotic break at this instant.

With Egtverchi for a therapist?

Preposterous. But who else . . . ?

"You're very gloomy tonight," the countess was complaining. "Won't you amuse anyone but children?"

"No one," Egtverchi said promptly. "Except, of course, myself. And of course I am also a child. There now: not only do I have mammals for parents, but I am myself my own uncle—these

3-V amusers of children are always everyone's uncle. You do not appreciate me properly, Countess; I become more interesting every minute, but you do not notice. In the next instant I may turn into your mother, and you will do nothing but yawn."

"You've already turned into my mother," the countess said, with a challenging, slumbrous look. "You even have her jowls, and all those impossibly even teeth. And the talk. My God. Turn into something else—and *don't* make it Lucien."

"I would turn into the count if I could," Egtverchi said, with what Michelis was almost sure was genuine regret. "But I have no affinity for affines; I don't even understand Haertel yet. Tomorrow, perhaps?"

"My God," the countess said again. "Why in the world did I think I should invite you? You're too dull to be borne. I don't know why I count on anything anymore. I should know better by now."

Astonishingly, Egtverchi began to sing, in a high, pure, *castrato* tenor: "*Swef, swef, Susa. . . .*" For a moment Michelis thought the voice was coming from someone else, but the countess swung on Egtverchi instantly, her face twisted into a Greek mask of pure rage.

"Stop that," she said, her voice as raw as a wound. Her expression, under the gilded gaiety of her party paint, was savagely incongruous.

"Certainly," Egtverchi said soothingly. "You see I am not your mother after all. It pays to be careful with these accusations."

"You lousy snake-scaled demon!"

"Please, Countess; I have scales, you have breasts; this is proper and fitting. You ask me to amuse you; I thought you might enjoy my jongleur's lullaby."

"*Where did you hear that song?*"

"Nowhere," Egtverchi said. "I reconstructed it. I could see from the cast of your eyes that you were a born Norman."

"How did you do it?" Michelis said, interested in spite of himself. It was the first sign he had encountered that Egtverchi had any musical ability.

"Why, by the genes, Mike," Egtverchi said; his literal Lithian mind had gone to the substance of Michelis' question rather than to its sense. "This is the way I know my name, and the name of my father. E-G-T-V-E-R-C-H-I is the pattern of genes on one of my chromosomes; the G, V and I alleles are of course from my mother, my cerebral cortex has direct sensual access to my genetic composition. We see ancestry everywhere we look, just as you see colors—it is one of the spectra of the real world. Our ancestors bred that sense into us; you could do worse than imitate them. It is helpful to know what a man is before he even opens his mouth."

Michelis felt a faint but decided chill. He wondered if Chtexa had ever mentioned this to Ruiz. Probably not; a discovery so fascinating to a biologist would have driven the Jesuit to talking about it. In any event, it was too late to ask him, for he was on the way to Rome; Cleaver was even farther away by now; and Agronski wouldn't know.

"Dull, dull, dull," the countess said. She had got back most of her self-possession.

"To be sure, to the dull," Egtverchi said, with his eternal grin, which somehow managed to disarm almost anything that he said. "But I offered to amuse you; you did not enjoy my entertainment. It is your doom to amuse me, too, you know; I am the guest here. What do you have in the subbasement, for instance? Let us go see. Where are my summer soldiers? Somebody wake them; we have a trip to take."

The packed guests had been listening intently, obviously enjoying the countess' floundering upon Egtverchi's long and multiple-barbed gaff. When she bowed her high-piled, gilded head and led the way back toward the trolley tracks, a blurred and almost animal cheer shook the lounge. Liu shrank back against Michelis; he put his arm tightly around her waist.

"Mike, let's not go," she whispered. "Let's go home. I've had enough."

THIRTEEN

Entry in Egtverchi's journal:

June 13th, 13th week of citizenship: This week I stayed home. Elevators on Earth never stop at this floor. Must check why. They have reasons for everything they do.

It was during the week Egtverchi's program was off the air that Agronski stumbled across the discovery that he no longer knew who he was. Though he had not recognized it for what it was at the time, the first forebodings of this vastation had come creeping over him as far back as that four-cornered debate in Xoredeshch Sfath, when he had begun to realize that he did not know what Mike, the Father and Cleaver were talking about. After a while, it had begun to seem to him that they didn't know, either; the long looping festoons of logic and emotion with which they so determinedly bedecked the humid Lithian air seemed to hang from nothing, and touch no ground on which he or any other human being he knew had ever stood.

Then, after he had come home, he had hardly even been angered—only vaguely irritated—when the *J.I.R.* had failed to include him in its invitation to prepare the preliminary article on Lithia. The Lithian experience had already begun to seem remote and dreamlike to him, and he already knew that he and the senior authors could have nothing more to say to each other on that subject which would make mutual sense.

So far, so good; but so far there was no explanation for the sensation of bottomless depair, loneliness and disgust which had swept over him here at the discovery, seemingly of no consequence in itself, that his favorite 3-V program would not be on tonight. Superficially, everything else was as it should be. He had been invited to a year of residency at Fordham's seismological laboratories on the basis of his previous publications of gravity waves—tidal and seismic tremors—and his arrival had been greeted with just the proper mixture of respect and enthusiasm by the Jesuits who ran the great university's science department. His apartment in the bachelor scientists' quarters was not at all monastic, indeed it was almost luxurious for a single man; he had as much apparatus as any geologist in his field could have dreamed of having under such an arrangement, he was virtually free of lecture duties, he had made several new friends among the graduate students assigned to him—and yet, tonight, looking blankly at the replacement program which had appeared instead of Egtverchi on his 3-V screen—

In retrospect, each of the steps toward this abyss seemed irrevocable, and yet they had all been so small! He had been looking forward to his return to Earth with an unfocussed but intense excitement, not directed toward any one aspect of Earthly life, but simply eager for the pat wink of all things familiar. But when he had returned, he found no reassurance in the familiar; indeed, it all seemed rather flat. He put it down to having been a relatively free-wheeling, nearly unique individual on a virtually unpopulated world; there was bound to be a certain jolt in readapting oneself to the life of one mole among billions.

And yet a jolt was precisely what it had not been. Instead, it had been a most peculiar kind of lack of all sensation, as though the familiar were powerless to move him or even to touch him. As the days wore by, this intellectual, emotional, sensual numbness became more and more pronounced, until it became a kind of sensation in itself, a sort of giddiness—as though he were about to fall, and yet could not see anything to grab hold of to steady himself, or indeed what kind of ground he was standing on at the moment.

Somewhere along in there he had taken up listening to Egtverchi's news broadcasts, out of simple curiosity insofar as he could remember any feeling so far removed in time. There had been something there that was useful to him, though he could not know what it was. At the very least, Egtverchi occasionally amused him. Sometimes the creature reminded him obscurely that on Lithia, no matter how divorced he had been from the thinking and the purposes of the other members of the commission, he had been almost unique; that was comforting, though it was a watery comfort. And sometimes, during Egtverchi's most savage sallies against Agronski's familiar Earth, he felt a slight surge of genuine pleasure, as though Egtverchi were his agent in acting out a long and complicated revenge against enemies hidden and unknown. More usually, however, Egtverchi failed to penetrate the slightly nauseating numbness which had closed around him; the broadcasts simply became a habit.

In the meantime, increasingly it came over him that he did not understand what his fellow men were doing or, in the minority of instances where he did understand it, it seemed to him to be something utterly trivial; why did people bind themselves to these regimes? Where were they going that was so important? The air of determined dull preoccupation with which the average troglodyte went to his job, got through it, and came away again to his cubby in his target area would have seemed tragic to him if the actors had not all been such utter ciphers; the eagerness, dedication, chicanery, short-cutting, brilliance, hard labor and total immersion of people who thought themselves or their jobs important would have seemed absurd had he been able to think of anything in the world more worth all this attention, but the savor was leaking rapidly out of everything now. Even the steaks he had dreamed of on Lithia were now only something else to be got through, an exercise in cutting, forking, swallowing, and disturbed cat naps.

In brief flashes of a few minutes at a time, he was able to envy the Jesuit scientists. They still believed geology to be important, an illusion which now seemed far in the past—a matter of weeks—to Agronski. Their religion, too, seemed to be a constant source of great intellectual excitement, especially during this Holy Year; Agronski had gathered from conversations with Ramon two years ago that the Jesuit order is the cerebral cortex of the Church, concerned with its knottiest moral, theological and organizational problems. In particular, Agronski remembered, the Jesuits were charged with weighing questions of polity and making recommendations to Rome, and it was here that the area of greatest excitement at Fordham was centered. Although he never did arouse himself sufficiently to find out the core of the issue, Agronski knew that this year was to mark the settlement by papal proclamation of one of the great dogmatic questions of

Catholicism, comparable to the dogma of the Assumption of the Blessed Virgin which had been proclaimed a century ago; from the hot discussions he overheard in the refectory, and elsewhere after working hours, he gathered that the Society of Jesus had already made its recommendation, and all that remained to be debated was the most probable decision which Pope Hadrian would arrive at. That there should still be any question about the matter surprised him a little, until a scrap of conversation overheard in the commissariat told him that there was nothing in the least binding about the Order's decisions. The doctrine of the Assumption had been heavily recommended against by the Jesuits of the time, despite the fact that it had been an obvious personal preference of the then incumbent Pope, but it had been adopted all the same—the decision of St. Peter's was beyond all appeal.

Nothing in the world, Agronski was learning with this feeling of general giddiness and nausea, was that certain. In the end his colleagues here at Fordham came to seem as remote to him as Ruiz-Sanchez had on Lithia. The Catholic Church in 2050 was still fourth in rank in terms of number of adherents, with Islam, the Buddhists and the Hindi sects commanding the greater number of worshipers, in that order; after Catholicism, there was the confusing number of Protestant groups, which might well outnumber the Catholics if one included all those in the world who had no faith worth mentioning—and it was probable that the agnostics, atheists and don't-cares taken as a separate group were at least as numerous as the Jews, perhaps more so. As for Agronski, he knew grayly that he belonged no more with one of these groups than with any other; he had been cut adrift; he was slowly beginning to doubt the existence of the phenomenal universe itself, and he could not bring himself to care enough about the probably unreal to feel that it mattered what intellectual organization you imposed on it, whether it was High Episcopalian or Logical Positivist. If one no longer likes steak, what does it matter how well it has been aged, butchered, cooked or served?

The invitation to Egtverchi's coming-out party had almost succeeded in piercing the iron fog which had descended between Agronski and the rest of creation. He had had the notion that the sight of a live Lithian might do something for him, though what he could hardly have said; and besides, he had wanted to see Mike and the Father again, moved by memories of having been fond of them once. But the Father was not there, Mike had been removed light-years away from him by having taken up in the meantime with a woman—and of all the meaningless obsessions of mankind, Agronski was most determined now to avoid the tyranny of sex—and in person Egtverchi had turned out to be a grotesque and alarming Earthly caricature of the Lithians that Agronski remembered. Disgusted with himself, he kept sedulously away from all of them, and in the process, quite inadvertently, got drunk. He remembered no more of the party except scraps of a fight that he had had with some swarthy flunkey in a huge dark room bounded by metal webwork, like being inside the shaft of the Eiffel Tower at midnight—a memory which seemed to include inexplicable rising clouds of steam and a jerky intensification of his catholic, nauseating vertigo, as though he and his anonymous adversary were being lowered into hell on the end of a thousand-mile-long hydraulic piston.

He had awakened after noon the next day in his rooms with a thousand-fold increase in the giddiness, an awful sense of mission before a holocaust, and the worst hangover he had

had since the drunk he had staged on cooking sherry in the first week of his freshman year in college. It took him two days to get rid of the hangover, but the rest remained, shutting him off utterly even from the things that he could see and touch in his own apartment. He could not taste his food; words on paper had no meaning; he could not make his way from his chair to the toilet without wondering if at the next step the room would turn upside down or vanish entirely. Nothing had any volume, texture, or mass, let alone any color; the secondary properties of things, which had been leaking steadily out of his world ever since Lithia, were gone entirely now, and the primary qualities were beginning to follow.

The end was clear and predictable. There was to be nothing left but the little plexus of habit patterns at the center of which lived the dwindling unknowable thing that was his *I*. By the time one of those habits brought him before the 3-V set and snapped open the switch, it was already too late to save anything else. There was nobody left in the universe but himself—nobody and nothing—

Except that, when the screen lighted and Egtverchi failed to appear, he discovered that even the *I* no longer had a name. Inside the thin shell of unwilling self-consciousness, it was as empty as an upended jug.

FOURTEEN

Ruiz-Sanchez put the much-folded, sleazy airletter down into his lap and looked blindly out the compartment window of the *rapido*. The train was already an hour out from Naples, slightly less than halfway to Rome, and as yet he had seen almost nothing of the country he had been hoping to reach all of his adult life; and now he had a headache. Michelis' sprawling cursive handwriting was under the best of circumstances about as legible as Beethoven's, and obviously he had written this letter under the worst circumstances imaginable.

And after emotion had done its considerable worst to Michelis' scrawl, the facsimile reducer had squeezed it all down onto a single piece of tissue for missile mail, so that only a man who knew the handwriting as well as Assyriologists know cuneiform could have deciphered the remaining ant tracks at all.

After a moment, he picked up where he had left off; the letter went on:

> Which is why I missed the subsequent debacle. There is still some doubt in my mind as to whether or not Egtverchi was entirely responsible—it occurs to me that maybe the

countess' smokes did affect him in some way after all, since his metabolism can't be *totally* different from ours—but you'd know much more about that than I would. It's perfectly possible that I'm just whistling past the graveyard.

In any event, I don't know any more about the subbasement shambles than the papers have reported. In case you haven't seen them, what happened was that Egtverchi and his bravoes somehow became impatient with the progress the serpentine was making, or with the caliber of the entertainment they could see from it, and went on an expedition of their own, breaking down the barriers between cells when they couldn't find any other way in. Egtverchi is still pretty weak for a Lithian, but he's big, and the dividing walls apparently didn't pose him any problems.

What happened thereafter is confused—it depends on which reporter you believe. Insofar as I've been able to piece all these conflicting accounts together, Egtverchi himself didn't hurt anybody, and if his *condottieri* did, they got as good as they gave; one of them died. The major damage is to the countess, who is ruined. Some of the cells he broke into weren't on the serpentine's route at all, and contained public figures in private hells especially designed by the countess' caterers. The people who haven't themselves already succumbed to the sensation-mongers—though in some instances the publicity is no more vicious than they had coming—are out to revenge themselves on the whole house of Averoigne.

Of course the count can't be touched directly, since he wasn't even aware of what was going on. (Did you see that last paper from "H. O. Petard," by the way? Beautiful stuff: he has a fundamental twist on the Haertel equations which makes it look possible to *see* around normal spacetime, as well as travel around it. Theoretically you might photograph a star and get a contemporary image, not one light-year old. Another blow to the chops for poor old Einstein.) But he is already no longer Procurator of Canarsie and, unless he takes his money promptly out of the countess' hands, he will wind up as just another moderately comfortable troglodyte. And at the moment nobody knows where he is, so unless he has been reading the papers it is already too late for him to make a drastic enough move. In any event, whether he does or he doesn't, the countess will be *persona non grata* in her own circles to the day she dies.

And even now I haven't any idea whether Egtverchi intended exactly this, or whether it was all an accident springing out of a wild impulse. He says he will reply to the newspaper criticism of him on his 3-V program next week—this week nobody can reach him, for reasons he refuses to explain—but I don't see what he could possibly say that would salvage more than a fraction of the goodwill he'd accumulated before the party. He's already half-convinced that Earth's laws are only organized whims at best—and his present audience is more than half children!

I wish you were the kind of man who might say "I told you so"; at least I could get a melancholy pleasure out of nodding. But it's too late for that now. If you can spare any time for further advice, please send it post haste. We are in well over our heads.

—*Mike*

P.S.: Liu and I were married yesterday. It was earlier than we had planned, but we both feel a sense of urgency that we can't explain—almost a desperation. It's as though something crucial were about to happen. I believe something is; but what? Please write.—*M.*

Ruiz groaned involuntarily, drawing incurious glances from his compartment-mates: a Pole in a sheepskin coat who had spent the entire journey wordlessly cutting his way through a monstrous and smelly cheese he had boarded the train with, and a Hollywood Vedantist in sandals, burlap and beard whose smell was not that of cheese and whose business in Rome in a Holy Year was problematical.

He closed his eyes against them. Mike had had no business even thinking about such matters on his wedding morning. No wonder the letter was hard to read.

Cautiously, he opened his eyes again. The sunlight was almost intolerably bright, but for a moment he saw an olive grove sweeping by against burnt-umber hills lined beneath a sky of incredibly clear blue. Then the hills abruptly came piling down upon him and the express shot screaming into a tunnel.

Ruiz lifted the letter once more, but the ant tracks promptly puddled into a dirty blur; a sudden stab of pain lanced vertically through his left eye. Dear God, was he going blind? No, nonsense, that was hypochondria—there was nothing wrong with him but simple eyestrain. The stab through the eyeball was pressure in his left sphenoid sinus, which had been inflamed ever since he left Lima for the wet North, and had begun to become acute in the dripping atmosphere of Lithia.

His trouble was Michelis' letter, that was plain. Never mind the temptation to blame eyes or sinuses, which were only surrogates for hands empty even of the amphora in which

Egtverchi had been brought into the world. Nothing was left of his gift but the letter.

And what answer could he give?

Why, only what Michelis obviously was already coming to realize: that the reason for both Egtverchi's popularity and his behavior lay in the fact that he was both mentally and emotionally a seriously displaced person. He had been deprived of the normal Lithian upbringing which would have taught him how fundamental it is to know how to survive in a predominantly predatory society. As for Earth's codes and beliefs, he had only half-absorbed them when Michelis forcibly expelled him from the classroom straight into citizenship. Now he had already had ample opportunity to see the hypocrisy with which some of those codes were served and, to the straight-line logic of the Lithian mind, this could mean only that the codes must therefore be only some kind of game at best. (He had encountered the concept of a game here, too; it was unknown on Lithia.) But he had no Lithian code of conduct to substitute or to fall back on, since he was as ignorant of Lithian civilization as he was innocent of experience of Lithia's seas, savannas and jungles.

In short, a wolf child.

The *rapido* hurled itself from the mouth of the tunnel as impetuously as it had entered, and the renewed blast of sunlight forced Ruiz to close his eyes once more. When he opened them he was rewarded by the sight of an extensive terraced vineyard. This was obviously wine country and, judging by the mountains, which were especially steep here, they must be nearing Terracina. Soon, if he were lucky, he might see Mt. Circeo; but he was far more interested in the vineyards.

From what he had been able to observe thus far, the Italian

states were far less deeply buried than was most of the rest of the world, and the people were on the surface for much greater proportions of their lifetimes. To some extent this was a product of poverty—Italy as a whole had not had the wealth to get into the Shelter race early, or on anything like the scale which had been possible for the United States or even the other continental countries. Nevertheless, there was a huge Shelter installation at Naples, and the one under Rome was the world's fourth biggest; that one had got itself dug with funds from all over the Western world, and with a great deal of outright voluntary help, when the first deep excavations had begun to turn up an incredible wealth of unsuspected archaeological finds.

In part, however, sheer stubbornness was responsible. A high proportion of Italy's huge population, which had never known any living but in and by the sun, simply could not be driven underground on any permanent basis. Of all the Shelter nations—a class which excluded only countries still almost wholly undeveloped, or unrecoverably desert—Italy appeared to be the least thoroughly entombed.

If that turned out to hold true for Rome in particular, the Eternal City would also be by far the sanest major capital on the planet. And that, Ruiz realized suddenly, would be an outcome nobody would have dared predict for an enterprise founded in 753 B.C. by a wolf child.

Of course, about the Vatican he had never been in any doubt, but Vatican City is not Rome. The thought reminded him that he had been commanded to an *udienza speciale* with the Holy Father tomorrow, before the ring-kissing, which meant before 1000 at the latest—probably as early as 0700, for the Holy Father was an early riser, and in this year of all years would be holding audiences of all kinds nearly around the clock. Ruiz had had nearly a month to prepare, for the command had reached him very shortly after the order of the College to appear for inquisition, but he felt unreadier than ever. He wondered how long it had been since any Pope had personally examined a Jesuit convert to an admitted heresy, and what the man had found to say; doubtless the transcript was there in the Vatican library, as recorded by some papal master of ceremonies—assiduous as always in his duty toward history, as masters of ceremonies had been ever since the invaluable Burchard—but Ruiz would not have time to read it.

From here on out, there would be a thousand petty distractions to keep him from settling his mind and heart any further. Just getting his bearings was going to be a chore, and after that there was the matter of accommodations. None of the *case religiose* would take him in—word had apparently got around—and he had not the purse for a hotel, though if worse came to worst he had a confirmed-reservation slip from one of the most expensive which just might let him into some linen closet there. Finding a *pensione*, the only other tolerable alternative, was going to be particularly difficult, for the one which had been contracted for him by the tourist agency had become impossible the moment he received the papal summons; it was too far from St. Peter's. The agency had been able to do nothing else for him except suggest that he sleep in the Shelter, which he was resolved not to do. After all, the agent had told him belligerently, it's a Holy Year—almost as though he were saying, "Don't you know there's a war on?"

And of course his tone had been right. There was a war on. The Enemy was presently fifty light-years away, but He was at the gates all the same.

Something prompted him to check the date of Michelis' letter. It was, he discovered with astonishment and disquiet, nearly two weeks old. Yet the postmark read today; the letter had been mailed, in fact, only about six hours ago, just in time to catch the dawn missile to Naples. Michelis had been sitting on it—or perhaps adding to it, but the facsimile process and the ensmallment, together with Ruiz' gathering eyestrain, all conspired to make it impossible to detect differences in the handwriting or the ink.

After a moment, Ruiz realized what importance the discrepancy had for him. It meant that Egtverchi's 3-V answer to his newspaper critics had been broadcast a week ago—and that he was due on the air again tonight!

Egtverchi's program was broadcast at 0300 Rome time; Ruiz was going to be up earlier than the pontiff himself. In fact, he thought grimly, he was going to get no sleep at all.

The express pulled into the *Stazione Termini* in Rome five minutes ahead of schedule with a feminine shriek. Ruiz found a porter with no difficulty, tipped him the standard 100 lire for his two pieces of luggage, and gave directions. The priest's Italian was adequate, but hardly standard; it made the *facchino* grin with delight every time Ruiz opened his mouth. He had learned it by reading, partly in Dante, mostly in opera libretti, and consequently what he lacked in accent he made up for in flowery phrases: he was unable to ask the way to the nearest fruit stall without sounding as though he would throw himself into the Tiber unless he got an answer.

"*Be' 'a!*" the porter kept saying after every third sentence from Ruiz. "*Che be' 'a!*"

Still, that was easier to get along with than the French attitude had been, on Ruiz' one visit to Paris fifteen years ago. He remembered a taxi driver who had refused to understand his request to be taken to the Continental Hotel until he had written the name down, after which the hackie had said, miming sudden comprehension: *"Ah, ah! Lee Con-ti-nen-TAL!"* This he had found to be an almost universal pretense; the French wanted one to know that without a perfect accent one is not intelligible at all.

The Italians, apparently, were willing to meet one halfway. The porter grinned at Ruiz' purple prose, but he guided the priest deftly to a newsstand where he was able to buy a news magazine containing a high enough proportion of text over pictures to insure an adequate account of what Egtverchi had said last week; and then took him down the left incline from the station across the Piazza Cinquecento to the corner of the Via Viminale and the Via Diocletian, precisely as requested. Ruiz promptly doubled his tip without even a qualm; guidance like that would be invaluable now that time was so short, and he might see the man again.

He had been left in the Casa del Passegero, which had the reputation of being the finest travelers' way station in Italy—which, Ruiz quickly discovered, means the finest in the world, for there are no other institutions precisely like the *alberghi diurni* anywhere else. Here he was able to check his luggage, read his magazine over a pastry in the *caffè*, have his hair cut and his shoes shined, have a bath while his clothes were being pressed, and then begin the protracted series of telephone calls which, he hoped, would eventually allow him to spend the coming night in a bed—preferably near by, but at least anywhere in Rome but in a Shelter dormitory.

In the coffee shop, in the barber's chair, and even in the tub, he pored again and again over the account of Egtverchi's broadcast. The Italian reporter did not give a text, for obvious reasons—a thirteen-minute broadcast would have filled an entire page of the journal in which he was limited to a single column of type—but he digested it skillfully, and he had an inside story to go with it. Ruiz was impressed.

Evidently Egtverchi had composed his rebuttal by weaving together the news items of the evening, just as they had come in to him off the wires beyond any possibility of his selecting them, into a brilliant extempore attack upon Earthly moral assumptions and pretensions. The thread which wove them all together was summed up by the magazine's reporter in a phrase from the *Inferno: Perche mi scerpi?/non hai tu spirto di pietate alcuno?*—the cry of the Suicides, who can speak only when the Harpies rend them and the blood flows: "Wherefore pluckest *thou* me?" It had been a scathing indictment, at no point defending Egtverchi's own conduct, but by implication making ridiculous the notion that any man could be stainless enough to be casting stones. Egtverchi had obviously absorbed Schopenhauer's vicious *Rules for Debate* down to the last comma.

"And in fact," the Italian reporter added, "it is widely known in Manhattan that QBC officials were on the verge of cutting off the outworlder in mid-broadcast as he began to cover the Stockholm brothel war. They were dissuaded by the barrage of telephone calls, telegrams and radiograms which began to pour down upon QBC's main office at precisely that moment. The response of the public has hardly diminished since, and it continues to be overwhelmingly approving. The network, encouraged by Signor Egtverchi's major sponsor, Bridget Bifalco World Kitchens, now is issuing almost hourly releases containing statistics 'proving' the broadcast a spectacular success. Signor Egtverchi is now a hot property, and if past experience is any guide (and it is) this means that henceforth the Lithian will be encouraged to display those aspects of his public character for which formerly he was being widely condemned, for which the network was considering taking him off the air in the middle of a word. Suddenly, in short, he is worth a lot of money."

The report was both literate and overheated—a peculiarly Roman combination—but as long as Ruiz lacked the text of the broadcast itself, he could not take exception to a word of it. Both the reporter's editorializing and the precise passion of his language seemed no more than justified. Indeed, a case could be made for a claim that the man had indulged in understatement.

To Ruiz, at least, Egtverchi's voice came through. The accent was familiar and perfect. And this for an audience full of children! Had any independent person called Egtverchi ever really existed? If so, he was possessed—but Ruiz did not believe that for an instant. There had never been any real Egtverchi to possess. He was throughout a creature of the Adversary's imagination, as even Chtexa had been, as the whole of Lithia had been. In the figure of Egtverchi He had already abandoned subtlety; already He dared to show Himself more than half-naked, commanding money, fathering lies, poisoning discourse, compounding grief, corrupting children, killing love, building armies—

—and all in a Holy Year.

Ruiz-Sanchez froze, one arm halfway into his summer jacket, looking up at the ceiling of the dressing room. He had yet to make more than two telephone calls, neither of them to the general of his Order, but he had already changed his mind.

Had he really failed, all this time, to read such obvious signs—or was he as crazed as heretics are supposed to be, smelling the *Dies irae*, the day of the wrath of God, in the steam of nothing but a public bath? Armageddon—in 3-V? The pit opened to let loose a comedian for the amusement of children?

He did not know. He could only be sure that he needed to hunt for no bed tonight, after all; what he needed was stones. He got out of the Casa del Passegero as quickly as he could, leaving everything he owned behind, and found his way alone back to the Via del Termini; the guidebook showed a church just off there, on the Piazza della Republica, by the Baths of Diocletian.

The book was right. The church was there: Santa Maria d'Angeli. He did not stop in the porch to cool off, though the early evening sunlight was almost as hot as noon. Tomorrow might be much hotter—unredeemably hotter. He went through the portals at once.

Inside, in the chill darkness, he knelt; and in cold terror, he prayed.

It did not seem to do him much good.

FIFTEEN

All about Michelis the jungle stood frozen in a riot of motionlessness. Filtered through it, the sourceless blue-gray daylight was tinged with deep green, and where the light fell on one or another clear reflection it seemed to penetrate rather than glance off, carrying the jungle on in an inversion of images to the eight corners of the universe. The illusion was made doubly real by the stillness of everything; at any moment it seemed as though a breeze would spring up and ruffle the reflections, but there was no breeze, and nothing but time would ever disturb those images.

Egtverchi moved, of course; though his figure was ensmalled as if by distance, he was about the right size for the rest of the jungle, and almost more convincingly colored and in the round. His circumscribed gestures seemed to be beckoning, as though he were attempting to lead Michelis out of this motionless wilderness.

Only his voice was jarring: it was at normal conversational volume, which meant that it was far too loud to be in scale with himself or his (and Michelis') surroundings. It seemed so loud to Michelis, indeed, that in his reverie he almost missed the content of Egtverchi's final speech. Only when Egtverchi had bowed ironically and faded away and his voice died, leaving behind only the omnipresent muted insect buzz, did the meaning penetrate.

Michelis sat where he was, stunned. A full thirty seconds of commercial for Mammale Bifalco's Delicious Instant Knish Mix went by before he remembered to put his finger over the 3-V's cut-off stud. Then this year's Bridget Bifalco in turn faded in mid-mix, smothered before she reached her famous brogue tag-line ("Give it t' me a minute, dharlin', till I give it a lhashin' "). The scurrying electrons in the phosphor complex migrated back to the atoms from which they had been driven by the miniature de Broglie scanner imbedded in the picture frame. The atoms resumed their chemical identity, the molecules cooled, and the screen became a static reproduction of Paul Klee's "Caprice in February." The principle, Michelis recalled with gray irrelevancy, had emerged out of d'Averoigne's first "Petard" paper, the count's only venture into applied math, published when he was seventeen.

"What does he mean?" Liu said faintly. "I don't understand him at all anymore. He calls it a demonstration—but what can he possibly demonstrate by that? It's childish!"

"Yes," Michelis said. For the moment he could think of nothing else to say. He needed to get his temper back; he was losing it more and more easily these days. That had been one of the reasons for his urgency in marrying Liu: he needed her calmness, for his own was vanishing with frightening rapidity.

No calmness seemed to be passing from her to him now. Even the apartment, originally such a source of satisfaction and repose for them both, felt like a trap. It was far above ground, in one of the mostly unused project buildings on the upper East Side of Manhattan. Originally Liu had had a far smaller set of rooms in the same building, and Michelis, after he had got used to the idea, had had them both installed in the present apartment with only a minimum of wire-pulling. It was not customary, it was certainly not fashionable, and they were officially warned that it was considered dangerous—the gangs raided surface structures now and then; but apparently it was no longer outright illegal, if one had the money to live that high up in the slums.

Given the additional space, the artist buried inside Liu's demure technician's exterior had run quietly wild. In the green glow of concealed light which washed the apartment, Michelis was surrounded by what seemed to be a miniature jungle. On small tables stood Japanese gardens with real Ming trees or dwarf cedars in them. An oriental lamp was fashioned out of a piece of fantastically sculptured driftwood. Long, deep, woven flower boxes ran completely around the room at eye level; they were thickly planted with ivy, wandering Jew, rubber plants, philodendron, and other non-flowering species, and behind each box a mirror ran up to the ceiling, unbroken anywhere except by the placidly witty Klee reproduction which was the 3-V set; the painting, made almost wholly of detached angles and glyphs like the symbols of mathematics, was a welcome oasis of dryness for which Liu had paid a premium—QBC's stock "covers" were mostly Sargents and van Goghs. Since the light tubes were hidden behind the planting boxes, the room gave an effect of extra-terrestrial exuberance kept under control only with the greatest difficulty.

"I know what he means," Michelis said at last. "I just don't know quite how to put it. Let me think a minute—why don't you get dinner while I do it? We'd better eat early. We're going to have visitors, that's a cinch."

"Visitors? But— All right, Mike."

Michelis walked to the glass wall and looked out onto the sun porch. All of Liu's flowering plants were out there, a real garden, which had to be kept sealed off from the rest of the apartment; for in addition to being an ardent amateur gardener, Liu bred bees. There was a colony of them there, making singular and exotic honeys from the congeries of blossoms Liu had laid out so carefully. The honey was fabulous and ever-changing, sometimes too bitter to eat except in tiny fork-touches like Chinese mustard, sometimes containing a heady touch of opium from the sticky hybrid poppies that nodded in a soldierly squad along the sun porch railing, sometimes sickly-sweet and insipid until, with a surprisingly small amount of glassware, Liu converted it into a liqueur that mounted to the head like a breeze from the Garden of Allah. The bees that made it were tetraploid monsters the size of hummingbirds, with tempers as bad as Michelis' own was getting to be; only a few of them could kill even a big man. Luckily, they flew badly in the gusts common at this altitude, and would starve anywhere but in Liu's garden, otherwise Liu would never have been licensed to keep them on an open sun porch in the middle of the city. Michelis had been more than a little wary of them at first, but lately they had begun to fascinate him: their apparent intelligence was almost as phenomenal as their size and viciousness.

"Damn!" Liu said behind him.

"What's the matter?"

"Omelettes again. That's the second wrong number I've dialed this week."

Both the oath—mild though it was—and the error were

uncharacteristic. Mike felt a twinge, a mixture of compassion and guilt. Liu was changing; she had never been so distractible before. Was he responsible?

"It's all right. I don't mind. Let's eat."

"All right."

They ate silently, but Michelis was conscious of the pressure of inquiry behind Liu's still expression. The chemist thought furiously, angry with himself, and yet unable to phrase what he wanted to say. He should never have got her into this at all. No, that couldn't have been prevented; she had been the logical scientist to handle Egtverchi in his infancy—probably nobody else could have brought him through it even this well. But surely it should have been possible to keep her from becoming emotionally involved—

No, that had not been possible either; that was the woman of it. And the man of it, now that he was forced to think about his own role. It was no use; he simply did not know what he should think; Egtverchi's broadcast had rattled him beyond the point of logical thought. He was going to wind up with his usual bad compromise with Liu, which was to say nothing at all. But that would not do either.

And yet it had been a simple enough piece of foolery that the Lithian had perpetrated—childish, as Liu had said. Egtverchi had been urged to be off beat, rebellious, irresponsible, and he had come through in spades. Not only had he voiced his disrespect for all established institutions and customs, but he had also challenged his audience to show the same disrespect. In the closing moments of his broadcast, he had even told them how: they were to mail anonymous, insulting messages to Egtverchi's own sponsors.

"A postcard will do," he had said, gently enough, through his grinning chops. "Just make the message pungent. If you hate that powdered concrete they call a knish mix, write and tell them so. If you can eat the knishes but our commercials make you sick, write them about that, and don't pull any punches. If you loathe *me*, tell the Bifalcos that, too, and make sure you're spitting mad about it. I'll read the five messages I think in the worst possible taste on my broadcast next week. And remember, don't sign your name; if you have to sign, use my name. Goodnight."

The omelette tasted like flannel.

"I'll tell you what I think," Michelis said suddenly, in a low voice. "I think he's whipping up a mob. Remember those kids in the uniforms? He's abandoned that now, or else he's keeping it under cover; in any event, he thinks he has something better. He has an audience of about sixty-five million, and maybe half of them are adults. Of those, another half is insane to some degree, and that's what he's counting on now. He's going to turn that group into a lynch gang."

"But why, Mike?" Liu said. "What good will that do him?"

"I don't know. That's what stops me. He's not after power—he's got too many brains to think he can be a McCarthy. Maybe he just wants to destroy things. An elaborate act of revenge."

"Revenge!"

"I'm only guessing. I don't understand him any better than you do. Maybe worse."

"Revenge on whom?" Liu said steadily. "And for what?"

"Well—on us. For making such a bad job of him."

"I see," Liu said. "I see." She looked down into her untouched plate and began to weep, silently. At that moment, Michelis would gladly have killed either Egtverchi or himself, had he known where to begin.

The Klee chimed decorously. Michelis looked up at it with bitter resignation.

"The visitors," he said. He touched the phone stud.

The Klee faded, and the chairman of the citizenship committee which had examined Egtverchi looked out from the wall at them from under his elaborate helmet.

"Come on up," Michelis said to the silently inquiring image. "We've been expecting you."

It took a while for the UN committee chairman to stop touring the apartment and exclaiming over Liu's decor, but this evidently was a ceremony. As soon as he had uttered the last amenity, he dropped his social manner so abruptly that Michelis could almost see it break on the carpetite. Even the bees had sensed something hostile about him; he had no sooner peered through the glass at them than they began butting their eye-bulging heads at him. Michelis could hear them thumping doggedly away at the transparent barrier all through the subsequent conversation, with a rising and falling snarl of angry wings.

"We've gotten more than ten thousand facsimiles and telegrams in the half hour between when Egtverchi went off the air and the first analysis of the response," the UN man said grimly. "That was enough to tell us what we're up against, and that's why I came to see you. We've had a good many decades of experience at assessing public response. In the next week, we are going to get about two million of these things—"

"Who's 'we'?" Michelis said, and Liu added: "That doesn't seem like a large figure to me."

" 'We' is the network. And the figure's large for us, since we're nearly anonymous in the public mind. The Bifalcos are going to get a little over seven and a half million such missives."

"Are they really so bad?" Liu said, frowning.

"They are as bad as they could be and still get through the

cables and the mail tubes," the UN man said flatly. "I've never seen anything like them, and I've been in QBC community relations for eleven years—this UN committee job is my other hat, you know how that goes. More than half of them are expressions of virulent, unrestrained hatred—pathological hatred. I have a few samples here, but I didn't bring the worst of them along. It's my policy not to show laymen anything that scares *me*."

"Let me see one," Michelis said promptly.

The UN man passed a facsimile over silently. Michelis read it. Then he gave it back.

"You're a little more calloused than you realize," he said in a gravelly voice. "I wouldn't have shown even that one to anyone but the director of research of an insane asylum."

The UN man smiled for the first time, looking at them both with quick, intelligent eyes. Somehow he seemed to be assessing them, not individually, but as a couple; Michelis had an overwhelming intuition that his privacy was somehow being violated, though there was nothing concrete in the man's behavior to which he could have taken exception.

"Not even to Dr. Meid?" the UN man said.

"To nobody," Michelis said angrily.

"Quite so. And yet I repeat that I didn't select it deliberately for shock value, Dr. Michelis. It's a bagatelle—very mild, compared to some of the stuff we've been getting. This Snake obviously has an audience of borderline madmen, and he means to use it. That's why I came to see you. We think you might have some idea as to what he intends to use it *for*."

"For nothing, if you people have any control over what you yourselves do," Michelis said. "Why don't you cut him off the air? If he's poisoning it, then you don't have any other choice."

"One man's poison is another man's knish mix," the UN

man said smoothly. "The Bifalcos don't see this the way we do. They have their own analysts, and they know as well as we do that they're going to get more than seven and a half million dirty postcards in the next week. But they *like* the idea. In fact, they're positively wriggling with delight. They think it will sell products. They will probably give the Snake a whole half hour, solely sponsored by them, if the response comes through as predicted—and it will."

"Why can't you cut Egtverchi off anyhow?" Liu said.

"The charter prevents us from interfering with the right of free speech. As long as the Bifalcos put up the money, we are obligated to keep the program on the air. It's a good principle at bottom; we've had experiences with it before that threatened to turn out nastily, but in every case we sweated them out and the public got bored with them eventually. But that was a different public—the broad public, which used to be mostly sane. The Snake obviously has a selected audience, and that's not sane at all. This time—for the first time—we are thinking of interfering. That's why we came to you."

"I can't help you," Michelis said.

"You can, and you will, Dr. Michelis. I'm talking from under both my hats now. QBC wants him off the air, and the UN is beginning to smell something which might prove to be much worse than the 1993 Corridor Riots. You sponsored this Snake, and your wife raised him from an egg, or damn near an egg. You know him better than anyone else on Earth. You will have to give us the weapon that we need against him. That's what I came to tell you. Think about it. You are responsible under the naturalization law. It's not often that we have to invoke that clause, but we're invoking it now. You'll have to think fast, because we have to have him closed out before his next broadcast."

"And suppose we have nothing to offer?" Michelis said stonily.

"Then we will probably declare the Snake a minor, and you his guardians," the UN man said. "Which will hardly be a solution from our point of view, but you would probably find it painful—you'd be well advised to come up with something better. I'm sorry to bring such bad news, but the news *is* bad tonight; that sometimes happens. Goodnight, and thank you."

He went out. He did not have to resume any of his three hats; he had never taken any of them off, visible or metaphorical.

Michelis and Liu stared at each other, appalled.

"We—we couldn't possibly have him as a ward *now*," Liu whispered.

"Well," Michelis said harshly, "we were talking about wanting a son—"

"Mike, don't!"

"I'm sorry," he said inadequately. "That officious son of a bitch. He was the man that passed on the application—and now he's throwing it right back in our laps. They must be really desperate. What are we going to do? I haven't an idea in my head."

Liu said, after a moment's hesitation: "Mike—we don't know enough to come up with anything useful in a week. At least I don't, and I don't think you do either. We've got to get through to the Father somehow."

"If we can," Michelis said slowly. "But even so, what good will that do? The UN won't listen to him—they've bypassed him."

"How? What do you mean?"

"They've made a *de facto* decision in favor of Cleaver," Michelis said. "It won't be announced until after Ramon's church has finished disavowing him, but it's already in effect. I knew about it before he left for Rome, but I didn't have the heart to tell him. Lithia has been closed; the UN is going to use it as a laboratory for the study of fusion power storage—not exactly what Cleaver had in mind originally, but close enough."

Liu was silent for a long time. She arose and went to the window, against which the huge bees were still butting like live battering-rams.

"Does Cleaver know?" she said, her back still turned.

"Oh yes, he knows," Michelis said. "He's in charge. He was scheduled to land back at Xoredeshch Sfath yesterday. I tried to tip Ramon off indirectly as soon as I heard about it—that's why I promoted that collaboration for the *J.I.R.*—but Ramon just didn't seem to hear any of my hints. And I just couldn't tell him outright that his cause was already lost, before he'd even had a hearing."

"It's ugly," Liu said slowly. "Why won't they announce it until after Ramon is officially excommunicated? Why does that make any difference?"

"Because the decision is tainted, that's all," Michelis said fiercely. "Whether you agree with Ramon's theological arguments or not, to decide for Cleaver is a dirty act—impossible to defend except in terms of raw power. They know that well enough, damn them, and sooner or later they're going to have to let the public see what the arguments were on the other side. When that day comes, they want Ramon's arguments discredited in advance by his own church."

"What precisely is Cleaver doing?"

"I can't say, precisely. But they're building a big Nernst generator plant inland on the south continent, near Gleshchtehk Sfath, to turn out the power, so that much of his dream is already realized. Later they'll try to trap the power raw, as it comes off, instead of stepping it down and throwing away ninety-five per cent of it as heat. I don't know how Cleaver proposes to do that, but I should guess he'd begin with a modification of the Nernst effect itself—the 'magnetic bottle' dodge. He'd better be damned careful." He paused. "I suppose I'd have told Ramon if he'd asked me. But he didn't, so I didn't say anything. Now I feel like a coward."

Liu turned swiftly at that, and came back to sit on the arm of his chair. "That was right to do, Mike," she said. "It's not cowardice to refuse to rob a man of hope, I think."

"Maybe not," Michelis said, taking her hand gratefully. "But what it all comes out to is that Ramon can't help us now. Thanks to me, he doesn't even know yet that Cleaver is back on Lithia."

Shortly past dawn, Ruiz-Sanchez walked stiffly into the vast circle of the Piazza San Pietro toward the towering dome of St. Peter's itself. The piazza was swarming with pilgrims even this early, and the dome, more than twice as high as the Statue of Liberty, seemed frowning and ominous in the early light, rising from the forest of pillars like the forehead of God.

He passed under the right arch of the colonnade, past the Swiss Guards in their gorgeous, *outré* uniforms, and through the bronze door. Here he paused to murmur, with unexpected intensity, the prayers for the Pope's intentions obligatory for this year. The Apostolic Palace soared in front of him; he was astonished that any edifice so crowded with stone could at the same time contrive to be so spacious, but he had no time for further devotions now.

Near the first door on the right a man sat at a table. Ruiz-Sanchez told him: "I am commanded to a special audience with the Holy Father."

"God has blessed you. The major-domo's office is on the first floor, to the left. No, one moment—a *special* audience? May I see your letter, please?"

Ruiz-Sanchez showed it.

"Very good. But you will need to see the major-domo anyhow. The special audiences are in the throne room; he will show you where to go."

The throne room! Ruiz-Sanchez was more unsettled than ever. That was where the Holy Father received heads of state, and members of the college of cardinals. Certainly it was no place to receive a heretical Jesuit of very low rank—

"The throne room," the major-domo said. "That's the first room in the reception suite. I trust your business goes well, Father. Pray for me."

Hadrian VIII was a big man, a Norwegian by birth, whose curling beard had been only slightly peppered with gray at his election. It was white now, of course, but otherwise age seemed to have marked him little; indeed, he looked somewhat younger than his photographs and 3-V 'casts suggested, for they had a tendency to accentuate the crags and furrows of his huge, heavy face.

Ruiz-Sanchez found his person so overwhelming that he barely noticed the magnificence of his robes of state. Needless to say, there was nothing in the least Latin in the Holy Father's mien or temperament. In his rise to the gestatorial chair he had made a reputation as a Catholic with an almost Lutheran passion for the grimmer reaches of moral theology; there was something of Kierkegaard in him, and something of the Grand Inquisitor as well. After his election, he had surprised everyone by developing an interest—one might almost call it a businessman's interest—in temporal politics, though the characteristic coldness of Northern theological speculation continued to color everything he said and did. His choice of the name of a Roman emperor was perfectly appropriate, Ruiz-Sanchez realized: here was a face that might well have been stamped on imperial coin, for all the beneficence which tempered its hardness.

The Pope remained standing throughout the interview, staring down at Ruiz-Sanchez with what seemed at first to be nine-tenths frank curiosity.

"Of all the thousands of pilgrims here, you may stand in the greatest need of our indulgence," he observed in English. Nearby, a tape recorder raced silently; Hadrian was an ardent archivist, and a stickler for the letter of the text. "Yet we have small hope of your winning it. It is incredible to us that a Jesuit, of all our shepherds, could have fallen into Manichaeanism. The errors of that heresy are taught most particularly in that college."

"Holiness, the evidence—"

Hadrian raised his hand. "Let us not waste time. We have already informed ourself of your views and your reasoning. You are subtle, Father, but you have committed a grievous oversight all the same—but we wish to defer that subject for the moment. Tell us first of this creature Egtverchi—not as a sending of the Devil, but as you would see him were he a man."

Ruiz-Sanchez frowned. There was something about the word "sending" that touched some weakness inside him, like an obligation forgotten until too late to fulfill it. The feeling was like that which had informed a ridiculous recurrent nightmare of his student days, in which he was not to graduate because he had forgotten to attend all his Latin classes. Yet he could not put his finger on what it was.

"There are many ways to describe him, Holiness," he said. "He is the kind of personality that the twentieth-century critic Colin Wilson called an Outsider, and that is the kind of Earthman he appeals to—he is a preacher without a creed, an intellect without a culture, a seeker without a goal. I think he has a conscience as we would define the term; he's very different from the rest of his race in that and many other respects. He seems to take a deep interest in moral problems, but he's utterly contemptuous of all traditional moral frames of reference—including the kind of rationalized moral automation that prevails on Lithia."

"And this strikes some chord in his audience?"

"There can be no doubt of that, surely, Holiness. It remains to be seen how wide his appeal is. He ran off a very shrewdly designed experiment last night, obviously intended to test that very question; we should soon know just how great the response will be. But it already seems clear that he appeals to all those people who feel cut off, emotionally and intellectually, from our society and its dominant cultural traditions."

"Well put," Hadrian said, surprisingly. "We stand at the brink of unguessable events, that is certain; we have had forebodings that this might be the year. We have commanded the Inquisition to put away its bell, book and candle for the time being; we think such a move would be most unwise."

Ruiz-Sanchez was stunned. No trial—and no excommunication? The drumming of events around his head had begun to remind him of the numbing, incessant rains of Xoredeshch Sfath.

"Why, Holiness?" he said faintly.

"We believe you may be the man appointed by our Lord to bear St. Michael's arms," the Pope said, weighing every word.

"I, Holiness? A heretic?"

"Noah was not perfect, you will recall," Hadrian said, with what might have been a half-smile. "He was merely a man who was given another chance. Goethe, himself more than a little heretical, reshaped the legend of Faustus to the same lesson: redemption is always the crux of the great drama, and there must be a peripataea first. Besides, Father, consider for a moment the unique nature of this case of heresy. Is not the appearance of a solitary Manichaean in the twenty-first century either a wildly meaningless anachronism—or a grave sign?"

He paused and fingered his beads.

"Of course," he added, "it will be necessary for you to purge yourself, if you can. That is why we have called you. We believe as you do that the Adversary is the moving spirit behind this whole Lithian crisis; but we do not believe that any repudiation of dogma is required. It all hinges upon this question of creativity. Tell us, Father: when you first became convinced that the whole of Lithia was a sending, what did you do about it?"

"Do about it?" Ruiz-Sanchez said numbly. "Why, Holiness, I did only what was recorded. I could think of nothing else to do."

"Then did it never occur to you that sendings can be banished—and that God has given that power into your hands?"

Ruiz-Sanchez had no emotions left.

"Banished. . . . Holiness, perhaps I have been stupid. I feel stupid. But as far as I know, exorcism was abandoned by the Church more than two centuries ago. My college taught me that meteorology replaced the 'spirits and powers of the air,' and neurophysiology replaced 'possession.' It would never have occurred to me."

"Exorcism was not abandoned, merely discouraged," Hadrian said. "It had become limited, as you have just pointed out, and the Church wished to prevent its abuse by ignorant country priests—they were bringing the Church into disrepute trying to drive demons out of sick cows and perfectly healthy goats and cats. But I am not talking about animal health, the weather or mental illness now, Father."

"Then . . . is Your Holiness truly proposing that . . . that I should have attempted to . . . *to exorcise a whole planet*?"

"Why not?" Hadrian said. "Of course, the fact that you were standing on the planet at the time might have helped to prevent you, unconsciously, from thinking of it. We are convinced that God would have provided for you—in Heaven certainly, and possibly you might have received temporal help as well. But it was the only solution to your dilemma. Had the exorcism failed, *then* there might have been some excuse for falling into heresy. But surely it should be easier to believe in a planet-wide hallucination—which in principle we know the Adversary has the power to do—than in the heresy of satanic creativity!"

The Jesuit bowed his head. He felt overwhelmed by his own ignorance. He had spent almost all his leisure hours on Lithia minutely studying a book which to all intents and purposes might have been dictated by the Adversary himself, and he had seen nothing that mattered, not in all those 628 pages of compulsive demoniac chatter.

"It is not too late to try," Hadrian said, almost gently. "That is the only road left for you to travel." Suddenly his face became stern, flinty. "As we have pointed out to the Inquisition, your excommunication is automatic. It began the instant that you admitted this abomination into your soul. It does not need to be formalized to be a fact—and there are political reasons, as well as spiritual ones, for not formalizing it now. In the meantime, you must leave Rome. We withhold our blessing and our indulgence from you, Dr. Ruiz-Sanchez. This Holy Year is for you a year of battle, with the world as prize. When you have won that battle you may return to us—not before. Farewell."

Dr. Ramon Ruiz-Sanchez, a layman, damned, left Rome for New York that night by air. The deluge of happenstance was rising more rapidly around him; the time for the building of arks was almost at hand. And yet, as the waters rose, and the words, *Into your hand are they delivered,* passed incessantly across the tired surfaces of his brain, it was not of the swarming billions of the Shelter state that he was thinking. It was of Chtexa; and the notion that an exorcism might succeed in dissolving utterly that grave being and all his race and civilization, return them to the impotent mind of the Great Nothing as though they had never been, was an agony to him.

Into your hand. . . . Into your hand. . . .

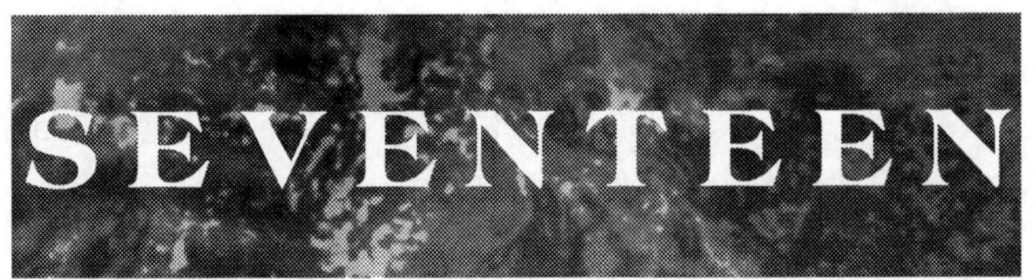

SEVENTEEN

The figures were in. The people who had taken Egtverchi as both symbol and spokesman for their passionate discontents were now tallied, although they could not be known. Their nature was no surprise—the crime and mental disease statistics had long provided a clear picture of that—but their number was stunning. Apparently nearly a third of twenty-first-century society loathed that society from the bottom of its collective heart.

Ruiz-Sanchez wondered suddenly whether, had a similar tally been possible in every age, the proportion would have turned out to be stable.

"Do you think it would do any good to talk to Egtverchi?" he asked Michelis. Over his protests, he was staying in the Michelis' apartment for the time being.

"Well, it hasn't done any good for *me* to talk with him," Michelis said. "With you it might be a different story—though frankly, Ramon, I'm inclined to doubt even that. He's doubly hard to reason with because he himself seems to be getting no satisfaction out of the whole affair."

"He knows his audience better than we do," Liu added. "And the more the numbers pile up, the more embittered he seems to become. I think they remind him continually that he can never be fully accepted on Earth, fully at home on it. He thinks he's of interest only to people who themselves don't feel at home on their own planet. That's not true, of course, but that's how he feels."

"There's enough truth in it so that he'd be unlikely to be dissuaded of it," Ruiz-Sanchez agreed gloomily.

He shifted his chair so as not to be able to see Liu's bees, which were hard at work in the shafts of sunlight on the porch. At another time he could not have torn himself away from them, but he could not afford to be distracted now.

"And of course he's also well aware that he'll never know what it means to be a Lithian—regardless of his shape and inheritance," he added. "Chtexa might get a shadow of that through to him, if only they could meet—but no, they don't even speak the same language."

"Egtverchi's been studying Lithian," Michelis said. "But it's true that he can't speak it, not even as well as I can. He has nothing to read but your grammar—the documents are still all classified against him—and nobody to talk to. He sounds as rusty as an iron hinge. But, Ramon, you could interpret."

"Yes, I could. But Mike, it's physically impossible. There just isn't time to get Chtexa here, even if we had the resources and the authority to do it."

"I wasn't thinking of that. I was thinking of CirCon—d'Averoigne's new circum-continuum radio. I don't know what shape it's in, but the Message Tree puts out a powerful signal—possibly d'Averoigne could pick it up. If so, you might be able to talk to Chtexa. I'll see what I can find out, anyhow."

"I'm willing to try," Ruiz-Sanchez said. "But it doesn't sound very promising."

He stopped to think, not of more answers—he had already hit his head against that wall more than often enough—but of what questions he still needed to ask. Michelis' appearance gave him the cue. It had shocked him at first, and he could still not quite get used to it. The big chemist had aged markedly: his face was drawn, and he had deeply cut, liverish circles under his eyes. Liu looked no better; while she had not seemed to age any, she looked miserable. There was a tension in the air between them, too, as though they had failed to find in each other sufficient release from the tensions of the world around them.

"It's possible that Agronski might know something that would be helpful," he said, only half-aloud.

"Maybe," Michelis said. "I've seen him only once—at a party, the one where Egtverchi caused such a stink. He was behaving very oddly. I'm sure he recognized us, but he wouldn't meet our eyes, let alone come and talk to us. As a matter of fact, I can't remember seeing him talking to anybody. He just sat in a corner and drank. It wasn't at all like him."

"Why did he come, do you suppose?"

"Oh, that's not hard to guess. He's a fan of Egtverchi's."

"*Martin?* How do you know?"

"Egtverchi bragged about it. He said he hoped to have the whole Lithia commission on his side eventually." Michelis grimaced. "The way Agronski was acting, he'll be of no use to Egtverchi or anybody else."

"And so we have still another soul on the way to damnation," Ruiz-Sanchez said grimly. "I should have suspected it. There's so little meaning in Agronski's life as it is, it won't take Egtverchi long to cut him off from any contact with reality at all. That is what evil does—it empties you."

"I'm none too sure Egtverchi's to blame," Michelis said, his voice steeped in gloom. "Except as a symptom. The Earth is riddled with schizophrenics already. If Agronski had any tendency that way, and obviously he did, then all he needed was to be planted here again for the tendency to flower."

"That wasn't my impression of him," Liu said. "From what little I saw of him, and from what you've told me, he seemed dreadfully normal—even simple-minded. I don't see how he could get deep enough into any question to be driven insane—or how he could be tempted to fall into your theological vacuum, Ramon."

"In this universe of discourse, Liu, we are all very much alike," Ruiz-Sanchez said dispiritedly. "And from what Mike tells me, I think we may be already too late to do much for Martin. And he's only—only a sample of what's happening everywhere within the sound of Egtverchi's voice."

"It's a mistake to think of schizophrenia as a disease of the wits, anyhow," Michelis said. "Back in the days when it was first being described, the English used to call it 'lorry-driver's disease.' When intellectuals get it, the results are spectacular only because they can articulate what they feel: Nijinski, van Gogh, T. E. Lawrence, Nietzsche, Wilson . . . it's a long list, but it's nothing compared to the ordinary people who've had it. And they get it fifty-to-one over intellectuals. Agronski is just the usual kind of victim, no more, no less."

"What has happened to that threat you mentioned?" Ruiz-Sanchez said. "Egtverchi got on the air again last night without his being made a ward of yours. Was your friend in the complicated hat just flailing the air?"

"I think that's partly the answer," Michelis said hopefully. "They haven't said another word to us, so I'm just guessing, but it may be that your arrival disconcerted them. They expected you to be publicly unfrocked—and the fact that you weren't has thrown their schedule for announcing the Lithia decision seriously out of joint. They're probably waiting to see what you will do now."

"So," Ruiz-Sanchez said grimly, "am I. I might just do nothing, which would probably be the most confusing thing I could do. I think their hands are tied, Mike. He's never mentioned the Bifalcos' products but that once, but obviously he must be selling them by the warehouse-load, so his sponsors won't cut him off. Nor can I see on what grounds the UN Communications Commission can do it." He laughed shortly. "They've been trying for decades to encourage more independent comment on 3-V anyhow—and Egtverchi is certainly a giant step in that direction."

"I should think he'd be open to charges of inciting to riot," Michelis said.

"He hasn't incited any riots that I've heard about," Ruiz-Sanchez said. "The Frisco affair happened spontaneously as far as anyone could see—and I noticed that the pictures didn't show a single one of those uniformed followers of his in the crowds."

"But he praised the rioters' spirit, and made fun of the police," Liu pointed out. "He as good as endorsed it."

"That's not incitement," Michelis said. "I see what Ramon means. He's smart enough to do nothing for which he could be brought to trial—and a false arrest would be suicide, the UN would be inciting a riot itself."

"Besides, what would they do with him if they got a conviction?" Ruiz asked. "He's a citizen, but his needs aren't like ours; they'd be chancing killing him with a thirty-day sentence. I suppose they could deport him, but they can't declare him an undesirable alien without declaring Lithia a foreign country—and until that report is released, Lithia is a protectorate, with a right to admission to the UN as a member state!"

"Small chance of that," Michelis said. "That would mean ditching Cleaver's project."

Ruiz-Sanchez felt the same sinking of the heart that had overcome him when Michelis first gave him that news. "How far advanced is it now?" he asked.

"I'm not sure. All I know is that they've been shipping equipment to him in huge amounts. There's another load scheduled to leave in two weeks. The scuttlebutt says that Cleaver has some kind of crucial experiment ready to go as soon as that shipment gets there. That puts it pretty close—the new ships make the trip in less than a month."

"Betrayed again," Ruiz-Sanchez said bitterly.

"Then is there *nothing* you can do, Ramon?" Liu asked.

"I'll interpret for Egtverchi and Chtexa, if anything comes of that project."

"Yes, but . . ."

"I know what you mean," he said. "Yes, there is something decisive that I can do. And possibly it would work. In fact, it is something that I *must* do."

He stared blindly at them. The buzzing of the bees, so reminiscent of the singing of the jungles of Lithia, probed insistently at him.

"But," he said, "I don't think that I'm going to do it."

Michelis moved mountains. He was formidable enough under normal conditions, but when he was desperate and saw a possible way out, no bulldozer could have been more implacable in crushing through an opening.

Lucien le Comte des Bois-d'Averoigne, late Procurator of Canarsie, and always fellow in the brotherhood of science, received them all cordially in his Canadian retreat. Not even the sardonically silent figure of Egtverchi made him blink; he shook hands with the displaced Lithian as though they were old friends meeting again after a lapse of a few weeks. The count himself was a large, rotund man in his early sixties, with a protuberant belly, and he was brown all over: his remaining hair was brown, his suit was brown, he was deeply tanned, and he was smoking a long brown cigar.

The room in which he received them—Ruiz-Sanchez, Michelis, Liu, and Egtverchi—was a curious mixture of lodge and laboratory. It had an open fireplace, rough furniture, mounted guns, an elk's head, and an amazing mess of wires and apparatus.

"I am by no means sure that this is going to work," he told them promptly. "Everything I have is still in the breadboard stage, as you can see. It's been years since I last handled a soldering iron and a voltmeter, too, so we may well have a simple electronic failure somewhere in this mass of wiring—but it wasn't a task I could leave to a technician."

He waved them to seats while he made final adjustments. Egtverchi remained standing in the rear of the room in the shadows, motionless except for the gentle rise and fall of his great chest as he breathed, and an occasional sudden movement of his eyes.

"There will be no image, of course," the count said abstractedly. "This giant J-J coupling you describe obviously doesn't broadcast in that band. But if we are very lucky, we may get some sound. . . . Ah."

A loudspeaker almost hidden in the maze crackled and

then began to emit distant, patterned bursts of hissing. Except for the pattern, it seemed to Ruiz-Sanchez to be nothing but noise, but the count said at once:

"I'm getting something in that region. I didn't expect to pick it up so soon. I don't make much sense of it, however."

Neither did Ruiz, and for a few moments he had all he could do to get over his amazement. "Those are—signals the Message Tree is broadcasting now?" he said, with a touch of incredulity.

"I hope so," the count said drily. "I have been busy all day installing chokes against any other possible signal."

The Jesuit's respect for the mathematician came close to awe. To think that this disorderly tangle of wiring, little black acorns, small red and brown objects like firecrackers, the shining interlocking blades of variable condensers, massively heavy coils, and flickering meters was even now reaching directly through the subether, around fifty light-years of space-time, to eavesdrop on the pulses of the crystalline cliff buried beneath Xoredeshch Sfath. . . .

"Can you tune it?" he said at last. "I think those must be the stutter pattern—what the Lithians use as a navigational grid for their ships and planes. There ought to be an audio band—"

Except he recalled suddenly, that that band couldn't possibly be an "audio" band. Nobody ever spoke directly to the Message Tree—only to the single Lithian who stood in the center of the Tree's chamber. How *he* got the substances of the message transformed into radio waves had never been explained to any of the Earthmen.

And yet suddenly there was a voice.

"—a powerful tap on the Tree," the voice said in clear, even, cold Lithian. "Who is receiving? Do you hear me? I do not understand direction your carrier is coming from. It seems inside the Tree, which is impossible. Does anyone understand me?"

Silently, the count thrust a microphone into Ruiz' hand. He discovered that he was trembling.

"We understand you," he said in Lithian in a shaky voice. "We are on Earth. Can you hear me?"

"I hear you," the voice said at once. "We understood that what you say is impossible. But what you say is not always accurate, we have found. What do you want?"

"I would like to speak to Chtexa, the metallist," Ruiz said. "This is Ruiz-Sanchez, who was in Xoredeshch Sfath last year."

"He can be summoned," said the cold, distant voice. There was a brief hashing sound from the speaker; then it went away again. "If he wishes to speak to you."

"Tell him," Ruiz-Sanchez said, "that his son Egtverchi also wishes to speak to him."

"Ah," said the voice after a pause. "Then no doubt he will come. But you cannot speak long on this channel. The direction from which your signal comes is damaging my sanity. Can you receive a sound-modulated signal if we can arrange to send one?"

Michleis murmured to the count, who nodded energetically and pointed to the loudspeaker.

"That is how we are receiving you now," Ruiz said. "How are you transmitting?"

"That I cannot explain to you," said the cold voice. "I cannot speak to you any longer or I will be damaged. Chtexa has been called."

The voice stopped and there was a long silence. Ruiz-Sanchez wiped the sweat off his forehead with the back of his hand.

"Telepathy?" Michelis muttered behind him. "No, it fits

into the electro-magnetic spectrum somewhere. But where? Boy, there sure is a lot we don't know about that Tree."

The count nodded ruefully. He was watching his meters like a hawk but, judging from his expression, they were not telling him anything he did not already know.

"Ruiz-Sanchez," the loudspeaker said. Ruiz started.

It was Chtexa's voice, clear and strong.

Ruiz beckoned at the shadows, and Egtverchi came forward. He was in no hurry. There was something almost insolent in his very walk.

"This is Ruiz-Sanchez, Chtexa," Ruiz said. "I'm talking to you from Earth—a new experimental communications system one of our scientists has evolved. I need your help."

"I will be glad to do whatever I can," Chtexa said. "I was sorry that you did not return with the other Earthman. He was less welcome. He and his friends have razed one of our finest forests near Gleshchtehk Sfath, and built ugly buildings here in the city."

"I'm sorry, too," Ruiz-Sanchez said. The words seemed inadequate, but it would be impossible to explain to Chtexa exactly what the situation was—impossible, and illegal. "I still hope to come some day. But I am calling about your son."

There was a brief pause, during which the speaker emitted a series of muted, anomalous sounds, almost yet not quite recognizable. Evidently the Lithian's audio hookup was catching some background noise from inside the Tree, or even outside it. The clarity of the reception was astonishing; it was impossible to believe that the Tree was fifty light-years away.

"Egtverchi is an adult now," Chtexa's voice said. "He has seen many wonders on your world. Is he with you?"

"Yes," Ruiz-Sanchez said, beginning to sweat again. "But he

does not know your language, Chtexa. I will interpret as best I can."

"That is strange," Chtexa said. "But I will hear his voice. Ask him when he is coming home; he has much to tell us."

Ruiz put the question.

"I have no home," Egtverchi said indifferently.

"I can't just tell him that, Egtverchi. Say something intelligible, in heaven's name. You owe your existence to Chtexa, you know that."

"I may visit Lithia some day," Egtverchi said, his eyes filming. "But I am in no hurry. There is still a great deal to be done on Earth."

"I hear him," Chtexa said. "His voice is high; he is not as tall as his inheritance provided, unless he is ill. What does he answer?"

There simply was not time to provide an interpretive translation; Ruiz-Sanchez told him the answer literally, word by word from English into Lithian.

"Ah," Chtexa said. "Then he has matters of import to his hand. That is good, and is generous of the Earth. He is right not to hurry. Ask him what he is doing."

"Breeding dissension," Egtverchi said, with a slight widening of his grin. Ruiz-Sanchez could not translate that literally; the concept was not in the Lithian language. It took him the better part of three long sentences to transmit even a dubious shadow of the idea to Chtexa.

"Then he *is* ill," Chtexa said. "You should have told me, Ruiz-Sanchez. You had best send him to us. You cannot treat him adequately there."

"He is not ill, and he will not go," Ruiz-Sanchez said carefully. "He is a citizen of Earth and cannot be compelled. This is why I called you. He is a trouble to us, Chtexa. He is doing us hurts. I had hoped you might reason with him; we can do nothing."

The anomalous sound, a sort of burring metallic whine, rose in the background and fell away again.

"That is not normal or natural," Chtexa said. "You do not recognize his illness. No more do I, but I am not a physician. You must send him here. I see I was in error in giving him to you. Tell him he is commanded home by the Law of the Whole."

"I never heard of the Law of the Whole," Egtverchi said when this was translated for him. "I doubt that there is any such thing. I make up my own laws as I go along. Tell him he is making Lithia sound like a bore, and that if he keeps it up I'll make a point of never going there at all."

"Blast it, Egtverchi—" Michelis burst in.

"Hush, Mike, one pilot is enough. Egtverchi, you were willing to cooperate with us up to now; at least, you came here with us. Did you do it just for the pleasure of defying and insulting your father? Chtexa is far wiser than you are; why don't you stop acting like a child and listen to him?"

"Because I don't choose to," Egtverchi said. "And you make me no more willing by wheedling, dear foster father. I didn't choose to be born a Lithian, and I didn't choose to be brought to Earth—but now that I'm a free agent I mean to make my own choices, and explain them to nobody if that's what pleases me."

"Then why did you come here?"

"There's no reason why I should explain that, but I will. I came to hear my father's voice. Now I've heard it. I don't understand what he says, and he makes no better sense in your translation, and that's all there is to it as far as I am concerned. Bid him farewell for me—I shan't speak to him again."

"What does he say?" Chtexa's voice said.

"That he does not acknowledge the Law of the Whole, and will not come home," Ruiz-Sanchez told the microphone. The little instrument was slippery with sweat in his palm. "And he says to bid you farewell."

"Farewell, then," Chtexa said. "And farewell to you, too, Ruiz-Sanchez. I am at fault, and this fills me with sorrow; but it is too late. I may not talk to you again, even by means of your marvelous instrument."

Behind the voice, the strange, half-familiar whine rose to a savage, snarling scream which lasted almost a minute. Ruiz-Sanchez waited until he thought he could be heard over it again.

"Why not, Chtexa?" he said huskily. "The fault is ours as much as it is yours. I am still your friend, and wish you well."

"And I am your friend, and wish you well," Chtexa's voice said. "But we may not talk again. Can you not hear the power saws?"

So that was what that sound was!

"Yes. Yes, I hear them."

"That is the reason," Chtexa said. "Your friend Xlevher is cutting down the Message Tree."

The gloom was thick in the Michelis apartment. As the time drew closer for Egtverchi's next broadcast, it became increasingly apparent that their analysis of the UN's essential helplessness had been correct. Egtverchi was not openly triumphant, though he was exposed to that temptation in several newspaper interviews; but he floated some disquieting hints of vast plans which might well be started in motion when he was next on the air.

Ruiz-Sanchez had not the least desire to listen to the broadcast, but he had to face the fact that he would be unable to stay away from it. He could not afford to be without any new data that the program might yield. Nothing he had learned had done him any good thus far, but there was always the slim chance that something would turn up.

In the meantime, there was the problem of Cleaver, and his associates. However you looked at it, they were human souls. If Ruiz-Sanchez were to be driven, somehow, to the step that Hadrian VIII had commanded, and it did not fail, more than a set of attractive hallucinations would be lost. It would plunge several hundred human souls into instant death and more than probable damnation; Ruiz-Sanchez did not believe that the hand of God would reach forth to pluck to salvation men who were involved in such a project as Cleaver's, but he was equally convinced that his should not be the hand to condemn any man to death, let alone to an unshriven death. Ruiz was condemned already—but not yet of murder.

It had been Tannhäuser who had been told that his salvation was as unlikely as the blossoming of the pilgrim's staff in his hand. And Ruiz-Sanchez' was as unlikely as sanctified murder.

Yet the Holy Father had commanded it; had said it was the only road back for Ruiz-Sanchez, and for the world. The Pope's clear implication had been that he shared with Ruiz-Sanchez the view that the world stood on the brink of Armageddon—and he had said flatly that only Ruiz-Sanchez could avert it. Their only difference was doctrinal, and in these matters the Pope could not err. . . .

But if it was possible that the dogma of the infertility of Satan was wrong, then it was possible that the dogma of Papal infallibility was wrong. After all, it was a recent invention; quite a few Popes in history had got along without it.

Heresies, Ruiz-Sanchez thought—not for the first time—come in snarls. It is impossible to pull free one thread; tug at one, and the whole mass begins to roll down upon you.

I believe, O Lord; help me in mine unbelief. But it was useless. It was as though he were praying to God's back.

There was a knock on his door. "Coming, Ramon?" Michelis' tired voice said. "He's due to go on in two minutes."

"All right, Mike."

They settled before the Klee, warily, already defeated, awaiting—what? It could only be a proclamation of total war. They were ignorant only of the form it would take.

"Good evening," Egtverchi said warmly from the frame. "There will be no news tonight. Instead of reporting news, we will make some. The time has come, it is now plain, for the people to whom news happens—those hapless people whose grief-stricken, stunned faces look out at you from the newspapers and the 3-V 'casts such as mine—to throw off their helplessness. Tonight I call upon all of you to show your contempt for the hypocrites who are your bosses, and your total power to be free of them.

"You have a message for them. Tell them this: tell them, 'Your beasts, sirs, are a great people.'

"I will be the first. As of tonight, I renounce my citizenship in the United Nations, and my allegiance to the Shelter state. From now on I will be a citizen—"

Michelis was on his feet, shouting incoherently.

"—a citizen of no country but that bounded by the limits of my own mind. I do not know what those limits are, and I may never find out, but I shall devote my life to searching for them, in whatsover manner seems good to me, and in no other manner whatsoever.

"You must do the same. Tear up your registration cards. If you are asked your serial number, tell them you never had one. Never fill in another form. Stay above ground when the siren sounds. Stake out plots; grow crops; abandon the corridors. Do not commit any violence; simply refuse to obey. Nobody has the right to compel you, as non-citizens. Passivity is the key. Renounce, resist, deny!

"Begin now. In half an hour they will overwhelm you. When—"

An urgent buzzer sounded over Egtverchi's voice, and for an instant a checkerboard pattern in red and black blotted out his figure: the UN's crash-priority signal, overriding the by-pass recording circuit. Then the face of the UN man looked out at them from under its funny hat, with Egtverchi underlying it dimly, his exhortations only a whisper in the background.

"Dr. Michelis," the UN man said exultantly. "He's done it. He's overreached himself. As a non-citizen, he's right in our hands. Get down here—we need you right away, before he gets off the air. Dr. Meid too."

"What for?"

"To sign pleas of *nolo contendere.* Both of you are under arrest for keeping a wild animal—a technicality only; don't be alarmed. But we have to have you. We mean to put Mr. Egtverchi in a cage for the rest of his life—a *soundproof* cage."

"You are making a mistake," Ruiz-Sanchez said quietly.

The UN man's face, a mask of triumph with blazing eyes, swung toward him briefly.

"I didn't ask what you thought, Mister," he said. "I have no orders concerning you, but as far as I'm concerned, you've been closed out of this case entirely. If you try to force your way back in, you'll get burned. Dr. Michelis, Dr. Meid? Do we have to come and get you?"

"We'll come," Michelis said stonily. "Sign off." He did not wait for the UN man, however, but killed the set himself.

"Do you think we should do it, Ramon?" he said. "If not, we'll stay right here, and the hell with him. Or we'll take you along if you want."

"No, no," Ruiz-Sanchez said. "Go ahead. No balking on your part will accomplish a thing but getting you both in deep trouble. Do me one favor, though."

"Gladly. What is it?"

"Stay off the streets. When you get to the UN offices, make them keep you there. As arrested citizens, you have the right to be jailed."

Michelis and Liu both stared at him. Then comprehension began to break over Michelis' face.

"You think it will be that bad?" he said.

"Yes, I do. Do I have your promise?"

Michelis looked at Liu and nodded grimly. They went out.

The collapse of the Shelter state had already begun.

EIGHTEEN

The beast Chaos roared on unslaked for three days. Ruiz-Sanchez was able to follow much of its progress from the beginning, via the Michelises' 3-V set. There were times when he would also have liked to look out over the sun porch rail, but the roar of the mob, the shots, explosions, police whistles, sirens, and unnamable noises had driven the bees frantic; under such conditions he would not have trusted Liu's protective garments for an instant, even had they been large enough for him.

The UN squads had made a well-organized attempt to bear Egtverchi off directly from the broadcasting station, but Egtverchi was not there—in fact, he had never been there at all. The audio, video and tri-di signals had all been piped into the station via co-axial cable from some unspecified place. The necessary connections had been made at the last minute, when it became obvious that Egtverchi was not going to show up, by a technician who had volunteered word of the actual situation; a sacrifice piece in Egtverchi's gambit. The network had sent an alert to the proper UN officers at once, but another sacrifice piece saw to it that the alert was shunted through channels.

It took nearly all night to sweat out of the QBC technician the location of Egtverchi's studio (the stooge at the UN obviously did not know) and by that time, of course, he was no longer there either. Also by that time, the news of the attempted arrest and the misfire was being blared and headlined in every Shelter in the world.

Even this much did not get to Ruiz-Sanchez until somewhat later, for the noise in the street began immediately after the first announcement had been made. At first it was disconnected and random, as though the streets were gradually filling with people who were angry or upset but were divided over what, if anything, they ought to do about it. Then there was a sudden change in the quality of the sound, and instantly Ruiz-Sanchez knew that the transformation from a gathering to a mob had been made. The shouting could not very well have become any louder, but abruptly it was a frightening uniform growl, like the enormous voice of a single animal.

He had no way of knowing what had triggered the change, and perhaps the crowd itself never knew either. But now the shots began—not many, but one shot is a fusillade if there have been no shots before. A part of the overall roar detached itself and took on an odd and even more frightening hollow sound; only when the floor shook slightly under him did he realize what that meant.

A pseudopod of the beast had thrust itself into the building. Ruiz-Sanchez realized that he should have expected nothing else. The fad of living above ground was still essentially a privilege, reserved to those UN employees and officials who knew how to get the necessary and elaborate permissions, and who furthermore had enough income to support such an inconvenient arrangement; it was the twenty-first century's version of commuting from Maine—*here* was where *they* lived—

Ruiz-Sanchez checked the door hastily. It had elaborate locks—left over from the last period of the Shelter race, when the great untended buildings had been natural targets for looters—but they had gone unused for years. Ruiz-Sanchez used them all now.

He was just in time. There was an obscene shouting in the corridor just outside as part of the mob burst into it from the fire stairs. They had avoided the elevator by instinct—it was too slow to sustain their thoughtless ferocity, too confined for lawlessness, too mechanical for men who were letting their muscles do their thinking.

Somebody rattled the door knob and then shook it.

"Locked," a muffled voice said.

"Break the damned thing down. Here, get out of the way—"

The door shuddered, but held easily. There was another, harder thump, as though several men had lunged against it at the same time; Ruiz-Sanchez could hear them grunt with the impact. Then there were five hammerlike blows.

"Open up in there! Open up, you lousy government fink, or we'll burn you out!"

The spontaneous threat seemed to surprise them all, even the utterer. There was a confused whispering. Then someone said hoarsely: "All right, but find some paper or something."

Ruiz-Sanchez thought confusedly of finding and filling a bucket, though he could not see how any fire could be introduced around the door—there was no transom, and the sill was snug—but at the same time a blurred shout from farther down the hall seemed to draw everyone outside stampeding away. The subsequent noises made it clear that they had found either an open, empty apartment, or an inadequately secured, occupied one where nobody was at home. Yes, it was occupied; Ruiz-Sanchez could hear them breaking furniture as well as windows.

Then, with a shock of terror, their voices began to come at him from behind his back. He whirled, but there seemed to be nobody in the apartment; the shouting was coming from the glassed-in sun porch, but of course there was nobody out there either—

"Jesus! Look, the guy's got his porch glassed in. It's a goddam garden."

"They don't let you have no goddam gardens in the Shelters."

"And you know who paid for it. Us, that's who."

He realized that they were on the neighboring balcony. He felt a surge of relief which he knew to be irrational. The next words confirmed its irrationality.

"Get some of that kindling out here. No, heavier stuff. Something to *throw*, you meathead."

"Can we get over there from here?"

"If we could throw a ladder across there—"

"It's a long way down—"

The leg of a chair burst through the glass on the sun porch. A heavy vase followed.

The bees came pouring out. Ruiz-Sanchez had not realized how many of them there were. The porch was black with them. For a moment they hovered uncertainly. They would have found the gaps in the glass almost at once in any event, but the men on the next porch, who could not have understood what it was they were seeing, gave the great insects the perfect cue. Something small and massive, possibly a torn-off piece of plumbing, shattered another pane and whirled through the midst of the cloud. Snarling like an old-fashioned aircraft engine, the bees swarmed.

There was an instant of dead silence across the way, and then a scream of agony and horror that made Ruiz-Sanchez' gut contort violently. Then they were all screaming. Briefly, he saw one of them, leaping straight out into space, his arms flailing, his head and chest swathed in golden-and-black furry bodies. Feet drummed past the door, and someone fell. The heavy buzzing threaded its way along the corridor after them.

From below, there were more screams. The great insects could not fly in the open air, but they were free in the building now. Some of them might even make it all the way down to the street, by descending the stairwell.

After a while, there were no human sounds left in the building, only the pervasive insect snarl. Outside the door, somebody moaned and was silent.

Ruiz-Sanchez knew what he had to do. He went into the kitchen and vomited, and then he crammed himself into Liu's beekeeper's togs.

He was no longer a priest; indeed, he was no longer even a Catholic. Grace had been withdrawn from him. But it is the duty of any person to administer extreme unction if he knows how, as it is the duty of any person to administer baptism if he knows how. What happened to the soul so ministered to when it departed would be disposed by the Lord God, Who disposes all things; but He had commanded that no soul come before Him unshriven.

The man before the door was already dead. Ruiz-Sanchez crossed himself out of habit and stepped over the body, his eyes averted. A man who has died of massive histamine shock is not an edifying sight.

The open apartment had been thoroughly smashed up. There were three bodies there, all beyond help. The door to the kitchen, however, was closed; if one of them had had the sense to barricade himself in there before the swarm got to him, he might have been able to kill the few bees who had come in with him—

As if in confirmation, there was a groan behind the door. Ruiz-Sanchez pushed at it, but it was partly locked. He got it open about six inches and wormed through.

The contorted man on the floor, his incredibly puffed, taut skin slowly turning black, his eyes glassy with agony, was Agronski.

The geologist did not recognize him; he was already beyond that. There was no mind behind the eyes. Ruiz-Sanchez fell to his knees clumsily in the tight protective clothing. He heard himself begin to mutter the rites, but he was no more hearing the Latin words than Agronski was.

This could be no coincidence. He had come here to give grace, if such a one as he could still give grace; and before him was the most blameless of the Lithian commission, struck down where Ruiz-Sanchez would be sure to find him. It was the God of Job who was abroad in the world now, not the God of the Psalmist or the Christ. The face that was bent upon Ruiz-Sanchez was the face of the avenging, the jealous God—the God Who made hell before He made man, because He knew that He would have need of it. That terrible truth Dante had written down; and in the black face with the protruding tongue which rolled beside Ruiz-Sanchez' knee, he saw that Dante had been right, as every Catholic who reads the *Divine Comedy* knows in his heart of hearts.

There is a demonolator abroad in the world. He shall be deprived of grace, and then called upon to administer extreme unction to a friend. By this sign, let him know himself for what he is.

After a while, Agronski was dead, choked to death by his own tongue.

But still it was not over. It was necessary now to make Mike's apartment secure, kill any bees that might have got in, see to it that the escaped swarm died. It was easy enough. Ruiz-Sanchez simply papered over the broken panes on the sun porch. The bees could not feed anywhere but in Liu's garden; they would come back there within a few hours; denied entrance, they would die of starvation an hour or so later. A bee is not a well-designed flying-machine; it keeps itself in the air by expending energy—in short, by pure brute force. A trapped bumblebee can starve to death in half a day, and Liu's tetraploid monsters would die far sooner of their freedom.

The 3-V muttered away throughout the dreary business. The terror was not local, that was clear. The Corridor Riots of 1993 had been nothing but a premonitory flicker, compared to this.

Four targets were blacked out completely. Egtverchi's uniformed thugs, suddenly reappearing from nowhere in force, had seized their control centers. At the moment, they were holding roughly twenty-five million people as hostages for Egtverchi's safe-conduct, with the active collusion of perhaps five million of them. The violence elsewhere was not as systematic—though some of the outbursts of wrecking must have been carefully planned to allow for the placing of the explosives alone, there seemed to be no special pattern to it—but in no case could it be described as "passive" or "non-violent."

Sick, wretched and damned, Ruiz-Sanchez waited in the Michelises' jungle apartment, as though part of Lithia had followed him home and enfolded him there.

* * *

After the first three days, the fury had exhausted itself sufficiently to permit Michelis and Liu to risk the trip back to their apartment in a UN armored car. They were wan and ghastly looking, as Ruiz-Sanchez supposed he was himself; they had had even less sleep than he had. He decided at once to say nothing about Agronski; that horror they could be spared. There was no way, however, that he could avoid explaining what had happened to the bees.

Liu's sad little shrug was somehow even harder to bear than Agronski.

"Did they find him yet?" Ruiz-Sanchez said huskily.

"We were going to ask you the same thing," Michelis said. The tall New Englander was able to get a glimpse of himself in a mirror above a planting box and winced. "Ugh, what a beard! At the UN everybody's too busy to tell you anything, except in fragments. We thought you might have heard an announcement."

"No, nothing. The Detroit vigilantes have surrendered, according to QBC."

"Yes, so have those goons in Smolensk; they ought to be putting that on the air in an hour or so. I never did think they'd succeed in pulling that operation off. They can't possibly know the corridors as well as the target area authorities themselves do. In Smolensk they got them with the fire door system—drained all the oxygen out of the area they were holding without their realizing what was going on. Two of them never came to."

Ruiz-Sanchez crossed himself automatically. Up on the wall, the Klee muttered in a low voice; it had not been off since Egtverchi's broadcast.

"I don't know whether I want to listen to that damn thing or not," Michelis said sourly. Nevertheless, he turned up the volume.

There was still essentially no news. The rioting was dying back, though it was as bad as ever in some shelters. The Smolensk announcement was duly made, bare of detail. Egtverchi had not yet been located, but UN officials expected a break in the case "shortly."

" 'Shortly,' hell," Michelis said. "They've run out of leads entirely. They thought they had him cold the next morning, when they found a trail to the hideaway where he'd arranged to tide himself over and direct things. But he wasn't there—apparently he'd gotten out in a hurry, some time before. And nobody in his organization knows where he would go next—he was *supposed* to be there, and they're thoroughly demoralized to be told that he's not."

"Which means that he's on the run," Ruiz-Sanchez suggested.

"Yes, I suppose that's some consolation," Michelis said. "But where could he run to, where he wouldn't be recognized? And *how* would he run? He couldn't just gallop naked through the streets, or take a public conveyance. It takes organization to ship something as *outré* as that secretly—and Egtverchi's organization is as baffled about it as the UN is." He turned the 3-V off with a savage gesture.

Liu turned to Ruiz-Sanchez, her expression appalled beneath its weariness.

"Then it's really not over after all?" she said hopelessly.

"Far from it," Ruiz-Sanchez said. "But maybe the violent phase of it is over. If Egtverchi stays vanished for a few days more, they'll conclude that he is dead. He couldn't stay unsighted that long if he were still moving about. Of course his death won't solve most of the major problems, but at least it would remove one sword from over our heads."

Even that, he recognized silently, was wishful thinking. Besides, can you kill a hallucination?

"Well, I hope the UN has learned something," Michelis said. "There's one thing you have to say for Egtverchi: he got the public to bring up all the unrest that's been smoldering down under the concrete for all these years. And underneath all the apparent conformity, too. We're going to have to do something about that now—maybe take sledgehammers in our hands and pound this damned Shelter system down into rubble and start over. It wouldn't cost any more than rebuilding what's already been destroyed. One thing's certain: the UN won't be able to smother a revolt of this size in slogans. They'll have to *do* something."

The Klee chimed.

"I won't answer it," Michelis said through gritted teeth. "I won't answer it. I've had enough."

"I think we'd better, Mike," Liu said. "It might be—news."

"News!" Michelis said, like a swearword. But he allowed himself to be persuaded. Underneath all the weariness, Ruiz-Sanchez thought he could detect something like a return of warmth between the two, as though, during the three days, some depth had been sounded which they had never touched before. The slight sign of something good astonished him. Was he beginning, like all demonolaters, to take pleasure in the prevalence of evil, or at least in the expectation of it?

The caller was the UN man. His face was very strange underneath his funny hat, and his head was cocked as if to catch the first word. Suddenly, blindingly, Ruiz-Sanchez saw the hat in the light of the attitude, and realized what it was: an elaborately disguised hearing aid. The UN man was deaf and, like most deaf people, ashamed of it. The rest of the apparatus was a decoy.

"Dr. Michelis, Dr. Meid, Dr. Ruiz," he said. "I don't know how to begin. Yes, I do. My deepest apologies for past rudeness. And past damn foolishness. We were wrong—my God, but we were wrong! It's your turn now. We need you badly, if you feel like doing us a favor. I won't blame you if you don't."

"No threats?" Michelis said, with unforgiving contempt.

"No, no threats. My apologies, please. No, this is purely a favor, requested by the Security Council." His face twisted suddenly, and then was composed once more. "I—volunteered to present the petition. We need you all, right away, on the Moon."

"On the Moon! Why?"

"We've found Egtverchi."

"Impossible," Ruiz-Sanchez said, more sharply than he had intended. "He could never have gotten passage. Is he dead?"

"No, he's not dead. And he's not on the Moon—I didn't mean to imply that."

"Then where *is* he, in God's name?"

"He's on his way back to Lithia."

The trip to the Moon, by ferry-rocket, was rough, hectic and long. As the sole space voyage now being made in which the Haertel overdrive could not be used—across so short a distance, a Haertel ship would have overshot the target—very little improvement in techniques had been made in the trip since the old von Braun days. It was only after they had been bundled off the rocket into the moonboat, for the slow, paddle-wheel-driven trip across the seas of dust to the Comte d'Averoigne's observatory, that Ruiz-Sanchez managed to piece the whole story together.

Egtverchi had been found aboard the vessel that was shipping the final installment of equipment to Cleaver, when the ship was two days out. He was half-dead. In a final, desperate improvisation, he had had himself crated, addressed to Cleaver, marked "FRAGILE—RADIOACTIVE—THIS END UP," and shipped via ordinary express into the spaceport. Even a normally raised Lithian would have been shaken up by this kind of treatment, and Egtverchi, in addition to being a spindling specimen of his race, had been on the run for many hours before being shipped.

The vessel, by no very great coincidence, was also carrying the pilot model of the Petard CirCon; the captain got the news back to the count on the first test, and the count passed it along to the UN by ordinary radio. Egtverchi was in irons now, but he was well and cheerful. Since it was impossible for the ship to turn back, the UN was now, in effect, doing his running for him, at a good many times the speed of light.

Ruiz-Sanchez found a trace of pity in his heart for the born exile, harried now like a wild animal, penned behind bars, on his way back to a fatherland for which no experience in his life had fitted him, whose very language he could not speak. But when the UN man began to question them all—what was needed was some knowledgeable estimate of what Egtverchi might do next—his pity did not survive his speculations. It was right and proper to pity children, but Ruiz-Sanchez was beginning to believe that adults generally deserve any misfortune that they get.

The impact of a creature like Egtverchi on the stable society of Lithia would be explosive. On Earth, at least, he had been a freak; on Lithia, he would soon be taken for another Lithian, however odd. And Earth had had centuries of experience with deranged and displaced messiahs like Egtverchi; such a thing had never happened before on Lithia. Egtverchi would infect that garden down to the roots, and remake it in his own image—transforming the planet into that hypothetical dangerous enemy against whose advent Cleaver had wanted to make it an arsenal!

Yet something like that had happened when Earth was a stable garden, too. Perhaps—*O felix culpa!*—it always happened that way, on every world. Perhaps the Tree of the Knowledge of Good and Evil was like the Yggdrasil of the legends of Pope Hadrian's birthland, with its roots in the floor of the universe, its branches bearing the planets—and whosoever would eat of its fruit might eat thereof. . . .

No, that must not be. Lithia as a rigged Garden had been dangerous enough; but Lithia transformed into a planet-wide fortress of Dis was a threat to Heaven itself.

The Count d'Averoigne's main observatory had been built by the UN, to his specifications, approximately in the center of the crater Stadius, a once towering cup which early in its history had been swamped and partially melted in the outpouring sea of lava which made the Mare Imbrium. What remained of its walls served the count's staff as a meteor-rampart during showers, yet they were low enough to be well below the horizon from the center of the crater, giving the count what was effectively a level plain in all directions.

He looked no different than he had when they had first met, except that he was wearing brown coveralls instead of a brown suit, but he seemed glad to see them. Ruiz-Sanchez suspected that he was sometimes lonely, or perhaps lonely all the time—not only because of his current isolation on the Moon, but in his continuing remoteness from his family and indeed the whole of ordinary humanity.

"I have a surprise for you," he told them. "We've just completed the new telescope—six hundred feet in diameter, all of sodium foil, perched on top of Mount Piton a few hundred miles north of here. The relay cables were brought through to Stadius yesterday, and I was up all night testing my circuits. They have been made a little neater since you last saw them."

This was an understatement. The breadboard rigs had vanished entirely; the object the count was indicating now was nothing but a black enamel box about the size of a tape recorder, and with only about that many knobs.

"Of course to do this is simpler than picking up a broadcast from a transmitter that doesn't have CirCon, like the Tree," the count admitted. "But the results are just as gratifying. Regard."

He snapped a switch dramatically. On a large screen on the opposite wall of the dark observatory chamber, a cloud-wrapped planet swam placidly.

"My God!" Michelis said in a choked voice. "That's—*is* that Lithia, Count d'Averoigne? I'd swear it is."

"Please," the count said. "Here I'm Dr. Petard. But yes, that's Lithia; its sun is visible from the Moon a little over twelve days of the month. It's fifty light-years away, but here we see it at an apparent distance of a quarter of a million miles, give or take ten thousand—about the distance of the Moon from the Earth. It's remarkable how much light you can gather with a six-hundred-foot paraboloid of sodium when there's no atmosphere in the way. Of course with an atmosphere we couldn't maintain the foil, either—the gravity here is almost too much for it."

"It's stunning," Liu murmured.

"That's only the beginning, Dr. Meid. We have spanned not only the space, but also the time—both together, as is only appropriate. What we are seeing is Lithia *today*—right now, in fact—not Lithia fifty years ago."

"Congratulations," Michelis said, his voice hushed. "Of course the scholium was the real achievement—but you threw up an installation in record time, too, it seems to me."

"It seems that way to me, too," the count said, taking his cigar out of his mouth and regarding it complacently.

"Are we going to be able to catch the ship's landing?" the UN man said intensely.

"No, I'm afraid not, unless I have my dates wrong. According to the schedule you gave me, the landing was supposed to have taken place yesterday, and I can't back my device up and down the time spectrum. The equations nail it to simultaneity, and simultaniety is what I get—neither more, nor less."

His voice changed color suddenly. The change transformed him from a fat man delighted with a new toy into the philosopher-mathematician Henri Petard as no disclaimer of his hereditary title could ever have done.

"I invited you to hold your conference here," he said, "because I thought you should all be witnesses to an event which I hope profoundly is not going to happen. I will explain:

"Recently I was asked to check the reasoning on which Dr. Cleaver based the experiment he has programmed for today. Briefly, the experiment is an attempt to store the total output of a Nernst generator for a period of about ninety seconds, through a special adaptation of what is called the pinch effect.

"I found the reasoning faulty—not obviously, Dr. Cleaver is too careful a craftsman for that, but seriously, all the same.

Since lithium 6 is ubiquitous on that planet, any failure would be totally disastrous. I sent Dr. Cleaver an urgent message on the CirCon, to be tape-recorded on the ship that landed yesterday; I would have used the Tree, but of course that has been cut down, and I doubt that he would have accepted any such message from a Lithian had it not been. The captain of the ship promised me that the tape would be delivered to Dr. Cleaver before any of the remaining apparatus was unloaded. But I know Dr. Cleaver. He is bullheaded. Is that not so?"

"Yes," Michelis said. "God knows that's so."

"Well, we are ready," Dr. Petard said. "As ready as we can be. I have instruments to record the event. Let us pray that I won't need them."

The count was a lapsed Catholic; his injunction was a habit. But Ruiz-Sanchez could no more pray for any such thing than the count could—and no more could he leave the outcome to chance. St. Michael's sword had been put into his hand now so unmistakably that even a fool could not fail to recognize it.

The Holy Father had known it would be so, and had planned for it with the skill of a Disraeli. Ruiz-Sanchez shuddered to think what a less politically minded Pope would have made of such an opportunity, but of course it had been God's will that this should happen in the time of Hadrian and not during any other pontificate. By specifically ruling out any formal excommunication, Hadrian had reserved to Ruiz-Sanchez' use the one gift of grace which was pertinent to the occasion at hand.

And perhaps he had seen, too, that the time Ruiz-Sanchez had devoted to the elaborate, capriciously hypercomplex case of conscience in the Joyce novel had been time wasted; there was a much simpler case, one of the classical situations, which applied if Ruiz-Sanchez could only see it. It was the case of the sick child, for whose recovery prayers were offered.

These days, most sick children recovered in a day or so, after a shot of spectrosigmin or some similar drug, even from the brink of the terminal coma. *Question:* Has prayer failed, and temporal science wrought the recovery?

Answer: No, for prayer is always answered, and no man may choose for God the means He uses to answer it. Surely a miracle like a life-saving antibiotic is not unworthy of the bounty of God.

And this, too, was the answer to the riddle of the Great Nothing. The Adversary is not creative, except in the sense that He always seeks evil, and always does good. He cannot claim any of the credit for temporal science, nor imply truthfully that a success for temporal science is a failure for prayer. In this as in all other matters, He is compelled to lie.

And there on Lithia was Cleaver, agent of the Great Nothing, foredoomed to failure, the very task to which he was putting his hand in the Adversary's service tottering on the edge of undoing all His work. The staff of Tannhäuser had blossomed: *These fruits are shaken from the wrath-bearing tree.*

Yet even as Ruiz-Sanchez rose, the searing words of Pope Gregory VIII trembling on his lips, he hesitated still again. What if he were wrong after all? Suppose, just suppose, that Lithia were Eden, and that the Earth-bred Lithian who had just returned there were the Serpent foreordained for it? *Suppose it always happened that way, world without end?*

The voice of the Great Nothing, pouring forth lies to the last. Ruiz-Sanchez raised his hand. His shaken voice resounded and echoed in the cave of the observatory.

"I, A PRIEST OF CHRIST, DO COMMAND YE, MOST FOUL SPIRITS WHO DO STIR UP THESE CLOUDS—"

"What? For heaven's sake, be quiet," the UN man said irritably. Everyone else was staring in wonder, and in Liu's glance there appeared to be a little fear. Only the count's glance was knowing and solemn.

"—THAT YE DEPART FROM THEM, AND DISPERSE YOURSELVES INTO WILD AND UNTILLED PLACES, THAT YE MAY BE NO LONGER ABLE TO HARM MEN OR ANIMALS OR FRUITS OR HERBS, OR WHATSOEVER IS DESIGNED FOR HUMAN USE.

"AND THOU GREAT NOTHING, THOU LUSTFUL AND STUPID ONE, *SCROFA STERCORATE,* THOU SOOTY SPIRIT FROM TARTARUS, I CAST THEE DOWN, *O PORCARIE PEDICOSE,* INTO THE INFERNAL KITCHEN:

"BY THE APOCALYPSE OF JESUS CHRIST, WHICH GOD HATH GIVEN TO MAKE KNOWN UNTO HIS SERVANTS THOSE THINGS WHICH ARE SHORTLY TO BE; AND HATH SIGNIFIED, SENDING BY HIS ANGEL; I EXORCISE THEE, ANGEL OF PERVERSITY:

"BY THE SEVEN GOLD CANDLESTICKS, AND BY ONE LIKE UNTO THE SON OF MAN, STANDING IN THE MIDST OF THE CANDLESTICKS; BY HIS VOICE, AS THE VOICE OF MANY WATERS; BY HIS WORDS, 'I AM LIVING, WHO WAS DEAD; AND BEHOLD, I LIVE FOREVER AND EVER; AND I HAVE THE KEYS OF DEATH AND OF HELL'; I SAY UNTO YOU, ANGEL OF PERDITION: DEPART, DEPART, DEPART!"

The echoes rang and dwindled. The lunar silence flowed back, underlined by the breathing of the people in the observatory and the sound of pumps laboring somewhere beneath.

And slowly, and without a sound, the cloudy planet on the screen turned white all over. The clouds and the dim oceans and continents blended into a blue-white glare which shone out from the screen like a searchlight. It seemed to penetrate their bloodless faces down to the bone.

Slowly, slowly, it all melted away: the chirruping forests, Chtexa's porcelain house, the barking lungfish, the stump of the Message Tree, the wild allosaurs, the single silver moon, the great beating heart of Blood Lake, the city of the potters, the flying squid, the Lithian crocodile and his winding track, the tall noble reasoning creatures and the mystery and the beauty around them. Suddenly the whole of Lithia began to swell, like a balloon—

The count tried to turn the screen off, but he was too late. Before he could touch the black box, the whole circuit went out with a puffing of fuses. The intolerable light vanished instantly; the screen went black, and the universe with it.

They sat blinded and stunned.

"An error in Equation Sixteen," the count's voice said harshly in the swimming darkness.

No, Ruiz-Sanchez thought; no. An instance of fulfilled desire. He had wanted to use Lithia to defend the faith, and he had been given that. Cleaver had wanted to turn it into a fusion-bomb plant, and he had got that in full measure, all at once. Michelis had seen in it a prophecy of infallible human love, and had been stretched on that rack ever since. And Agronski—Agronski had wanted nothing to change, and now was unchangeably nothing.

In the darkness, there was a long, ragged sigh. For a moment, Ruiz-Sanchez could not place the voice; he thought it was Liu. But no. It was Mike.

"When we have our eyesight back," the count's voice said, "I propose that we suit up and go outside. We have a nova to watch for."

That was only a maneuver, an act of misdirection on the count's part—an act of kindness. He knew well enough that that nova would not be visible to the naked eye until the next Holy Year, fifty years to come; and he knew that they knew.

Nevertheless, when Father Ramon Ruiz-Sanchez, sometime Clerk Regular in the Society of Jesus, could see again, they had left him alone with his God and his grief.

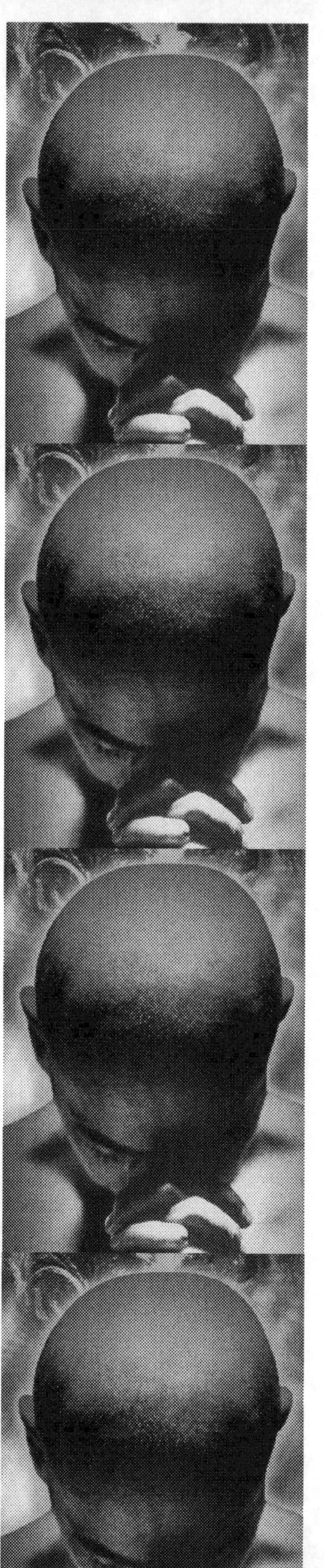

APPENDIX

The Planet Lithia (from Michelis, D., and Ruiz-Sanchez, R.: Lithia—a preliminary report. *J.I.R.* 4:225, 2050; abstract).

Lithia is the second planet of the solar type star Alpha Arietis, which is located in the constellation Aries and is approximately 50 light-years from Sol.[1]

It revolves around its primary at a mean distance of 108,600,000 miles, with a year of approximately 380 terrestrial days. The orbit is definitely elliptical, with an eccentricity of 0.51, so that the long axis of the ellipse is approximately 15 percent longer than the short axis.

The axis of the planet is essentially perpendicular to the orbit, and the planet rotates on its axis with a day of about 20 terrestrial hours. Hence, the Lithian year consists of 456 Lithian days. The eccentricity of the orbit produces mild seasons, with long, relatively cold winters, and short, hot summers.

The planet has one moon with a diameter of 1,256 miles,

1. An earlier figure of 40 light-years, often quoted in the literature, arose from application of the so-called Cosmological Constant. Einstein's reluctance to allow this "constant" into his scholium has now been fully justified. v. Haertel, *J.I.R.* 1:21, 2047.

which revolves about its primary at a distance of 326,000 miles, twelve times in the Lithian year.

The outer planets of the system have not yet been explored.

Lithia is 8,267 miles in diameter, and has a surface gravity of 0.82 that of Earth. The light gravity of the planet is accounted for by the relatively low density, which in turn is the result of its composition. When the planet was formed there was a much lower percentage of the heavy elements with atomic numbers above 20 included in its make-up than was the case with the Earth. Furthermore, the odd-numbered elements are even rarer than they are on Earth; the only odd-numbered elements that appear in any quantity are hydrogen, nitrogen, sodium and chlorine. Potassium is quite rare, and the heavy odd-numbered elements (gold, silver, copper) appear only in microscopic quantities and never in the elemental form. In fact, the only uncombined metal that has ever appeared on the planet has been the nickel-iron of an occasional meteorite.

The metallic core of the planet is considerably smaller than that of the Earth, and the basaltic inner coating correspondingly thicker. The continents are built, as on Earth, basically of granite, overlaid with sedimentary deposits.

The scarcity of potassium has led to an extremely static geology. The natural radioactivity of K^{40} is the major source of the internal heat of the Earth, and Lithia has less than a tenth of the K^{40} content of the Earth. As a result, the interior of the planet is much cooler, vulcanism is extremely rare, and geological revolutions even rarer. The planet seems to have settled down early in life, and nothing very startling has happened since. The major part of its uneventful geological history is at best conjectural, because the scarcity of radioactive elements has led to great difficulties in dating the strata.

The atmosphere is somewhat similar to that of the Earth.[2] The atmospheric pressure is 815.3 mm at sea level, and the composition of dry air is as follows:

Nitrogen	66.26 percent by volume
Oxygen	31.27
Argon, &c.	2.16
CO_2	0.31

The relatively high CO_2 concentration (partial pressure about 11 times that of the gas in the Earth's atmosphere) leads to a hothouse type of climate, with relatively slight temperature differences from pole to equator. The average summer temperature at the pole is about 30° C., at the equator near 38° C., while the winter temperatures are about 15° colder. The humidity is generally high and there is a lot of haze; gentle, drizzling rain is chronic.

There has been little change in the climate of the planet for about 700 million years. Since there is little vulcanism, the CO_2 content of the air does not rise appreciably from that cause, and the amount consumed in photosynthesis by the lush vegetation is compensated for by the rapid oxidation of dead vegetable matter induced by the high temperature, high humidity, and high oxygen content of the air. In fact, the climate of the planet has been in equilibrium for more than half a billion years.

As has the geography of the planet. There are three continents, of which the largest is the southern continent, extending roughly from latitude 15° south to 60° south, and two-thirds of the way around the planet. The two northern

2. Clark, J.: The climate of Lithia. *J.I.R.*, in press.

continents are squarish in shape, and of sizes similar to each other. They extend from about 10° south to about 70° north, and each one about 80° east and west. One is located north of the eastern end of the southern continent, the other north of the western end. On the other side of the world there is an archipelago of large islands, the size of England and Ireland, running from 20° north to 10° south of the equator. There are thus five seas or oceans: the two polar seas; the equatorial sea separating the southern from the northern continents; the central sea between the two latter, and connecting the equatorial sea with the north polar sea; and the great sea, stretching from pole to pole, broken only by the archipelago, extending a third of the way around the planet.

The southern continent has one low mountain range (highest peak 2,263 meters) paralleling its southern shore, and moderating the never very momentous effect of the south winds. The northwestern continent has two ranges, one paralleling the eastern and one the western sea, so that the polar winds have a free run, and give this continent a more variable climate than that of the southern one. The northeastern continent has a slight range along its southern shore. The islands of the archipelago have few hills, and possess an oceanic type of climate. The trade winds are much like those of Earth, but of lesser velocity, due to the lesser temperature differentials between the different parts of the planet. The equatorial sea is nearly windless.

Except for the few mountain ranges, the terrain of the continents is rather flat, particularly near the coasts, and the lower reaches of all the rivers are of the meandering type, bordered with marshes, and with low plains that are flooded, miles wide, every spring.

There are tides, milder than on Earth, producing an appreciable tidal current in the equatorial sea. As the coastal terrain is generally quite flat, except where the mountain ranges come to the sea, wide tidal flats separate the shore from the open sea.

The water is similar to that of Earth, but considerably less salty.[3] Life began in the sea, and evolved much as it did on Earth. There is a rich assortment of microscopic sea life, types resembling such forms as seaweed and sponges, and many crustacea and mollusklike forms. The latter are very highly developed and diversified, particularly the mobile types. Quite familiar fishlike forms have emerged and dominate the seas as they do on Earth.

Present-day Lithian land plant life would be unfamiliar, but not surprising, to a terrestrial observer. There are no plants exactly like those of Earth, but most of them have a noticeable similarity to those with which the visitor would be familiar. The most surprising aspect is that the forests are of a remarkably mixed type. Flowering and non-flowering trees, palms and pines, tree ferns, shrubs and grasses all grow together in remarkable amity. Since Lithia never had a glacial period, these mixed forests, rather than the uniform type prevailing on Earth, are the rule.

In general the vegetation is lush and the forests can be considered as typical rain-forests. There are several varieties of poisonous plants, including most of the edible-looking tubers. Their roots resemble potatoes and they produce extremely toxic alkaloids, whose structure has not yet been worked out, in large quantities. There are several types of bushes which grow thorns impregnated with glucosides which are extremely irritating to the skins of most vertebrates.

3. Ley, W.: The ecologies of Lithia. *J.I.R.*, in press.

The grasses are more prevalent on the plains, shading into rushes and similar swamp-adapted plants in the marshes. There are few desert areas—even the mountains are rounded and smooth, and covered with grasses and shrubs. Seen from space, the land areas of the planet are almost entirely green. Bare rock is found only in the river valleys, where the streams have cut their way down to the lime and sandstone, and in ligneous outcroppings where flint, quartz and quartzite are frequently found. Obsidian is rare, of course, because of the lack of volcanic activity. There is clay to be found in some of the river valleys, with an appreciable alumina content, and rutile (titanium dioxide) is not uncommon. There are no concentrated deposits of iron ore, and hematite is almost unknown.

The land-living animal forms include orders similar to those found on Earth. There is a large variety of arthropods, including eight-legged insectlike forms of all sizes, up to a pseudo dragonfly with two pairs of wings and a wingspread which has been recorded at 86.5 cm. maximum. This variety lives exclusively on other insects, but there are several types dangerous to higher forms of animals. Several have dangerous bites (the poison is generally an alkaloid) and one insect can eject a stream of poisonous gas (reputed to be largely HCN) in quantity sufficient to immobilize a small animal. These insects are social in nature, like ants, living in colonies which are usually left severely alone by otherwise insectivorous organisms.

There are also many amphibians, small lizardlike forms with three fingers on each limb instead of the five that are common to terrestrial land vertebrates. They form an extremely important class, and there are some species that are as large as a St. Bernard dog at maturity. Except for some small and unimportant forms, however, the amphibians are confined to the marshy lowlands near the sea, and the rest of the land is dominated by a class resembling Earthly reptiles. Among these is the dominant species, a large, highly intelligent animal with a bipedal gait which balances itself with a rather stiff, heavy tail.

Two groups of the reptiles went back to the sea and engaged in successful competition with the fish. One adopted a completely streamlined form and is, outwardly, just another 30-foot fish. But its tail fin is in the horizontal plane and its internal structure shows its ancestry. It is the fastest thing in the waters of Lithia, doing nearly 80 knots when pressed (as it usually is by its insatiable appetite). The other group of returned reptiles resembles crocodiles, and is competent either in the open sea or on the mud flats, although it is not very fast in either situation.

Several genera of the reptiles have taken to the air, as did the terrestrial pteranodons. The largest of these has a wingspread of nearly three meters, but is very lightly built. It roosts mainly on the sea cliffs of the southern coast of the northeastern continent, and lives mainly on fish, and such of the gliding cephalopods as it can manage to catch above water. This flying reptile has a large assortment of sharp, backward-curving teeth in its long beak. One other species of flying reptile is of special interest, because it has developed something resembling feathers, in a many-colored crest down its long neck. They appear only on the mature reptile; the young are completely naked.

Some 100,000,000 years ago the land-living reptiles were almost completely wiped out by one of the smallest of their own family, which adopted the easiest method of making a living: eating the eggs of its larger relatives. The larger forms almost completely disappeared, and those that survived (such as the

Lithian allosaur) are now almost as rare as the terrestrial elephant (as compared, for instance, with the many elephant species of the Pleistocene). The smaller forms survived better, but are not nearly so abundant now as they once were.

The dominant species is an exception. The female of this species has an abdominal pouch in which the eggs are carried until they hatch. This animal is about twelve feet tall at the crown, with a head shaped for bifocal vision. One of the three fingers on the free forelimb is an opposable thumb.

About the Author

James Blish (1921–1975) received a B.A. in microbiology from Rutgers in 1942. He served in World War Two as a medical technician, then resumed his studies at Columbia after the war. During this time, he joined the Futurians—a group of science fiction writers, fans, editors, and publishers—and married literary agent Virginia Kidd, whom he divorced in 1963.

In 1959, he received the Hugo Award for his science fiction novel *A Case of Conscience*, and by 1967, he'd written 27 books and over 175 smaller pieces. He moved to England in 1968, where he could live comfortably as a full-time writer.

In his final years, Blish became a major contributor to the *Star Trek* saga, rewriting scripts into anthologies and contributing original stories and screenplays.

About the Type

Minion is a 1990 Adobe Original typeface by Robert Slimbach. Minion is inspired by classical, old style typefaces of the late Renaissance, a period of elegant, beautiful, and highly readable type designs. Created primarily for text setting, Minion combines the aesthetic and functional qualities that make text type highly readable with the versatility of digital technology.

Over the course of more than twenty years, Del Rey has built its reputation as a publisher of trailblazing science fiction and fantasy works that have withstood the test of time to become acknowledged classics of their genres. *Fahrenheit 451, Ringworld, Dragonflight, Childhood's End, Lord Foul's Bane, The Sword of Shannara, The Mists of Avalon*—all breakthrough works of their respective eras—continue to enthrall each new generation of readers that discovers them. And Del Rey remains dedicated to keeping these, and all the mainstays it has introduced over the years, prominent in the pantheon of speculative fiction.

But even the occasional masterpiece can slip through the cracks and become buried treasure until, after years of unfair neglect, its immense value is rediscovered—by happy accident or through the efforts of a lone champion able to recognize a mislaid gem—and it is restored to its rightful glory. Now, for an extraordinary selection of books, Del Rey is that champion. And it is with great pride that I introduce Del Rey Impact: a new imprint for a gathering of vintage works long overdue for rediscovery—and eminently worthy of the honor.

From high-tech science to epic fantasy, the classic titles bearing the Del Rey Impact imprimatur will appeal to speculative fiction readers of every taste. *The King of Elfland's Daughter, The Man Who Fell to Earth,* and *The Drawing of the Dark*—to name just a few—are works that touched and transformed readers in their time and paved the way for many a bestseller that would follow in their trendsetting footsteps. All of us at Del Rey are thrilled to be returning these long unsung masterworks to the spotlight, in splendid new trade paperback editions. We hope that Del Rey Impact will reacquaint many readers with the old favorites they remember and introduce many more readers to new wonders they never dreamed existed.

—Shelly Shapiro
Editorial Director
Del Rey Books

Printed in the United States
by Baker & Taylor Publisher Services